BRADFORD HONIGSBERG

SITUATION BARNEGAT LIGHT

A. C. T. PUBLICATIONS, INC.
FLANDERS, NEW JERSEY

A. C. T. Publications
4 Goldmine Road
Flanders, New Jersey 07836

For distribution information call: 1-800-765-2769

This is the First Edition, Published December 1995.

Library of Congress No. 94-070774

ISBN 0-964342-1-3

Author's Note: This is a work of fiction. The Soclarians are an
imaginary people created for the purposes of this work alone. A
fictionalized account of fictional events regarding Saddam Hussein
are intended for fiction only. However, this fictionalized rendition
is predicated upon proven and demonstrated behaviors as they
relate to villainy, atrocities and crimes against humanity as
historically performed and perpetrated by Saddam Hussein.
Where other people of notoriety are alluded to or mentioned, no
historic accuracy concerning them is intended. This book contains
no intentional portrayals of any person living or dead with
exceptions noted above. Any other references to actual individuals
living or dead; any such resemblance(s) or similarities that may be
discerned are individually and severally coincidental and without
purposeful intention on the part of the author.

DEDICATION

This book is dedicated to my late grandfather,
Henry (Pop) Feid, whose love for Barnegat Bay
and my love for him both must surely survive
and transcend the limitations imposed by death

TABLE OF CONTENTS

Kevin Murdock .... Owner of Yacht in Barnegat Bay

Peter Murdock .... Kevin's Four-year Old Son

Andrew Murdock .... Kevin's Nine-year Old Son

Ensign Hall .... Coast Guard Ensign

Ted Painedast .... Marina Manager

General Edwards .... Marines 105th Intel.

Major Richard Taylor .... General's Aide

Hank Feidor (Pop) .... Kevin's Grandfather

Joseph Feidor .... Hank's Grandfather

Moses Senecus .... Captain of Star Seeker III

Lieutenant Lasamar .... 1st Officer of Star Seeker III

Adrienne Slater .... Kevin's Girlfriend

Gerta Slater .... Adrienne's Mother

Winston Tanderoth .... Kevin's Friend

Joshua Leotor .... Commander Earth Station IV

Justinian Fairborne .... High Counsel Ambassador

Daramer Mostrale ... Kevin's Guide in the Middle East

Jenifer Tanderoth .... Winston's Wife

Brendon Tanderoth .... Winston's Son

Susan Harmon .... Shipwrecked Mother

Stacey Harmon .... Shipwrecked Daughter

-CHAPTER ONE-

Why was the lighthouse's warning beacon of light pulsating with increasing "on-off" frequency; the light stabbing into the night sky like an insistently scolding finger?

From his vantage point, standing on the dock of the marina directly across from the lighthouse, Kevin Murdock watched this strange phenomenon. He had heard reports of these occurrences throughout the years, but he had simply believed them to be manifestations of local lore.

There it was now...directly in front of him... blinking...challenging his doubt. It was, in some inexplicable way, ominous in its staccato performance. Then, after just ten or fifteen seconds, it stopped. The beacon returned to its commissioned navigational assignment, guiding ships with its familiar pattern of rotation.

The reports he had heard stated that no one was ever able to explain the cause of these code like interruptions of the light's beam. State engineers had inspected the structure to try to verify or debunk the reports. They came up with excuses of everything from sea birds flying directly in front of the light's path, to breeze blown coastal fog repeatedly dipping down, then retreating back into the sky, to college kids getting in and fooling around with the switches as part of some kind of fraternity initiation ceremony.

It was a clear, cloudless night, and Kevin didn't

buy any of that mumbo-jumbo. The birds, clouds and college kids were all somewhere else at that particular moment.

The reports of these occurrences normally came in conjunction with troubled times or world crises: the death of Kennedy, the Cuban missile crisis, Vietnam, the invasion of Kuwait, the slaughter of the Kurds and the Kurds' subsequent plight as they retreated from the murderous vengeance of Iraq's leadership; even with the mass starvation deaths in Somalia. The reports went back to the times of the First World War.

Was this simply coincidental? Was the lighthouse some kind of world barometer? Did the flashing phenomenon mark the passage of souls or somehow concentrate and manifest the universal outpouring of concern and emotion regarding these horrible events? Or was this a warning to humanity to change its ways?

Kevin toyed with these ideas, realizing that he was being somewhat whimsical and somewhat more than a little foolish. Yet, it seemed that there were just too many of these **coincidences** for there not to be some connection with what was going on in the world and this imposing monument of guidance and warning.

Kevin felt that the pulsations spoke to him succinctly, bullet like, crisply, purposely, deliberately...but what was the connection?

The world was still technically at war with Iraq. No lasting or permanent peace treaty had been signed. The crises in the Gulf and elsewhere were on everyone's mind. Fears of a world war or a cataclysmic Iraqi retaliation were paramount of all concerns for most people. Would this one be the fulfillment of Revelation, predicting the total fiery destruction of the world? Would the killings at the Dome of the Rock herald Armageddon? Or was the fulfillment of that fiery prophesy the now extinguished six hundred catastrophic oil well fires

10

in the Kuwaiti desert; fires caused by a madman, the environmental assassin...Saddam Hussein?

Saddam had nuclear capability as did several other tin horn dictators around that part of the world. The destabilization of the area made cataclysmic confrontation seem more and more likely each day.

Muslim worshipers at the Dome of the Rock who had provoked the Israelis were slaughtered by inexperienced and panicked troops who over reacted to rocks being thrown at Jewish worshipers. A blood bath ensued. This was the worst possible reaction at a time when cool heads were needed on every front.

The dictator of Iraq knew this was grist for his mill of hatred and untruth. It was a helpful perverse justification for his attack on Kuwait and for further atrocities after the cease-fire went into effect. He called for a jihad, a "holy war" against the infidels of western civilization to serve his own perverse, paranoid, hateful, and selfish ends.

The supposed barbarity and unfairness of Israel provided his rallying cry to inflame and incite the other area leaders and populations. He and others like him ignored the reality that the territories occupied by Israel after the Six Day War were in fact spoils of war taken by the victor after Israel itself was the invaded party.

Unfortunately, the Palestinian civilians who became victims of the United Nations' actions creating Israel in 1947, became further victimized by the 1967 war. They unwittingly became a permanent underclass, a cheap labor force for Israel's agricultural industry and for other industries.

This did not occur by design; it was a by-product. They became an oppressed people through no real fault of Israel's. Yet Israel became a perennial target, left with no real alternative other than that of self-defense. A **no win** situation.

These were truly dangerous times. The Persian Gulf was in turmoil; Kurds were being victimized and slaughtered without mercy. The Baltics and other former Soviet states were in rebellion, striving for an identity and independence. South Africa was in revolt. Terrorism was rampant throughout the world. It seemed like no one cared about anyone anymore.

Man's increasingly brutal interaction with his fellow man coupled with world events seemed to be taking on a consciousness of its own. How could it be stopped, let alone reversed? War and the technology of war were so beyond the control of the generals and the world leaders that the potential of experiencing the annihilation of civilization was a real possibility.

Aside from the day-to-day struggle just to live and survive; aside from the anxieties caused by just trying to **make it** from one day to the next, this new element, the specter that each day might be the last for civilization as we know it, ominously loomed in the consciousness of every person who loved family, life, country, the world.

Each person was forced to find his own refuge, his own escape, his own oasis in the desert of a world going mad. Barnegat Bay and the area surrounding the Barnegat Inlet along the New Jersey coast was such a place for Kevin Murdock.

Illuminated by lights at its base, the red and white monolithic structure silhouetted against the jet black backdrop of the pleasantly temperate Jersey shore summer evening, shouted its presence with each revolution of its penetrating and guiding beacon. This beacon slicing through the seemingly tangible darkness came from a lighthouse appropriately named **Barnegat Light.**

Barnegat Light commanded the landscape of the

coastline along the twenty mile stretch between Seaside Heights and Ship Bottom. "Old Barney," as the local residents fondly referred to it, represented to Kevin Murdock all that was good and memorable about his childhood.

After over one hundred years, the lighthouse was badly in need of a face lift. Work was continuing on the lighthouse and on the inlet whose waters ceaselessly undulated and raced along the side of it.

The inlet was often vicious and sometimes deadly. It was rated the third most treacherous inlet on the East Coast. It was feared by most and respected by all for its unpredictable and violent moods.

A breakwater of unparalleled proportions was being built to tame this intimidating challenge to navigation. Cranes and other heavy equipment ringed the lighthouse and lined up on the man-made peninsula that was forming straight out into the ocean.

Mountains of rock of various sizes reached eastward. First a bed of small rocks was poured at its base. Next, rocks of intermediate size were put down. Finally, the largest boulders that one could imagine were meticulously placed by the huge cranes.

Behind the lighthouse on the bay side, nestled in a large cove, the flat barges laden with the huge rocks remained at anchor, silently awaiting their turns to be towed to the spot where their cargo would remain in perpetuity. It was a sight to behold when these barges were ultimately cajoled, aimed, and set into forward motion by the gargantuan tugs toward their passengers' appointments with permanence.

It was now thirty years later, during the revitalization of this landmark and the surrounding recreational area, that Kevin returned with his two sons, almost to the foot of that very symbol that had meant so much to him as a boy. His new sixty foot motor

13

yacht occupied a rather overpriced boat slip at the Sandbar Yacht Club. Well, the yacht was new to him anyway. It was the fulfillment of a boyhood dream.

Business was slow for this new marina. He was one of four slip occupants. On this particular night his was the only occupied boat. It was Sunday night and the weekend sunseekers had gone home.

Kevin had requested and received the very last slip on the point of the marina nearest the channel along the marina's breakwater. It was the most remote slip in the marina, and it was just what Kevin wanted; near enough, yet far enough.

The slip extended outward from the marshy protected wetlands area of Sandbar Island for about fifty yards into a large cove that was home for the commercial fishing fleet of the town of Barnegat Light. To get to the slip, one had to walk 200 yards along a planked floating walkway over a 110 foot arching extension bridge. Nothing could be built on the wetlands because the area had been preserved as a wildlife sanctuary. There was also another floating walkway extending out toward the town of Barnegat Light and the U.S. Coast Guard station.

The slip happened to be not only the deepest slip in the marina, but also the deepest part in all of Barnegat Bay. In this one part of the bay the depth dropped off to 200 feet. This was the primary reason and determining factor behind the decision to construct floating docks secured by weighted cables. Nothing else could be secured with that kind of depth. The water was too deep for poles.

No one could ever explain the enormous hole below the slip. There was no known natural reason for its being there (its existence). Although there was a channel another 150 yards toward the town of Barnegat Light, the tidal flow did not course its way through

14

that small waterway fast enough to cause such a hole under a boat slip so removed from that channel. The hole was just there. But it was not the only unusual phenomenon for that general area surrounding the lighthouse.

Compared with any other section of the bay, the area's marshes were greener. The water was cleaner. The clams were tastier. The crabs were larger. The sea gulls were beefier. The fish were more plentiful. Cranes, egrets, sea birds of every description made the area their home and breeding ground. The air was more refreshing and a good night's sleep was easier to come by.

"Why is this place so idyllic?" Kevin wondered out loud. It didn't make sense. What was it about this place? In an area that was within 50 miles of New York City, one of the world's most populated and polluted areas, how could such a place exist?

He knew there was an energizing, invigorating feeling in the air. It defied further description. He thought that it should be left at that. Yet, he felt there was more...something else... something he couldn't quite put his finger on.

The **ACT I** was a "love at first sight" purchase. The teak woodwork provided the warm lush setting that almost every boat enthusiast dreams of for his dream boat. At sixty feet in length, standing twenty-two feet tall and having a beam of seventeen feet, this flush-deck motor yacht provided everything necessary for that out-of-the-way summer escape. It was self-contained. It even had a full laundry room.

Not bad for the little fatherless "Jew boy" (a taunt he had never forgotten), who had to learn to run fast and fight hard thirty years before on the western side of the bay in Port-Town.

After enduring such harsh prejudice as a little boy

and having moved to Port-Town from Miami Beach the summer after his father's death in 1955, Kevin reflected and thanked God for the peace, tranquility, passive companionship and just plain great fun and adventure that the bay and its creatures below and above provided. Just being there helped Kevin get through a very tough time after being cheated out of the benefit of a normal childhood and having to understand the hatred of children and adults alike.

These rather less-than-informed individuals were commonly referred to as "Pineys" by those living a little closer to New York City. These people (naturally not all of them, just enough to make a difference) hated blacks, Jews, and almost everyone else who was either not just like them, revered education, aspired to greater heights or just plain acted more refined than they did. The latter were referred to by the Pineys as "out-of-towners who put on airs."

Kevin's grandfather taught him how to be alone and that it was OK to be alone with yourself; to escape with yourself when you are cast into a situation that you can't do much about. He taught him that the greatest joys come from people, but that your greatest disappointments, also, come from people.

He did not mean one should withdraw from humanity when the world was cruel, but to take a sabbatical; to recharge on a moment's notice, right out of of your own backyard door on Barnegat Bay. The day's events, people, and family all fell into perspective after "recharge." Somehow, he knew the secret. He felt, acknowledged, and learned from that intangible force emanating from that body of water.

Everyone in town called Kevin's grandfather, Hank, "Pop". He was a happy, gregarious, and loving man who probably spent too much of his money buying everyone rounds of drinks at the local tavern. He was a slender, wiry man with a prominent, dimpled chin and a deeply etched leather like face.

He taught Kevin that, sure, we are all a part of the family of man. Certainly, we all need each other; but it's OK to be alone. Hank was happiest when he was on Barnegat Bay, alone. It was this legacy, this ability to draw solace from the bay, this treasure that Hank passed along to his grandson. But these were not the only secrets about the bay that they shared.

There are few experiences on earth eerier than being on Barnegat Bay in a thick fog just as dawn approaches. That is exactly how Kevin and his grand-father found themselves one early August morning in 1959. At the mouth of Barnegat Inlet they had just cut the Gray Marine engine of Hank's thirty-foot wooden cabin cruiser, **Sanctuary**, so that they could start a drift for fluke.

Suddenly, almost from nowhere, a strange fog rolled in from the sea behind the lighthouse. It was a cold, chilling, alarming fog. Neither of them had ever seen one quite like it before.

The fog rolled its way toward them; reaching about twenty feet into the air. Before they could get the killies out of the bait box and onto their hooks they were completely surrounded by it. They baited their lines and dropped them into the water. It was slack tide. There was no wind. It was as if they were at anchor. The water was glassy flat; not a ripple could be seen.

Their lines hung limply down, not having moved an inch along the bay's bottom. Then, barely percep-tible at first, coming from deep inside the dense fog, the sound of the soft rushing of air met their ears; a sound like that of a growing wind rushing through pine trees.

Their skin tingled, but it was not from excitement,

although excited they were. Kevin looked at Pop to find that what was left of Pop's thinning hair was standing straight out from his head. Kevin reached for his head to find that his own hair was doing the same. It was then that they saw it.

Not more than fifty feet off their starboard side a huge airborne object gently glided past them with a whoosh and an electric like crackle. The object moved at about fifteen miles an hour. The fog tumbled behind the object to fill the vacuum left by its transit, obscuring the object immediately. Pop and Kevin both sat down dumbfounded, in awe and at the same time humbled by such an event. What great technology could be responsible for this? They started comparing notes on what they had just witnessed.

The object was wing-shaped, like the flying-wing bomber design of World War II that never really made it into mass production. From tip-to-tip it measured about one hundred feet. It was about twenty feet thick at its thickest point in the middle. It measured about forty feet from front to back. There were no visible engines nor was there any fiery exhaust emanating from the back of the object. There was one large window that was dome shaped, centered in the middle of the object and extending, sloping, and tapering to a point in the rear of the object. There were no visible seams. Through the clear dome three humanoid figures could be seen silhouetted against a faint blue background light.

The craft traveled about three feet above the water with the same bluish glow reflecting against the glassy water's surface. Electrical discharges from the object bounced off the water's surface forming an erratic lacework of bluish-white lines on the mirrored water's surface. The lacework hung on the surface of the water, crackled and danced for a few seconds, then dissipated.

There were little nodes of light at the junctions of each of these lines. They wiggled to and fro at varying rates of speed intermittently bouncing off one another.

After the craft had passed, there remained a sauna like moist ozone smelling vapor. The temperature change of the air was noticeable. Ten seconds later there was the thunderous crack of a sonic boom off in the direction in which the object had disappeared into the fog. Through a break in the fog created by the object's passage, Pop and Kevin saw the object coursing its way through the pre-dawn sky at an incredible speed before disappearing into the heavens.

After their hair went back down and they had time to sufficiently calm themselves, Pop started offering explanations about what they had just seen. He desperately wanted to rationalize in a manageable fashion something that challenged reason. He wanted to categorize the experience not only so that his grandson could deal with it, but so that he also could come to grips with it himself.

Pop came up with the plausible explanation that it was a new airplane being tested by the armed forces and that it was probably based out of McGuire Air Force Base or the Lakehurst naval facility. Kevin shook his head in agreement. But he knew that the technology represented by what he had just seen was way beyond the reach of any military facility in the world.

Pop admonished Kevin not to leak word of this chance encounter because, first of all, no one would believe it and second of all, the government needed their help in keeping sensitive information regarding experiments away from the Communists.

A few days later Pop went out on what he said would be a two day fishing trip. He said he wanted to fish for marlin and mahi-mahi in the ocean and that the water would be too rough for Kevin to go along.

Kevin never really believed this, but out of respect for his grandfather, he kept his thoughts to himself. He felt that Pop sensed there was something (perhaps dangerous) out there and that Pop wanted to find out just what it was, alone.

That Saturday afternoon after coming back from the two-day trip, Pop walked in with the most serene gaze on his face. He seemed at peace, not saying much for the rest of the day. That Monday he went to see his lawyer without telling anybody just why. He was in a strange happy-yet-sad mood, like he wanted to tell everybody something but couldn't. Somehow, he seemed healthier and more vigorous. On Tuesday evening of that same week, after an unusually long round of visiting all of his favorite haunts, Pop went to bed and slept a drunk and deep sleep for the last time. Pop died in his sleep that night or early Wednesday morning.

The doctor came to the house and declared Pop dead. A hearse was sent for and it arrived just seconds before a very strange call came to the house from Pop's lawyer. It seems that Pop wrote a new will when he had visited the lawyer's office that Monday. Pop must have had some type of premonition about his death, because he asked the lawyer to check up on him that very morning.

It was then that the family learned Pop had put into his will that under no circumstances was he to have an autopsy performed on his body after his death. Because Pop cashed in his life insurance policy, there was no suspicion that he had taken his own life.

The laws were different back then. No autopsy was performed against a family's wishes or if a person had indicated in a will that he or she didn't want one. However, if a crime (such as life insurance fraud or foul play) were suspected, then there would be a man-

20

datory autopsy. Pop had covered all bases in order to avoid an autopsy.

He had placed a further request in his will that his body be placed intact, without embalmment, into a weighted canvas shroud and that it be delivered to the depths of the ocean five miles east of Barnegat Light near the bell buoy in forty feet of water. This was to be done as close as possible to dawn on the day following his death.

This request was strange for those times. The weddings and funerals on the water that did not conform to convention were not yet in vogue. However, since Pop was a former Navy man, the family believed that his request was a reflection of his love for the sea and they acquiesced to the request. His body was commended to the sea during a brief predawn service the following morning.

The sunrise was a particularly beautiful one that morning. The day was particularly pleasant and crisp; one of the nicest days that anyone could recall in the recent weeks. That was good, because Kevin wanted to remember good days with Pop. Probably Pop wanted it to be the same way. It was Pop's last voyage on the *Sanctuary*.

These thoughts from years gone by raced through Kevin's head as he stood on the floating dock at the stern of his boat and breathed deeply of the intoxicating night air. The piercing beam of the lighthouse was preparing another stab in the direction of the marina when Kevin's macaw parrot, Matey, bellowed a loud and uncharacteristic after-dark "S-Q-U-A-W-K." Scores of nearby sea gulls responded in kind. Then in blind flight hundreds of birds of different varieties thundered into the night sky. The frogs stopped calling. The locusts and crickets stopped their concert. This was not normal behavior. Something was wrong...very wrong.

21

Maybe an earthquake or some other surprise of nature was about to occur.

The rotating beacon atop Old Barney suddenly slowed. The beacon itself, the inlet lights, house lights, street lights and all other lights to either side of Barnegat Inlet ominously lost their intensity. They yellowed, and dimmed further. Then, suddenly, as if eerily conducted by the wand of the diminishing beam of Barney's fenced and white capped dome...they vanished.

Stark and profound darkness shrouded the area. The birds settled back into the marshes. Kevin's eyes started to adjust to the darkness while he postulated that one hell of a transformer must have blown.

Strange though, the lights of the few structures on the north side of the inlet also went out. There is no cable under the inlet. The power for that side comes in from the Toms River-Seaside section. Maybe the Crab Creek nuclear generating station located at four rivers went down. Who knows?

Kevin remembered Pop telling him that shortly after he had gotten out of the Navy and had built and launched the *Sanctuary*, he had witnessed a similar phenomenon in 1943 while night fishing. Pop claimed that just before the blackout he had seen glowing objects in the eastern sky off Barnegat Inlet.

Pop explained that he had heard loud booms and saw multiple flashes of light. Ten minutes later the lights came back on. Almost at the same moment military helicopters raced across the sky toward the direction of the action.

The next day the radio news explained that there was a mock battle exercise off the coast, along with a surprise blackout to fortify and brace the population and the armed services against the possibility of a combined submarine, commando, and naval assault by the Nazis along the New Jersey coastline. There was so much industry and so many oil refineries within a naval strike force's reach that this precaution became necessary.

It was believable. The war had made everyone petrified of the Nazis almost to the point of hysteria; fearing from day-to-day that the coastline would be attacked. Everyone in Port-Town bought the explanation. Pop didn't believe it. He knew the naval armaments. He had recently separated from the Navy. Nothing in the arsenal as he knew it had anything that would come close to explaining away the glowing objects in the sky. He kept his mouth shut, but he never stopped wondering.

It was now a few minutes after midnight. Kevin was glad that his two boys were asleep in their bunks. Suddenly being cast into darkness might have frightened four year old Peter and nine year old Andrew. They had had it hard enough after their parents' recent divorce. They certainly did not need an upsetting experience on their first night on the boat and their first reunion with their father since the divorce became final.

However, Kevin knew that with the shore power off, it would get pretty stuffy below decks without the air conditioning system working. Even though the night was temperate, moisture from the bay would make the cabin rather sultry if the air conditioner stayed off. He knew that before the boys started to stir and shake their blankets off, he'd better get below and start the generator while they were still in a relatively deep sleep.

He noticed that the battery powered lights were alarmingly low when he climbed aboard. He checked the battery gauges. There was no reading. Why wasn't the constant voltage system doing its job? It was supposed to put a constant charge on the vessel's batteries from the shore while in port.

He went below decks and checked the port side engine room where the constant voltage charge box was bolted to the bulkhead. The batteries of his flashlight were dead. He lit a match, which wasn't the brightest thing to do in an engine room. There were no fumes, and since the flash point of diesel fuel is pretty high, he took a chance. He struck the match and held it to the box. The charge box was on, but showed no activity on the gauges.

Almost at the same instant he noticed a faint bluish glow outside the engine room porthole. The boat started to rock violently as if an ocean liner had passed. The boat strained at its mooring ropes. The strange light grew brighter and brighter. The vessel and the floating docks were heaving straight up and down by this time, as if there were a giant piston under the boat.

Water surged through the open engine room portholes. The water rushed into the bilges. The unfastened porthole doors snapped off their hinges. If this continued, it wouldn't be long before the water reached the floorboards. They needed electricity and fast. He climbed out into the hallway and slammed the door. The boys started screaming, "Daddy, Daddy, help! Please, Daddy, please!"

Kevin's arms bristled. His skin tingled. He got his bearings and bolted for the boys' room. They had both been thrown from their bunks onto the floor.

He had heard no crashes other than dishes and loose objects. He judged that there was no hull damage. The boat continued its strange ride. In the bluish glow he saw that the boys' hair was standing straight out from their heads. His hair was doing the same.

"Boys, stay here. Don't move. I am going topside to see what this is all about. Don't move. Do you understand?"

Peter screamed after him, "Daddy don't leave,

don't leave me here!" His older brother gathered him in close to himself protectively.

Kevin held onto the rail of the boat as best he could and peered toward the light, which had greatly increased in intensity. The bronco ride continued. The water of the bay boiled and surged.

Kevin reached for the radio to call "Mayday!"...but the boat's batteries were dead. Damage to the boat was imminent and the boys were in peril. As Kevin raced back toward the boys' cabin, the undulating stopped. The lights came back on as mysteriously as they had faded. The boys were terrified; sobbing, sitting between their beds, with their backs pressed against a built-in night table.

"Is G-God mm-mad at us, Daddy? Did we do something wrong, Da-Daddy?" Andrew sobbed.

For some reason, both boys felt guilty that they had done something that might have caused the divorce. They had definite feelings of guilt that carried over into many areas. It would take time to make them understand there was nothing that they did or didn't do to contribute to the divorce.

"Of course not, Bonker. You're the best. God is not mad at you. Something just happened in the bay currents that caused us to have a wild ride, that's all."

Andrew believed his father as much as Kevin had believed Pop some thirty-plus years back. It had to do for now. Kevin got the boys into the galley to give them some milk and a couple of cookies. After getting the boys settled and comfortably munching, he returned topside to try to sort this thing out.

Kevin saw that all the lights on Long Beach Island and north of the lighthouse were on again. He tried the ship-to-shore radio again. It was working. He called out to the Barnegat Light Coast Guard Station, which was slightly south of the lighthouse. He figured they could respond faster than the police who were some distance away. Anyway, this was a maritime related incident.

Who cared how they were going to respond or what jurisdiction covered this? He needed some assurances from somebody. He had to show the boys he was doing *something* about all of this.

"Mayday, Mayday, Mayday, Barnegat Light Coast Guard. This is the vessel **ACT I**. Please respond."

A pleasant yet firm female voice responded. "This is United States Coast Guard responding to the vessel calling Mayday. What is the nature of your emergency Captain?"

Kevin, trying to fight his impulse to babble like an idiot, asked that a patrol boat come out immediately to investigate the occurrence.

"There is something going on under my boat. I have no idea what happened. My boat was thrown up and down violently by some underwater activity. There was a bluish light under the water while it was going on. I'm worried that it might happen again and do some real damage.

"We have already taken on considerable water. I do not know the condition of the hull for a certainty at this time. I have two young boys on board. Do you copy?"

The response came rapidly, "Yes, Captain, we copy. Tell us your present location and whether anyone is injured. Over."

Thank God. She was taking him seriously. "There are no injuries. We are located about one third of a mile across from you in the Sandbar Marina. It's the one with the floating docks."

She assured him over the radio, "We are on the way. Sir, at this time I am requesting that you and your passengers put on life vests. Inspect your vessel. If you find that you are not taking on any additional water, stay on board with your boys until our crew arrives at your location to investigate and assess your situation. Your report of a blue light has been verified from this location. United States Coast Guard Group Barnegat Light standing by on channel one-six. Out!"

Seconds later over the radio came the alarm, "Pan pan...pan pan...pan pan...Hello, all stations, hello, all stations, hello, all stations. This is United States Coast Guard Group Barnegat Light. Break!" "The vessel **ACT I**, located at Sandbar Marina approximately one third mile west south west of the inlet, reports being in jeopardy with possible hull damage and was last reported as having taken on water. Break!

"There are three people on board reporting no injuries at this time. The vessel is tied at the dock at this time. However, there are extreme and unusual circumstances reported. Break!"

"All on-hand and available Coast Guard and Marine Police traffic in the area of Sandbar Marina are requested to proceed with caution to that location. Render assistance as necessary and report to this station. United States Coast Guard Group Barnegat Light. Out!"

As he awaited the arrival of the Coast Guard, Kevin gazed down over the port rail to find that there was scarcely a visible hint of the bluish light left. It flickered two or three times and then was gone. It was clear while this was going on that this was no wave action. It was a column of water rising straight up. It was like a misguided river trying to find its course, but was able only to flow straight up. Could it be an underground river?

"Nah!!" Kevin said to himself. It couldn't have that kind of pressure behind it from so far down. It has to be something else; but what?

Ironically, the patrol boat from the State Police arrived with its sirens blaring and lights flashing atop its canopy just moments before the Coast Guard arrived in similar fashion. Evidently, they were monitoring Kevin's transmission and started toward the light he described while he was still talking to the Coast Guard dispatcher.

Unknown to Kevin, the light during its brightest emission shot straight up into the clear night sky more intensely than its navigational competitor across the cove.

State Police cars started swarming into the parking lot. What was going on here? He didn't ask them to respond. The newly arrived patrol boats tied off in two of the remaining seven slips on "A" dock.

None of the troopers attempted to approach the boat. They first cordoned off the entrance gates to the floating docks. Then they roped off the entrances to the two parking lots.

Fighter jets screamed overhead to some point offshore. They must have come out of McGuire Air Force Base. Was the coast under attack?

Seemingly, events were taking on a direction of their own at this point. It was like a well-rehearsed drill that had become almost automatic.

"My God, they're back!" Kevin said aloud to himself as the impact of the event started settling in. The secret memory he shared with his grandfather was rushing back to his consciousness as if it had happened yesterday.

The boys were up in the boat's salon now looking out of the window at all the activity. "Stay inside, boys, while I talk to these gentlemen." He couldn't share with the boys that he was convinced something not of this world had disturbed their slumber.

Amidst the crackling of the marine radios, the

police radios, the flashing multicolored lights, and the bullhorn commands, Kevin could see that the police from the patrol boats were walking away from the dock of the **ACT I** to confer with the officers in the parking lot. The leader of the contingent from the Coast Guard was walking toward his boat. Kevin climbed down the ladder located off the aft deck and then stepped onto the dock to meet the man.

The officer, dressed in a blue work uniform and orange life vest, walked toward him extending his hand. "Good evening sir", he greeted with a stiff military bearing. "I am Lieutenant Hall from the Barnegat Light Coast Guard Station. I am the commanding officer of the group. I was in the station this evening and wanted to answer your call personally."

The Coast Guard officer was an erect, slender individual with a crew cut. He had a square jaw and, despite his obvious boyish looks, had a no-nonsense way about him that said "I am in command here."

He asked if Kevin had called the State Police. The officer was as surprised as Kevin regarding the unusually rapid and large response by land and water by the State Police. Kevin assured him that he did not ask them to come.

No sooner had they made this observation then a huge helicopter of the Sea Stallion variety thundered down the coast from the north. It arched around Old Barney with intense search beams cutting the darkness of the entire area with a wide swath of light. It circled once around Kevin's boat, then hovered off the stern about seventy-five yards toward the main channel and about ten feet above the water. Scuba divers with lights and various kinds of equipment started repelling down ropes from the craft in groups of two, until a total of eight had descended into the depths below.

The marina manager arrived back at the marina after a night out with his girlfriend. Ted lived alone in an apartment at the marina. Perhaps, he was going to get lucky this particular night. Kevin hoped so. It might calm him down.

He was a wiry sort, with a perpetual red hue to his complexion. You didn't want to cross him or suggest that you might know something more about the ocean or boats than old Ted. This overbearing man knew it all. He was hot tempered and defensive; given to bouts of rage and heavy drinking from time to time. This night was such a night.

Ted stormed onto the scene in his full glory, because he was convinced that this new upstart boat owner, Kevin, had committed some transgression against marine law, etiquette, tradition, common sense, nature, the government, the Shriners or something. He wanted to be able to say "I told you so" so badly that he could taste it (and the owners of the marina wondered why business was so bad).

"Murdock!" he screamed from the parking lot. "What have you done now?" Ted Painedast had to embarrass people in order to stroke his own ego. You could almost hear him praying out loud that 'please, this time, let it be something serious. I can finally see this thorn in my side get what's coming to him.' Customers were problems to him. They interrupted his whole day.

Simply stated, Ted hated Kevin's guts. Ted was not happy about where he was at that point in his life and projected his insecure and angry feelings about himself and his own perceived shortcomings on anyone else around him who had achieved a measure of success in life. He made his feelings toward Kevin quite plain right from the start stating, "Just because you have a large yacht, you think you can do anything you want around here." He was in one of his many ugly drunken fits at the time as well.

This former government engineer had problems far beyond whose boat was bigger. The only reason Kevin stayed at the marina was that God made a perfect spot for a boat right there and good old Ted could be ignored and avoided. It was a shame for a customer to have to try to avoid someone whose salary the customer was helping to pay.

The marina owners put up with him because they knew nothing about boats and boating themselves and were convinced by Ted that they could never find anyone as knowledgeable as he.

The fact of the matter is that anyone with a resentful and ugly disposition is inherently replaceable if any business wishes to survive. A business with that type of atmosphere of an employee "riding herd" over clients and upper management doing nothing about such behavior is doomed to mediocrity at best and failure at worst. You promote what you permit.

Some people live for someone (most of the time it's not important who) to knock the chip off their shoulders. Ted Painedast was such an individual. Kevin cringed every time this annoying and alarming pain-in-the-stern crossed his path.

As Kevin joked to himself that now his night was completely made by the arrival of this disruptive and pompous sot, another helicopter of vast proportions landed on the flat area off the starboard side of the **ACT I**, just beyond the parking lot on land that was being prepared for a state park picnic area. It landed with remarkable grace for such an awesome and powerful craft.

A door on the right front of the helicopter shot open. Six soldiers in full battle gear rushed from the extended ramp. Four of them ran to positions located at the front and rear of the craft and stood guard with machine guns at the ready.

The two remaining soldiers helped extend and secure the middle third of the craft which had opened to form an awning. This was obviously some kind of military mobile command post.

With speed and quick efficiency, the soldiers remaining inside the aircraft started unloading satellite dishes, cameras, lights, antennas and other sophisticated looking electronic gadgetry.

Amid this organized bustle stood a lumbering, cigar-smoking, animated gentleman who was obviously the authority figure of the group and projected a visage reminiscent of General George Patton. With an armed guard and an aide at his side he approached Kevin and reached him at the same time as Ted.

Obviously "half in the bag", Ted made an uncharacteristically wise decision to allow the officer to speak first. "I am Brigadier General Clayton Edwards of the 105th Marine Intelligence Division. This is my aide Major Richard Taylor. This area has been declared a military priority site and must be evacuated temporarily and immediately. I apologize for the inconvenience. However, this exercise must not be compromised by extraneous personnel."

It was then that Ted decided to assert himself in his inimitable and uniquely distinctive fashion. "Excuuusse me" he interjected pointedly and pompously. "I am the manager here, and I say what goes on or not on these premises. You are the trespassers here."

Kevin thought, 'What cajones this lush has. But you have to give him credit for being consistent, if nothing else.' For the first time Kevin felt as if he was on Ted's side, as unlikely as that might seem. He didn't especially feel like relocating his sons and himself in the middle of the night.

"What has Murdock done to get you guys here?"

The general gave him a patient and contemplative look as if to say, 'should I take valuable time and debate this interruption to my task or just have him ushered off under guard?' He chose the first.

"We have had an unexplained event here," he started. "There may be possible national security matters involved of which I am not at liberty to discuss at present. We will be in a better position to provide you with an explanation and quite possibly access to your property after noon tomorrow. At this juncture, time is of the essence. We must perform our examinations without interruption. Quite frankly, you may be in danger here. This event may reoccur during the night. We just don't know at this point.

"So, for your own safety, I ask that you take a few things you might need and let the United States Government treat you to a night at the hotel of your choice in the area. We will want to talk to you in the morning, Mr. Murdock, since you were here during the event.

"Please make your arrangements with Major Taylor here and let him know where we can get in touch with you. Thank you for your cooperation."

Kevin thought it strange that they didn't want a report right then and there. They apparently didn't need one...strange.

The general turned to Lieutenant Hall and commanded: "Lieutenant, this site is under direct Pentagon control. Please, contact your regional commander and ask him to call our command desk in Washington. Tell him to ask the Pentagon operator to patch him through to *Situation Barnegat Light*. That is our operation's designation here.

"He will know the procedure. We will need Coast Guard support tonight to keep curiosity seekers and the press away. Thank you. That will be all, Lieutenant."

The lieutenant said, "Yes, sir, right away," saluted, turned on his heels and walked off smartly toward his boat.

Kevin addressed the major: "I will get my boys, and a few things and meet you in the parking lot."

Ted gave a "harumphhh" and walked off in a snit toward his apartment with the major in tow.

The general folded his arms, puffed on his cigar, and stared down into the dark depths below as the underwater lights of the divers came closer to the **ACT I**.

The Pelican's Roost Hotel and Restaurant just over the bridge at the easternmost terminus of Route 72 in Ship Bottom was always the favorite place for Kevin and his boys when they fished at the shore before he bought the boat. The place was always cozy, the food always good, the pool always clean and the owner was always there to make certain things were going just right.

It was now almost 2:00 am. The boys were zonked. Kevin put them both into one of the two queen-sized beds. Kevin turned out the lights, slipped under the covers of the other bed, reached for the remote control, turned on the TV, and lowered the volume.

The late night-early morning edition of the news was on one of the New York stations. They were just ending their news broadcast when Ginger Chang, the pretty and personable reporter, started, "Finally, tonight, we have a report from Barnegat Bay in New Jersey that a strange light was seen near Barnegat Lighthouse. Officials are investigating and taking the incident quite seriously. The area has been sealed off. However, officials at the scene seem to believe at this point that magnetic flux in the earth's crust detected earlier in the day caused electrically charged emissions of swamp gas from the local marshes to phosphoresce for a time.

34

"More on this phenomenon will follow on *Good Morning, New Day* tomorrow morning. Until then, have a pleasant evening; goodnight."

Kevin whispered to himself, "Ri...ght! Damndest active swamp gas I ever saw. It nearly killed us and sunk our boat."

Who would believe him? He looked over at his boys, thankful to God that those dearest to his heart were spared from injury (or worse) that night. He turned off the TV. Exhausted, he rolled over and fell into a deep sleep.

-CHAPTER TWO-

Peter and Andrew were the first to awaken. Kevin woke up to find he had kicked all his sheets and blankets off and had his pillow in a headlock. He blinked the sleep from his eyes and rolled over to find the boys watching cartoons. This was like old times. Did last night really happen?

It was 10:00 am. The reality again settled in and motivated Kevin's feet. He jumped in and out of the shower, dried, had the boys brush their teeth, packed their few things, got them into the car and started heading down the road back toward the marina. Kevin was not prepared for what he saw when he got there.

It was a serene morning belying the activities of the night before. The sun was out. The day was clear. The sea birds were soaring above. Not a trace of the scores of men, trucks, cars, the helicopter and other equipment remained. A few reporters and two camera crews were just finishing packing up their equipment and were pulling away from the curb outside of the marina grounds. Only the general's aide, Major Taylor, remained out by the **ACT I**.

Kevin started walking with the boys along the floating docks toward the major. Suddenly, from under the floating pontoon sections, came an abrupt eruption of noise and churning water.

The boys clung to Kevin's legs as his heart

37

pounded in his chest. From between the pontoons startled wood ducks thundered from their secret shelter into the open water of the marina.

"That was a dirty trick!" Kevin called after the fleeing ducks.

With a shared sigh of relief the threesome continued toward Major Taylor. He had a grin on his face as they approached. He extended his hand to shake Kevin's.

"You know, Mr. Murdock, I got the ducks to queue in your honor. If you weren't awake before you are now, right? Tough night for all of us last night, huh?" said the major, establishing common ground and a common frame of reference between them.

In the past Kevin thought that the term "military intelligence" had the same homogeneous sound as "oil" and "water". However, encountering this affable and outgoing army officer made him realize that perhaps he should change some of his thinking. Previously, he had ascribed to all military officers such characteristics as flat personality, bland, gung-ho, tunnel-visioned, rule book automatons, egomaniacs, self-satisfied, self-centered and self-righteous.

Now in one fell swoop, with his disarming grin and glib tongue the major challenged Kevin's preconceptions. This was a regular guy.

"Well, Major," Kevin asked, "did you find any little green men and can I have my boat back?"

Taylor gave a chuckle and said, "Yes, you may have your boat back. We found no little green men. However, our geo-scientist whiz kids are fairly certain that we do know what happened here last night. Your boat happens to be sitting over a very special place on this planet. Try to follow me. I am going to explain to you what I explained to the reporters."

Taylor continued, "I realize that you are questioning why the authorities arrived on the scene so soon after your call for help. I realize, also, that you are probably wondering why no one asked you about your experience last night."

Kevin said to himself 'this guy's name in his last life must have been Clara Voiant. Get to something I don't already know.'

"Well Kevin, the fact is, you could not have told us anything last night that we didn't already know. Last night our geo-stationary satellite system detected a strong electromagnetic flux in the earth's core. This flux concentrated its activity at a point under your boat. This caused ionization of the gases trapped underground. Those gases were created by rotting vegetative and other organic material. The molecular excitation and ionization experienced by the gases resulted in their phosphorescing and being channeled straight up into the sky by the magnetic path created by the core flux.

"Mr. Murdock, this ultimately resulted in the distinct and directed luminous beam emanating from under your boat. Also, the accompanying gaseous release accounted for the turbulent and violent water activity you experienced.

"So, you see, in short this whole thing was a perfectly natural phenomenon. We all lost sleep over nothing really. If anything else should happen, give me a call. Here is my card. Good-bye, and have a good stay with your boys." With that the major turned and walked off.

"You actually believe that crap yourself?" Kevin muttered to himself. Why was this explanation reminiscent of Kevin's grandfather trying to explain away the inexplicable?

Intellectually, sure...what Taylor was describing was possible. Kevin knew, however, that where there is a gas release underwater there are bubbles. Anyone who has ever farted in a bathtub knows that. There were no bubbles underwater the night before. It was a stream, a column of water...rising and falling.

He knew that for some reason the government wanted to cover up the true cause of the event, but why? What harm would the truth do? Even if there were little green men, so what? People could handle that unless, of course, the powers that be didn't want the populace to know that we were vulnerable to or at the mercy of a greater technology.

This day was a beautiful one. It was the end of the summer. School was going to start in two weeks. Kevin had been promising the boys that they could spend one full and uninterrupted week with him on the boat. He planned on keeping that promise. At the moment, he was quite content to allow the government to worry about whatever happened the night before.

If there were any imminent danger or hot steaming secret, the NASA boys and the military types would not allow anyone to come within ten miles of the place let alone spend the week on the site. Kevin and the boys got onto the boat, got settled back in, lowered the fifteen foot Boston Whaler tender into the water, got their fishing gear, and loaded their sodas and snacks.

All of a sudden, Kevin saw something that made his heart leap into his throat. He gazed transfixed at what confronted him at the end of the pier, not seventy-five feet from the boat, as his blood burned his ear rims, flushed his face, and pounded a primal alert behind his eardrums. His dead grandfather stood staring at him with a calm, benign, and almost loving gentility. He was wearing a bluish, silvery gray one piece flight suit or wet suit. He looked as if he was about ten years younger than he looked just before he died.

Kevin choked trying to regain his breathing. The figure walked toward him. In panic Kevin attempted to hop off the Boston Whaler onto the dock to find the boys who were down in the galley fixing their own peanut butter and jelly sandwiches.

Falling backward, Kevin lost his footing, twisting and careened into the water of the marina. When he surfaced and pulled his head up over the side of the Whaler, the figure was gone.

Weakened by the fright, Kevin could barely pull himself out of the water. He sat on the hardwood bench of the boat shaking and dripping as the boys scurried off the yacht toward him.

They called, "Dad, Dad, are you OK? What happened? We heard you yelling."

He replied, "I'm OK, boys. I just lost my balance and fell into the water." What else was he going to say, ---'You see, boys, I just saw a ghost in broad daylight'? Yeah, right! That should go over big.

He needed some time to calm down and think. He told the boys, "Go to the clubhouse for a little while and play some Ping-Pong, OK? I have to dry off and change my clothes. When I'm ready, I'll toot the horn twice and we'll give those fluke some trouble."

Andrew glanced at Peter and said, "Come on, I'll race you to the clubhouse."

They were off like a shot, leaving Kevin mumbling to himself as he got back into the **ACT I**. When he got to the aft cabin he propped the two large back windows open and breathed deeply to clear his head. He stripped off his wet clothes and hopped into the warm shower to rinse off the salt water.

Leaning both hands against the wall of the shower and putting his face directly into the stream of water, he tried to convince himself that he wasn't crazy.

"Have I missed my grandfather that much? Did

41

he mean so much to me that I am having hallucinations twenty-seven years after his death?"

He gave himself credit for being of sound mind. He dismissed the notion that he may have been fantasizing due to some kind of psychological response to the events of the night before.

"I saw what I saw," he announced. There was something going on beyond his reach of comprehension; but whatever it was, it had to be explainable.

He climbed out of the shower and toweled himself off. He threw the towel over his head to rub his hair dry as he walked from the bathroom into the center of the stateroom. He peeled the towel off looping it on his shoulders behind his head and stood practically nose-to-nose with his grinning grandfather.

"Well, just don't stand there bare-assed looking as if you've seen a ghost, boy! Where are your manners? Take a breath. Blue isn't your color.

"Well, hell then, if you're not going to ask me to sit down, I'll just find a spot over here on your bed," quipped this talking apparition from a past generation.

Whoever this was, he was certainly enjoying himself (or itself) at Kevin's expense. "There, that's better."

"Hu-hu-wh---whooo---who are you and what do you want with me? Who put you up to this? Who are you?" Kevin repeated, "And how the hell did you get in here?" He demanded.

"Is that any way to talk to your dear departed old grandfather who bounced you on his knee and took you fishing when you were no larger than a good sized bluefish? I should say not. Just hold on and keep taking long, slow, deep breaths and I'll come clean with you. Is that a fair deal?" His grandfather chided.

"You've got my full attention, Pop. I'm either dead or dreaming. Either way, you've got the floor."

42

His knees were weak and shaking as he sat down.

"First of all, Kevin, I'm real. Here, touch my arm. See? I'm flesh and blood. I'm not a ghost. I don't walk through walls or boat hulls. Your windows back here are wide open. I climbed on your swim platform and in I came. I am alive. I never died. I couldn't tell anyone what I was up to before my death or at least my staged death.

"What I am about to tell you now and in the days to come must be confidential. The survival of this planet depends on it. If you breach this confidentiality, we will know. All evidence involving our presence here will either disappear or be destroyed. Do you understand me and follow me to this point?"

Kevin gave a dumbfounded nod of his head and a grunt of acknowledgment.

Pop could see the pained and confused look on Kevin's face. Before he could make any headway at all in getting through to Kevin he had to humanize himself more and gain a common ground, continuing, "Will you please put your robe on? Nobody wants to see your shortcomings." Kevin obeyed.

Pop stopped his talking and walked over to the opposite double bed. He put his arm around Kevin and said, "I'm sorry for the fright, son. It's just that I'm so used to being alive for all these years that I can't really stand in the shoes of someone who has believed that I have been dead for so long. I'm going to take this one step at a time and I am going to start at the beginning. Please don't say squat until I'm finished. Deal?

"When you were a boy, you didn't need a wall to fall on your head to let you know that your grandmom was one hell of a bitch."

Kevin flashed back. It was true. Nothing ever made her happy. She was the most contrary, bigoted, complaining, condemning, opinionated, inspiration and soul killing battle-ax a man could ever hope to avoid, let alone marry. Other than that she was a gem.

"I smoked and drank. I womanized. I fished, worked, went to gin mills and did almost anything just to keep out of the way and sight of that oppressive witch.

"Other than our three daughters, our home was a lifeless, lonely, and practically loveless place where I simply went when I had to put my head down to sleep. In short she was killing me and I was letting her.

"People didn't divorce back in those days. It just wasn't done. My health was going down the tubes. So you could pretty well guess that if someone offered me happiness, health, longevity, purpose, camaraderie, community, acceptance, and love, I would jump at it.

"Well, it was offered and that's exactly what I did. I didn't give it a second thought. I didn't even look back. Except, I looked back to you.

"My daughters were grown. To them I wasn't much of a father. I spent so much time trying to avoid their mother that I wound up avoiding them too. So it's no wonder that they thought of me as simply the guy who earned the money, got home after they had gone to bed, and got up and went to work after they had gone to school.

"But, you and I, well, we had something special. We both needed human affection...the way that humans should need each other. You needed a father figure, and I never had a son. Having to leave you was one of the few regrets I had. You know what though? I would have been dead within six months anyway. So, I did what I had to do and took advantage of an offer that only happens in dreams.

"Kevin, you knew in your heart of hearts that

44

what you and I saw flash by the boat when you were a boy was nothing that could have been produced on this earth. You were respectful enough not to tell me I was nuts for suggesting that it was something that the military was experimenting with. I am thanking you for that now.

"As you know, that wasn't my first experience with strange phenomenon on Barnegat Bay. I had to find out more. It became an obsession with me. I know that you had your suspicions when I insisted that I go out on the boat alone after our encounter with the craft.

"Kevin, I found them. They are our ancestors. They are not gods. But they are god like in their treatment of others, their outlook on the universe, their passion to help and nurture and their inclination toward forgiveness.

"Their continuing mission is mandated by God. Christ was one of them. Mary and Joseph were actually settlers who had conceived Jesus prior to their departure. Their mission was mandated even back then by God as the Almighty's ambassadors. In that sense Christ was the son of God for he went about his Father's work and in fact spoke directly with him throughout his time on this world.

"He was to be the seed for hope, a fresh outlook and inspiration for a race comprised of unwitting pioneers raised in isolation on their own planet, then resettled on this one long before the time of Moses or even Abraham. But things got out of control. The people descended from the original settlers lost touch with their faith. The experiment of total isolation prior to colonization had a fatal flaw.

"Although there was an inherent, inbred, timeless concept of right and wrong, of the Almighty and of the design, intent, meaning and course of the universe, people developed a need to *see* their God, to touch Him, to hear Him. In that socially acceptable and perceived need rested the fatal flaw.

"They looked to each other to find their gods, selecting one man after another; time after time, not realizing or simply not being in tune with their own internal God-given intuition that we all hold the candle of God and the capacity for good and magnanimity within the innermost recesses of our own God-given miracle that we refer to as the human soul.

"When Egypt, Rome, and other communities of humans generated one murderous madman leader after another, whom the people revered and feared, Christ was sent to get civilization back on track; to bring it back into step with the universe and the will of God with simple and basically common sense redirection...to remind them of what was already there within each of them."

"You've heard it said that you can't keep a good idea down. One might be able to kill the messenger but you can never kill a good idea. It grows like a fragrantly flowered meadow. That's the way it was with Christ.

"It is those people, yes, people - humans, they're the ones I live with now. They took me in and offered me peace in the knowledge and direction of the universal consciousness. They have given me new life and with their God given technology, perpetual life if I choose to live forever.

"Personally, I think two or three hundred years should just about do it for me. I know that this is all incredible to you. Your head must be swimming with questions, doubt, and probably fears.

"So, first off, no one's here to hurt you. Second, our station is one and a half miles directly beneath Barnegat Lighthouse. Third, I have been sent to the surface many, many times but this time I have been instructed to contact you.

"It is much easier to be on the surface now because most of my contemporaries have passed on. I always ran the risk of being recognized. Now, only a few remain. Other than two of my daughters and you, there remains only one of my dear old friends who would surely recognize me.

"Percy Gladcris is past ninety now and still fishes the bay and ocean every day. Bless his heart. I know, I've watched him. God, how I have wished I could just show up on the dock one day and say 'Percy, let's go out and nail some blues today.' He is another one who has a love and devotion for the peace, tranquility, and healing properties of the bay.

"We always shared that unspoken feeling every time we sat out on the bay or drifted along the oceanside beaches near Barnegat Inlet. But, you see Kevin, if I broke security, that would be a breach of my contract with my benefactors. You, though, are a different story. I had to come to you at this time.

"Haven't you ever wondered why you have done so well in business? In the past eight years hasn't it seemed as if everything was going your way? Hasn't it all seemed a little too easy? You have had help. I know that you have felt that something was pushing for you. You know full well that you instinctively have been drawn to this place like a salmon to its river.

"Year after year, decade after decade, you have come back to these waters, and now to this exact spot directly over one of our rejuvenation water vents. There is a plan for you and a role for you to play just as it has been for me and had been for my grandfather before me.

"Every other generation has been skipped. You and I are descended from one of several families who have always been the direct contacts of the original settlers. This chain of contact was set up just before the death of Christ. Two of the seven original operatives were in fact disciples of Christ.

"They and I and many more earthlings like us represent the local Earth council of the planet Soclar. The events of the world dictated that you should be contacted earlier than had been anticipated. I will explain all of this to you later."

Kevin found himself taking this all in as if it were the most natural thing in the world for him to be sitting side by side with his "born again" grandfather. He blurted out, "Fine, now I have three things for you.

"If I am to take all of this on face value I'm telling you here and now that I have a life to live. I do not need complications. I have a family that depends on me and I'm just beginning to enjoy life.

"Second, how did you do it? How did you fake death and come back after almost thirty years down the pike, looking more like sixty than seventy-three and a fit sixty at that?

"Third, in a few minutes the boys are going to be back. Just what am I going to tell them? 'Boys, I want you to meet your great-grandfather who has a new career as the *creature from the deep*?'"

Hank chuckled and said, "I'm glad you can joke about this. That's good. You are going to need a sense of humor to see you through during the next few days. You're going to have to have perspective. A sense of humor is going to be a big part of that, son. But, you've always had one, and it's something you don't lose.

"Let me answer your questions the best I can. One thing though, you mustn't tell the children. I must have your word on that. So much depends on secrecy and discretion in our work. The story of my staged death and my return is going to take some time. I have to be able to sit down with you for a couple of undisturbed hours. I am going to lay it all out for you from soup to nuts. But, I need your undivided attention for that."

With that, the thumping clatter of the boys scurrying aboard resounded through the deck to the aft cabin below. Hank followed Kevin up the spiral staircase from the galley to the wheelhouse to find the boys puffing and out of breath.

"Beat ya."

"Did not."

"Did so," they argued.

Kevin interrupted, "Hey, hey, whoa, you race horses. Don't you see we have a guest?"

Andrew piped up, "Sorry, dad, but we came back to see if you were OK. We didn't hear the horn. Are we going to go fishing or not?"

"We sure are, Bonzo-burger," started Kevin. "In fact we are going to do better than that. We'll take the big boat out, drift for fluke in the ocean, and then camp out in the middle of the bay on the boat tonight. It's supposed to be clear, warm and calm for the next couple of days. What do you say about that, guys?"

"Now, you're talking Dad! Great!!!" The boys chimed. Kevin introduced Hank, "Boys, this is a very old friend of mine. In many ways I feel like we are family. This is Mr..."

Hank extended his hand abruptly and said, "Just call me Pop, boys."

Turning to Kevin, Pop seized the opportunity. "Well, Kevin, since we are old friends, how about if I tag along on this adventure? Do you have room?"

Kevin was caught off guard, but caught Hank's look, knowing that he wanted to talk further. "Sure, Pop. After all this time, I would have it no other way."

The few things on the boston whaler were transferred over to the yacht. The boys helped Kevin and Pop secure everything that was loose. The televisions were tied down with rubber stretch cords, the plates and glasses were put away, and all the little decorative ornaments were put down on couches or into drawers. Kevin started up the generator and switched from shore to on-board power. The heavy power cables were pulled onto the deck. Next the cable TV line and the telephone line were gathered in.

Kevin started up the twin 220-horsepower diesel engines so that they could warm up for a few minutes. The boat cruised at ten knots and topped out at thirteen knots. Perhaps, it wasn't the fastest of boats, but it sure could cruise for long distances. It held 1,200 gallons of fuel. It consumed a miserly ten gallons every hour. It could make it nonstop to Florida on one fill-up if the need ever arose. Also, it could stay at anchor in the middle of the bay for almost two months if necessary. The generator could go and keep on going with that 1,200 gallons of fuel on board.

Kevin was now on the flying bridge. The last of the ropes were cast off. He put the gear shifts into forward. The boat inched forward out of the slip with the throttles completely pulled back to dead slow. Once clear of the marina, Kevin throttled up and headed for the nearby inlet. They set a course that was an hour and a half down the coast toward Beach Haven.

Hank climbed the ladder to the flying bridge with ease. He showed no sign of stiff muscles or joints. Just before Hank died (or had everyone believing that he had died) he was bent from arthritis and was weak and stiff from inactivity and chronic emphysema.

After the group cleared the inlet, the boys quickly retreated to their cabin to play video games. Pop, seeing that everyone was settling in for the trip, turned to Kevin and said, "Keep an open mind, Kevin. What I'm about to tell you is going to be difficult for you to comprehend.

"When I first met these guys there was none of this modern technology or science-fiction junk that you folks have now. What mankind has achieved in space and science in the last thirty years will give you a perspective that I never had. Just give me a chance to go through the whole magilla. Don't make any value judgements about what I decided and did until you hear me out."

Pop leaned up against the flying bridge wall and unfolded his incredible tale to the drone of the humming diesels.

-CHAPTER THREE-

The dew was still clinging to the windshield of the *Sanctuary* on this particular morning in August 1959. Hank flipped on the windshield wipers as he made his way toward the channel and his destiny with the unknown that he sought that morning.

He knew that he was not a fisher of game or food that morning but rather of truth and maybe even hope. He wasn't sure of what hope he was looking for or what truth...hope for mankind, hope for the future, hope for his family, hope for himself?

Ever since the encounter with the flying object several days before, Hank realized that he had witnessed something very special. He also felt instinctively that what he saw not only wanted to explore but wanted to be seen as well.

It was too convenient. The closeness of the encounter and the speed of the passage told Hank that someone or something inside the craft wanted to be visible, wanted to make an impression. But why? Why didn't it stop and make contact?

Perhaps if he had been alone, it might have made a difference. Perhaps they thought it would be too much for the boy. This was intuited by Hank. He felt it as the craft passed. He didn't know how, but he had a strange and unexplainable sense that was exactly what the inhabitants intended.

Hank cleared the inlet twenty minutes later. He headed for the bell buoy five miles out. He could hear the clanging slow rhythm of the buoy riding over the waves almost two miles before he reached it.

The buoy was like a welcome friend to those who navigated those waters. When night crept up a little too quickly or if an unexpected fog rolled in, you could always get a bearing from the bell buoy. It was a comforting sound as Hank approached.

Suddenly, Hank felt a sharp rap on the hull of his boat. He must have struck a log or other floating debris in the water. He looked behind the boat and saw nothing. There was no apparent damage, but he thought that he'd better make sure. He put the engine into idle and went below. Everything was fine. He throttled up the engine again and returned to his course. It was then that he heard it.

The rushing sound of water, like the cascading roar of a river over a precipice reached Hank's ears. It was nearly deafening him as he whirled his head around with an ever increasing sense of panic.

He yelled, "Shoot, it's a damn submarine, and it's going to ram me!" as the object raced to catch up behind his boat. The rounded top of the object was the only thing visible above the water's surface. The displaced water rushing in to fill the vacuum left by this thing as it rocketed through the water was the cause of the thunderous intrusion of the morning's serenity.

Hank turned the wheel hard to port. The object followed him. He knew that if he went much further to port he would run hard aground at the speed he was going. He turned the wheel hard to starboard and thrust the throttle as far forward as he could. The engine strained. He could not keep this up for long. The old worn Gray Marine engine would start overheating soon. He looked again behind himself just as the pursuing object dipped below the water's surface.

Beads of perspiration were dripping down Hank's

face and soaked the back of his shirt. He cut the engine and drifted, gasping for breath. His lungs and heart could not take this stress. He fell dizzily back into his wheelhouse chair thinking that he had escaped whoever was playing tag with him.

"Damned Russian sons of bitches. They have nothing better to do than to play tag with an old man, scaring him half to death? What the hell's wrong with them?" The thought of Russians he could deal with. He was looking for something flying in the sky...not for what had just happened or for what appeared next.

Again, the hard thud on his hull. The boat leaned acutely to one side. Hank saw nothing to either side except water. In back he saw what he thought was the large conning tower of a submarine. It was huge. The superstructure was made of a mirrored black metallic substance fading to a dull sandy color toward the top of the rounded tower. It looked like an upside-down soup bowl with no windows.

But it was too far back to be affecting his boat like this. It must have been back a hundred yards or so. His boat was being lifted out of the water inch by inch. The conning tower like structure kept rising as well.

Hank again looked down. This time he saw that the water was draining away rapidly from whatever was lifting him up. The same metallic substance appeared underneath the boat. An outline of the object started to appear.

Hank swooned. The enormity of what was happening around him started to sink in. This object could not have been of this earth. It extended back another hundred yards behind the conning tower. That rounded tower was the only raised portion of the object's surface. The overall shape appeared to be round with a diameter of 250 yards; bigger than anything that Hank ever saw afloat. It certainly dwarfed any submarine that he had ever seen.

Hank's heart raced to the point that he thought that it would quit on him. His blood pressure was up so high that his ears rang. He tried to tell himself that if they wished to kill him he would have been dead already. They could have just rammed him. What did they want with him? Was it possible that they actually knew he was looking for them?

But this wasn't what he was looking for. What he sought was much smaller and was airborne. Hank knew that he was about to black out but he fought to stay conscious.

Suddenly, a warm orange glow emanated from the object, surrounding the boat. It was like a calming drug to Hank. His heart stopped pounding. Inside his head he could sense something telling him, "shhh...calm, calm...shhh. You're going to be all right," as his mother calmed him as a boy.

From the surface of the object a clear globe like shield, seemingly made from Plexiglass, started to rise from left to right. The shield was about eighty feet in diameter. It completed its semicircular transit over the top of the boat and then closed with an echoing and clicking hollow thud.

Hank could feel that the air around him was being pressurized. He had to pinch his nose and blow to pop his ears. It was like being in an airplane that was pressurizing its cabin. But, he saw that he hadn't moved, yet.

Without warning the craft went down, slowly at first. Then the craft accelerated forward and downward with Hank and the *Sanctuary* in tow under the bubble. He saw fish all around him that rapidly turned to blurry streaks as he went faster and faster, deeper and deeper.

Hank estimated that they had descended at least ninety feet into the depths of the Atlantic when the craft finally came to rest on the bottom.

A sense of excitement had replaced the sense of panic that Hank had felt at the surface. It was a nurturing entity, not a malevolent entity that he was confronted with. He knew this in his gut.

Something was going to happen, something that Hank had felt was going to happen for a long, long time, something good. It was as if he had had an appointment with this day for his entire life. He began to feel as if this were his birthday, Hanukkah, Christmas, New Year's Eve, and Thanksgiving Day rolled into one.

The **Sanctuary** started going down again. This time it was going down on the platform under the dome. Hank was going below the deck. It was a lot like an aircraft carrier platform with the floor closing above him becoming the ceiling.

As he dropped, he saw considerable activity below. Men and women were rushing around working and pushing equipment. With the whooshing sound of air escaping from a pressure valve, the platform came to rest on the inner working deck of the most technologically advanced, gargantuan craft that mankind could ever hope to see, (at least mankind of this century).

Everyone on the deck was in uniform. The uniforms were all one piece, certainly not of any nation that Hank knew of. The activity was like sailors being called to general quarters. The platform that his boat was on folded into a V, supporting the boat in a level position. The crew disappeared behind round doors that opened and closed like the shutter of a camera.

The craft started moving again. There were several windows that Hank could see from. There was one large one that was closest to Hank just outside the clear dome in which he was being held captive. It appeared that they were turning and heading back toward land. Yes, he was certain of it. He first saw the chain and weight for the bell buoy and then the two chains of the two buoys marking the beginning of the approach to the inlet. The rounded craft moved very smoothly across the bottom. The craft then turned forty-five degrees to the left on its own axis while still going in the same direction. Then, almost like an afterthought, it changed the direction of motion to coincide with the orientation of the completed spin maneuver.

The craft traveled slowly, almost at a creep for about five minutes. A tone sounded much like a hospital's overhead pager, and a pulsing blue light flashed simultaneously on the ceiling. Men and women hurried in from several opening doors. They took up positions at work station consoles that were separated by huge pipes and valve like configurations.

A barely perceptible vibrating shudder could be felt. Then a powerful humming of turbines or other type of engines along with the rushing sound of water could be heard from every direction.

Hank looked out the windows again and saw a storm of sand swirling in every direction. The massive turbulence was causing the craft to sink into the sand. A resounding metallic clank rang through the entire chamber. They had struck something. There was a secondary sound, like metal sliding over metal, under the area of the original contact noise.

Hank could see occasional miniature avalanches of sand cascade from the upper rim of the craft. The rim had to be only a few inches above the sandy bottom.

"The damn thing covered itself up like a damn manta ray," Hank commented to himself. With the craft's smooth rounded mound of a conning tower, that's how it must have looked from above.

The V platform that held the *Sanctuary* sank further down toward the deck floor until the handrail of the boat was level with the floor that closed in almost flush around the vessel. Taking this as an invitation, Hank walked out onto the floor and over to the perimeter of the dome.

Some of the humanoid occupants walked toward him with a strange mixed expression of indifference and curiosity. The rest walked toward a cylinder that was rising from the floor. With a diameter of ten feet, the monolithic presence stood impassively and motionless for a moment. Then the cylinder with its door half facing Hank rotated to the right. The door disappeared within the wall of the cylinder like a door of an elevator disappearing behind the wall.

Transfixed with a mixture of fear, awe, and confusion, Hank watched three men emerge from the strange cylinder. One of them was his grandfather Gross Pop, who had disappeared from this life in what was thought to have been a boating accident in the Atlantic off the beach of Seaside Heights, New Jersey, almost thirty-six years before.

The hard bubble like dome around the boat vanished into thin air as the three men walked toward him with a deliberate yet cordial demeanor. "Gross Pop, how can it be? You look so much younger than I remember you. What happened to you? Please, what strange ship is this and why are you with these men? Why have I been captured?"

Gross Pop stood patiently, waiting for Hank to finish. He put his right arm around Hank's shoulders. "Welcome to the **Star Seeker III**. Come, walk with me."

They walked through one of the strangely configured doors down a corridor that was lit by the metal itself. The structural material had its own luminosity. He was to later learn that this metal had elements in it that actually phosphoresced brightly as a result of the electromagnetic fluxes generated by both the planet and by the craft's gravity condensers.

"I know this is all very foreign and confusing to you. I will answer all of your questions. First, however, let me get you something to eat. We will sit and talk this all out."

Gross Pop faced Hank, put his arms around him and gave him a loving hug. "My son, I've missed you and I love you. Back when I was among you and the rest of the family, such feelings between father, son, grandfather, grandson, or brothers were just not shown or expressed. That type of demonstration expressed between men in America was considered to be a sign of weakness at that time.

"You see, it wasn't discouraged, but it sure wasn't encouraged because it would bring one's manhood into question. I am sorry for that. Thank God that at least now I have been given a second chance to tell you these things; although late and from what you might consider to be a ghost."

The other two men walked behind Hank and his grandfather. "First thing, son, they call me by my name here. You might as well call me Joseph, too."

Hank thought that this seemed appropriate, since his grandfather looked much younger than he looked himself. They sat down in what appeared to be normal, cushioned armchairs in what looked like a cafeteria. The exception was that everything was prepared by machinery that hummed behind the luminous structural metal.

"First things first. Let's order something," Joseph offered. Out from a sliding panel came two plates with a metallic covering over them. After prying the magnetized plates free, they walked back to the table where the other two gentlemen were already seated.

For the first time one of the other two spoke. They were so unobtrusive and calm in their deportment that Hank nearly forgot they were even seated at the same table. The black man spoke first.

"The fish is fresh grouper. They are raised right below our feet. Go ahead and chow down. We have already eaten, but we'll keep you company.

"I can see that we can't depend upon Joseph to make the formal introductions. He's been practicing for this day for a week, so he thinks that we all know each other already."

Joseph flushed red and apologized.

The black man continued, "I am Captain Moses Senecus. I am the captain of this earth based spacecraft. The station itself is commanded by Commander Joshua Leotor. He is currently preoccupied, but wishes to send his regards. I am sure you will meet in the future.

"I am actually from Earth and have lived between Earth and what is now my home planet for 415 earth years."

Hank's mouth dropped open as the captain continued: "I was born on a spacecraft much like this one. My mother was from Earth. My father was an officer from our home planet, Soclar, and was part of our ongoing interplanetary liaison with Earth and its people.

"This is our first officer Lieutenant Abdul Lasamar. Abdul, why don't you tell our guest a little about yourself?"

The second man looked Egyptian. His complexion was coppery tan. His eyebrows were thick. His eye sockets were deep. His hair was black and wavy.

His cheekbones were high and pronounced. He had a broad forehead and large cranium. His nose was romanesque and his lips were full. His chin was pronounced, broad, angular, and dimpled. He was erect and erudite. Another thing was obvious, he was taking everything in without comment or change of expression.

"Mr. Feidor, I am one hundred percent Soclarian. I am 681 years of age. My furlough from this tour is long overdue and I am counting the days for my vacation back on Soclar, if the truth must be known."

This guy is getting a bad case of foreign port burnout, Hank reflected. Hank saw this in the Navy and was a victim of it himself. You miss the familiar when you are away. When you are a stranger in a foreign land (even with many of your own people around you), you feel like a stranger and yearn for the comfort within your home community (if that place was peaceful and the memories were happy and pleasant ones).

Abdul continued, "My ancestors and their colleagues were among the original ambassadors to the Nile region here on Earth. Much of the culture and civilization of what you call ancient Egypt resulted from the technical and academic interactions and, I may add, intermarriages between the original settled stock and our educated and totally briefed liaisons."

Captain Senecus picked it up from there. "After we stopped today, there was a loud thud you must have heard. That was the point at which we attached this craft to our Atlantic coast underground operations and wildlife rejuvenation base. We call it Earth Station Barnegat Light.

"There are six of these bases on Earth. The others are located in Alaska, close to Kodiak, near the North Pole, the South Pole, under a reef off Australia's

Queensland Coast and under the Persian Gulf near the Strait of Hormuz.

"The Persian Gulf installation was our first. Colonists were established along the Tigris and Euphrates rivers in the area that is now called Iraq. The settlements were responsible for fostering the seeds of civilization on this planet. This area has historically been our most active area and coincidentally has always proven to service our most recalcitrant charges. We are laboring not to have to write this portion of the planet off. Time is short in that regard, I am afraid. Also, it looks like they could take the rest of the planet with them, given enough time.

"This particular one that is under us now is approximately the size of New York City and has twelve levels. By elevator tube the first of the levels is about one mile below this craft. The other five locations are more or less the same size."

Joseph interrupted. "Abdul, at this point I have to fill in some background for Hank. I'm sure he's confused about the difference between original settled stock from our planet and further population interventions effected by Soclar."

Joseph went on to tell the story that Hank was destined to repeat to Kevin almost thirty years later on Kevin's boat. After finishing most of the background, Joseph went on; "So, you see Hank, we have really been here from the beginning. We've just been out of sight most of the time.

"In any event, tonight might be one of those times when a UFO will be sighted, because you are going with us to our planet for a short visit."

This made Hank sit up and take exception. "I might have some kind of destiny with you guys according to your scheme of things, but I have a life and a choice about what I want to do and where I want to go. I have people who love me and depend on me up top. I really don't want to go flying off to never-never land without carefully considering this and at least being able to say good-bye."

"Hold on, hold on there a minute," Joseph said with his hands in front of himself urging Hank to stop for a moment.

"No one is going to force you to do anything. However, there are several things about yourself I think you have to know right now...things you probably already know deep down that must be considered during your deliberations.

"When you were first under our neutrino shield, our scanning sensors detected something that we have suspected for some time now. You have emphysema, high blood pressure, cardiovascular disease, and, topping the list, cirrhosis of the liver.

"For God's sake, Hank, your heart muscle is like a bag of tissue paper. In a matter of weeks you are going to develop an esophageal varicosity. You will bleed out.

"In short, you can pop off now at any time, without notice. Your brain is on the verge of being turned into a pickled marshmallow between the booze, the ammonia levels, and other chemical buildups going on in your body. It's just a matter of time before you turn into a bedwetting gork if the other stuff doesn't get you first."

Tears from the recognition of the truth being spoken welled up in Hank's eyes. "What can I do? I've been through so much pain in my life. I just want it to stop. I love life, but the stress from my family and other things is just too much for me to bear sometimes without the booze. I'm not a strong man. I'm not made of steel."

Hank never did recover from the Great Depression, when he and his family were reduced to having to eat dandelion leaves for dinner because there was no money to buy anything at all to eat. What toll does this take on a man with a family? What toll does it take on the love and respect for the man of the house in a marriage?

Alcoholics look for any reason to keep drinking. They blame their drinking on others, saying it's someone else's fault. At least that's what they have to believe in order to give themselves permission to slowly kill themselves.

Hank's subsequent job with a brewery, where the average worker consumed twelve bottles of beer a day, got him started down the road to alcoholism. The pattern of spiteful treatment from his wife that began during the Depression plus the alcoholism sent Hank well on his way to poor health. His end was predictable years in advance.

Joseph counseled, "The flesh is weak, Hank. I have met someone who has made me realize that and that it is OK. However, neither self-effacement nor self-reproach nor altering your lifestyle at this point are going to save your life.

"The time of your corporeal presence on this Earth is nearly at an end now. You asked me what you can do. There is salvation and life for as long as you want it. But before you decide, I want you to understand our mission more completely. I want you to feel good about it and your possible role in the scheme of things before you jump.

"This is not just an **out** to save your butt from a nagging wife and a dying body. Although these benefits will be a by-product of your choice, you must realize that you are going to have responsibilities with us.

"We need you as an emotionally strong person, able to stand on your own feet in order for you to be of any use to us. Your excuses will be taken away. The lies you have been telling yourself along with the real hardships that have helped shape your life will disappear and will no longer be a factor. You must come to grips with that right here and now.

"**Total responsibility** for self is the credo of our society and must be realized and adopted by you if you are going to fit in and function in your new role. I have something to show you. Follow me."

They walked back to the cylinder from which the three men originally emerged. The captain and the lieutenant opted to stay on board, and they bid Hank and Joseph farewell at the door of the lift. When the door closed, Joseph explained that they were first going to go down through the three levels of the craft through the air lock and then down into the nerve center located on the third level of Earth Station Barnegat Light.

As the lift came to a soft and quiet stop, the door rotated open. Walls of a transparent material held back millions, perhaps billions of gallons of water. Fish of every variety were in aquariums of unfathomable proportions. The crystal clear water and the eerie self-illuminating structural material made it evident to Hank that the tanks on this level extended for miles. What technology could make this possible he wondered?

Technicians were busily performing their functions. There was instrumentation everywhere.

"Hank, we are *THE KEEPERS* of this planet in every respect. It starts with the oceans. The oceans sustain the life of this planet, atmospherically, climatically and agriculturally. Between this station and the other five we effectively filter the waters of the oceans. Much of what you believe to be currents caused by the rotation

66

of the planet is not that at all.

"The primary impetus for these currents is our gravitational pumps. These pumps are essentially constructed of flat plates that extend for miles here underground. These plates are composed of a material developed on Soclar eons ago.

"The basic principle behind the material and the operation of the pump itself is the polarity reversal of the gravitational field concentrators used in these heavy plates.

"In the first of the two modes, the up mode, the material actually amplifies and concentrates the gravitational pull of the matter of the universe directly above and straight out into the heavens from each of our base locations around the world. The down mode depends mostly on the increased natural gravitational pull of the Earth. The plates, together with the two opposing forces, create an extremely powerful, rhythmic, slow, and perpetual pump. **We are the heart of this planet's life blood system.**

"Any energy can be concentrated, channeled or bent. Electricity can be made to flow through conductive wires. Steam, with its heat energy can be guided through pipes. Sound can be amplified, radio waves can be dispersed and collected. The rays of the sun can be bent and concentrated by a magnifying glass.

"It is the same with gravity. It can be concentrated and bent. Not only is there a down but an up and a side-to-side. It's all a matter of the direction we turn our concentrators.

"In theory, these plates, if proper polarity switching does not take place, are capable of concentrating gravity from the cosmos to the point of lifting themselves right out of the ground, destroying all land above them as they pull themselves toward the land masses of other galaxies.

"To this point we have chosen not to leak this information, mainly because it is the principle behind our ability to achieve light speed and beyond in our spacecraft. However, there is other technology involved. The inhabitants of this planet are not yet psychologically ready for this. Plus, quite frankly, their developed bellicose nature makes the inhabitants of this planet a threat to the rest of the universe.

"One might think that your military would have detected the seismic activities of our pump plates. However, they existed long before sensing devices were discovered by Earth's scientists.

"Your military and scientific community believe that the *white noise* seismic and other background created by these plates are manifestations of normal subterranean magma activity and normal geo-magnetic flux impulses. The x-ray impulses, radio wave impulses and various other phenomenon emanating from outer space and concentrating here on Earth as a result of our pumps' activities has been attributed to quasars, novas and other phenomenon.

"It would probably take decades before your own space probes would find that these phenomenon are less concentrated as one leaves the influences of the Earth's periphery. Even then, the weaker impulses that may register would be attributed to weaknesses due to diffuse signal transmissions, being that they would have no standard with which to compare. In other words, it would probably be a long--long time before they figure it out.

"We must insure that any knowledge of this technology never falls into the wrong hands or else much could be lost. Entire worlds could become runaway renegades affecting the gravitational influences of entire systems and the eventual balance of the universe as a whole. This is much like one atom striking another, causing a chain reaction, or like one billiard ball striking a racked set of balls causing them to bounce off the cushions of the table.

"However, in the vacuum of space this bouncing could go on and on, given the added feature of the inherent property of stars' and planets' mass attraction. The whole kettle of the universe is just calming down from such an event after six hundred fifty million years. We were not the first to experiment with this technology. Thank God we were the ones who could control it though. We have shared this technology with other civilizations. We just are not ready to share it with this one.

"There are many factors affecting the gene pool of each and every species of plant and animal on this planet. Radon gas, ultraviolet rays, gamma rays, radio waves from the stars, and other natural phenomenon collectively serve as mutating factors in the environment.

"We must constantly guard against the destruction of species of plants and animals by protecting, storing and breeding the existing successful gene pools of these organisms. The ocean is the most susceptible ecosystem because the species that are contained therein are the most fragile and vulnerable.

"When depletions of fish become critical to the point that the species may disappear, we make controlled releases along with the supply of staple food sources that they depend upon. This dual release is made in exacting proportions.

"If dangerous or unnecessary mutations start to take hold in a population, we then capture large quantities of the species and perform genetic engineering. We then, likewise, effect releases from our rejuvenation zoos and aquariums through vents and caves located at different points around each base station.

"One such vent from this station is located about one quarter of a mile west of the Barnegat Lighthouse. Another such vent is on the other side of the light house in deep water about one mile from where we now stand. This first vent is for the release of fry from various aquatic species or for bait fish that need protected waters to establish themselves.

"The byproducts of the filtration process are disposed of by molecular disruption caused by particle beam and laser light recombinant techniques. The resulting raw materials are reintroduced into the marine environment in diluted quantities. Our job has become harder and harder. Especially around this neck of the woods.

"As I have explained to you earlier today, we also send our agents to the surface to affect moderation of mankind's more destructive instincts and behaviors when those characteristics raise their ugly heads to threaten the world. Not all our agents are public figures. In fact very few are. They simply influence and advise those who are.

"Sometimes we are more successful than at other times. Sometimes, we fail. This is where you and I and others like us fit in. How does this sound to you? Are you in or out?"

Hank's response was immediate. "I'm in, Gross Pop. If I can look half as good as you and do God's work and some good for this world and mankind, then what more noble mission may I ever hope for?"

Joseph faced Hank and clasped his hands on his shoulders. "Good, then there is no time to lose. You must first visit Soclar for your initial cellular rejuvenation treatment.

"The first treatment will only arrest deterioration. A second treatment will be required in approximately eight to nine days, depending on the recommendation

70

of our physicians. Booster treatments must take place once every seventy-five years on Soclar for as long as you wish to remain among the living.

"Barring rare complications, accidents, and the like, how long you wish to live will remain your choice. The longest corporeal presence that I am aware of is that of one of our Earth ambassadors who chose not to rejuvenate twenty years ago. He was 2,657 years old. He wanted to move on.

"The technology for these treatments must never leave the home planet. That is why we must go there without delay. We really do not know how long you've got. We must leave this evening. The destiny to which you were born is too important for it to be lost down the neck of a whiskey bottle. If we act now, we won't have to worry about that."

The men walked together to the lift. They were transported to the level on which the *Sanctuary* rested. They walked toward the back of the craft through another camera-shutter door. Once through that door there was another lift that took them up into the conning tower section.

Once there, they found the rest of the crew already strapped in, ready for departure. There were about 150 crew members organized in rows facing forward. Instrumentation blinked information all around them.

The damndest thing was that the dome's walls, which were opaque and sandy colored from the outside, were completely transparent from the inside. They were in a huge fish bowl. Except that the fish were on the outside.

"Sit here and strap yourself in." Joseph gestured to a rather commodious chair located directly behind the command console chair occupied by Captain Senecus. In front of him on the left Lieutenant Lasamar

71

was seated. To the right of the lieutenant Joseph sat down and strapped himself in.

"We are very pleased with your decision, Hank" the Captain commented. "We need you and your special social abilities of which you are not even aware of yet. We will be leaving the ocean floor and making our way toward Soclar very soon now.

"Just as the veil of darkness descends upon the New Jersey coast, we will be making our departure. In a moment we will be taxiing, so to speak, along the ocean floor until we get to the Canyon."

The Canyon off the Jersey coast is an area much like the Grand Canyon, only underwater, located about 180 miles out.

"We are going to the Canyon in order to take advantage of the optimum geo-magnetic and gravitational influences that exist in that location in order to propel this craft out of the atmosphere with the least likelihood of detection. We don't like publicity.

"Within two and one-half seconds we will have passed the speed of light. Your seat is designed to compensate and to protect you from the effects of such rapid acceleration. In fact, the gravity-reversal technology will be working in a cone around each of these chairs in this chamber. You know, like you folks like to keep a refrigerator in a warm room in a house while it is below zero outside. The same analogous principle applies.

"After four seconds we will have reached a speed of three hundred times the speed of light. Although we will be on Soclar for a number of days, we will return you to this point with your boat with only one and a half days having gone by on Earth.

"Our dual-dimensional spatial time compensator apparatus will see to it that you will return to your home when you are expected. I know that this is hard for you to comprehend in total at this point, but are you following me in principle?" Hank gave a rather half-hearted nod.

"Hank, you are going to have some strange sensations before, during, and, for a few seconds, after light-speed attainment. This will be caused by the built-in protective shroud that will encircle you.

"The effects of this shroud will manifest themselves by a warm tingling sensation on the surface of your skin. You will feel euphoric for a moment, with a false sense of exaggerated well being and giddiness.

"Don't let these feelings frighten you. They are normal and will pass. For now, relax and enjoy the ride. Do you have any questions?" The craft started to glide forward.

Hank asked, "What if we hit something at that speed? Won't we be splattered all over kingdom come?"

The captain replied, "A reasonable question. This craft is constructed of the absolute hardest material in the entire universe. Nothing can penetrate it whatsoever after the final catalysts have been added. If we were hit broadside by a comet we would just be knocked to the side as if we were standing still. However, we will not be standing still.

"We go at such a high speed that we would vaporize any small objects and go clean through any larger ones, even if we did not have the help of the molecular transponder field.

"This field operates much like a television signal. It takes molecules instead of radio waves, scrambles them in front of the craft and rearranges them directly behind the craft on a constant basis so that nothing that we come into contact with is damaged in any way; life forms included.

"It is much like water filling in behind your hand as you move it through the water. At the speeds we go

73

and at the rate the transponder field functions, a bird would not miss a flap of its wings if we invaded its space. However, we always set courses to avoid large bodies of matter."

The water around them was now dark. Soon there was the calm announcement from Lieutenant Lasamar, "Six seconds to field-reversal convergence."

With a blinding light, a very slight sensation of being pulled backward and the symptoms described by the captain, Hank could see star after star passing by the observation command chamber in a blurring progression. There wasn't even time to get a glimpse of Earth as they departed.

"Our departures are generally abrupt like that, sorry. We take precautions like that so we are not seen. I hope you understand. You will probably hear of this when you get back, Hank," Joseph explained.

"What will be reported is a flash of light in the eastern sky accompanied by the deafening crack of an explosion. Some will say that it was night ballistic practice at Fort Dix. Some will say that it was an atmospheric disturbance. Others will swear that it was a UFO. You must remain silent, keeping our pact."

After what seemed like a half an hour, the blur of the rapid passage of stars past the dome slowed so that each star could be seen as a point of light. Smaller objects passed by. They appeared to be planets and asteroids. As the craft slowed, an emerald green and blue planet loomed directly in front of them. It hung in the heavens before them like a jeweled pendant.

A voice crisply announced over a speaker; "Welcome back home, **Star Seeker III**. Captain, you are cleared for landing on Approach 32 Alpha. Your designated field will be on land at Quad 4. Please proceed. Copy?"

Captain Senecus responded in the affirmative.

Things happened so fast after that point that Hank barely had time to assimilate it all. He remembered being taken to a hospital like facility where he was poked, probed, examined, injected and scanned. He knew that he had been sedated, but did not know how long he was out for. After, he vaguely remembered being put back into his seat on the **Star Seeker III** in a semi-stupor state, like he was just coming out of anesthesia.

It seemed almost moments later that he woke up at the helm of the *Sanctuary*. He found a good haul of fish in his iced fish box that was open behind him. The engine was idling in gear. The wheel was pulled completely to the right causing the boat to make wide lazy circles.

"Hank?" Joseph's voice questioned over the marine radio.

"This is the *Sanctuary* back to the vessel calling on channel ten. What happened? What do I do now?" He was still a little woozy.

Joseph responded: "Hank, only you can hear me on this radio. We are right under you. You have had your first treatment and accompanying injections. You have three days to make your good-byes without letting the cat out of the bag before you go into a death like state.

"Make certain that you place in your will that you must be buried at sea completely nude except for a sheet covering your body and that your body must not be mutilated in any way: no embalmment nor any other invasive procedure may be done.

"You must insist in your will that your burial at sea take place early in the morning the day following what will appear to be your death. That will make it this coming Thursday morning. You must be specific that you wish this burial to take place near the bell buoy where you now are. We will be waiting for you. Your burial shroud must be weighted so that you do not somehow get lost in the current. Do you understand me?"

Hank indicated over the radio that he did.

"Hank, if this is not done, you will in fact die. The salt water will serve as the electrolytic medium by which your life force will be recharged and restored to you. Never mind the physiology behind it; you just have to know that it works. With what you have floating around in your bloodstream, it is important that the sea water soak your skin completely.

"Early on Wednesday morning at about 3:00 am you will enter the death like state, but you won't be dead. You might as well have a few drinks Tuesday night 'for the road' so to speak. It will probably help you cope with what you have to face. There is no reason whatsoever to be afraid. However, this is something you don't go through every day. Just be careful not to get too talkative.

"One more thing. You must find some pretense to make absolutely certain that your lawyer calls you first thing on Wednesday morning. If he does not, then your family may start normal burial and embalming procedures. That will mean curtains and all bets will be off.

"OK, I want you to repeat these instructions back to me."

Hank repeated the instructions accurately. When he was finished, Joseph informed him, "There is no turning back now. The course is set and your destiny with it. Good luck, Hank. God bless you.

"You know that you will be missed and that you will also miss those whom you are leaving behind. But now you have another chance and you are grasping that chance. Let there be no second thoughts.

You must be resolute in the notion that you have no other choice.

"If you were not going to come with us, you soon would be dead to them and to yourself. Now you will only be dead to them. However, you will be part of a greater whole; a destiny that will ultimately aid those you are leaving and their children for generations to come. Take solace and comfort from that thought and hold it in your heart for the next few days. See you on Thursday."

Joseph's voice cut off with a crackling of the radio. Hank turned it off, turned the boat toward home and headed in.

- CHAPTER FOUR -

Kevin turned from Pop, took a deep breath, and exhaled with a whistle as he leaned forward over the fly bridge wheel with his hands clenched tightly around the stainless steel wheel.

"What do you do for an encore, Pop? I thought I was *driving* the only tough *ACT* to follow. Let me have a little time to digest this.

"I always knew deep down in my being that intelligent life was out there. I had no idea that one of those societies was playing an active role in our destiny. It's simply incredible. But, you know what? It's comforting to know, in a way.

"Why not go public with it? What's the big deal? I think the world would welcome such intervention in our screwed-up affairs. Look at the world today. God knows that we could be on the brink of Armageddon right here and now. What harm would there be in revealing the existence of Soclar and its agents? They should have faith in their progeny here on earth.

"If the children have the capacity for destroying the world and the capacity for evil that surrounds that possibility, don't they, also, have the ability to create and embody the antithesis of that and possess the collective communal ability for good?

"Why not let us out of our cage with the freedom of truth that you possess and allow their charges to show you how we can soar?

"You know, Pop...I'm not sure of **what** you have or have not witnessed with your friends...with your heads under the water or under the sand. But, you know what? There's something I've found out here in the *real* **world**...my world...OK, our world. Your greatest pain comes from people, even the ones you love. But, your greatest joys come from people too. If you let the pain rule your day-to-day dealings, your life, your destiny, then you never see the true nature of people. You guys should trust us.

"Sure, people lie, steal, kill, cheat on their spouses and their taxes, but that is not humanity. A person, humanity as a whole, **is not a deed** and cannot be written off as being that one deed. The collective and deep-routed nature of mankind is a good nature. I just know it. I feel it.

"There are forces loose on this planet that cater to, pander to, and unfortunately control the communal consciousness of the masses. Those forces exhort the individual to deny his inner nature and his inherent God-given concept of right and wrong...of good and evil.

"I have found, though, that if you go one-on-one with each member of any group that has engaged in evil crowd behavior, such as the taunting and beating of the only Jew in a small town school as was my case, you remember, or even those who get caught up in the KKK, those people don't want to be known as bad. They just are being defensive, shallow, ignorant, and are pursuing the love of some surrogate family, you know, the group.

"That doesn't make them evil or bad. It makes them human; seeking human comfort, acceptance, pride, fulfillment, and, yes, a sense of love within a very inappropriate framework and at the expense of their fellow man. Yet they are God's children.

"At times, the overwhelming need to be loved and accepted within a wider scope outside of self and self-awareness overshadows the inherent concept of **good** and one's awareness of the rights of those outside '**the group**' one wishes to impress and be loved and accepted by...the extended or surrogate family. Whether or not they stand for right or wrong is not the issue.

"I have had pain from the ones I love and from people that I had grown to trust. So have most people. I have found that, if I withdraw from people so I don't get hurt, I never experience the joy of the benign, loving and good side of humanity. One can't experience intimacy without risking vulnerability.

"I submit to you, Pop, that you guys have become as jaded as many of the defensive charges you claim to be protecting. If you truly wanted to make the most significant and positive impact, you would come clean with the dwellers of this planet... now.

"Clearly, there are nuts out there leading frightened people. Sure, there are those who have been warped by a deprived childhood or other experience. Certainly, there is much to mistrust about humanity. But, guess what? If you're all that fired advanced and almighty, then give these sheep you are shepherding a different drum to march to.

"What are you afraid of? Are you afraid that once the curtain is raised that there really will remain little or no difference between Earthlings and Soclarians? Take a chance. What do you really have to lose? Or is there something I don't know about?"

Hank started, "Well, if you would get off your self-righteous soap box for just one damn minute, maybe I can get a word in edgewise and answer that question. The answer is, we *are* ready for that.

81

"The world is on the brink of a nuclear holocaust. That is where you fit in, Kevin. You are way ahead of me even before I make my pitch to you. I am heartened to realize that you harbor these thoughts regarding your fellow man, because there isn't much time. You have confirmed to me that you are the man for the job. It will be you, Kevin, who will be the catalyst, the link between our two societies.

"The tensions in the Persian Gulf right now make it clear to us that either people come together soon and realize their place in the universe and in the scheme of the universal consciousness, or all will be lost.

"If everyone keeps on insisting that their position is cut and dry or that they have the only *right* position, then everyone on the surface of this planet will be right, *dead right*... permanently.

"We'll talk tonight. Let's have some fun. I have new great-grandsons to get to know. For the time being, I think the best thing for me to do is play the roll of your friend, Pop. I'll let you tell them in your own time and own way. However, for the moment I must insist that confidentiality be the byword.

"How come their mother isn't here? I want to get to know her, too, or is there a reason why she isn't here today? After all this time I still know you well enough to tell something just ain't right. We might be high-tech, but, we don't eavesdrop on people's bedrooms. What's up? Come clean with me."

Kevin related the abbreviated version of a failed marriage story. He was too overwhelmed with the events of the last two days to be able to rehash what seemed like a very bad dream.

After a time he realized that the going over and over again of the same old story even bored him. It took him so long of listening to his own complaining about how bad things were, how little sex he had, how things were going from bad to worse before he had the guts to do anything about it, that he just wanted to let it drop after a brief "It just didn't work out" comment. He knew old Pop wouldn't accept that, but it would have to do for now.

The **ACT I** arrived at Kevin's choice for a fishing spot one-half mile off the beach of Long Beach Island's southern shore. He blew the horn to let the boys below know that it was time to drop their fishing lines into the water. He killed the engines and got down from the bridge.

There was a steady gentle wind blowing up the coast from the south. It allowed the **ACT I** to drift parallel to the coast right back to the inlet. It was 11:30 am; a little late to get started fishing, but with a leisurely drift they could have three hours of fishing and talking before choosing a nice isolated spot to anchor out in the bay for the night.

The bait box went overboard. Everybody lent a hand getting the fishing tackle to the front of the boat. The **ACT I** was built for cruising, not really for fishing. But if you are on the water anyway, the fish don't know the difference. The boat had a long, broad forward exposed deck with a railing. That's all you need. Put a large cooler on the deck and there's the required fish box.

The boys put some squid and killies on their hooks, played out their lines until the sinkers skimmed along the bottom of the ocean floor and sat back in their deck chairs. They were set for the day and were in seventh heaven. What would make it just perfect would be some fluke.

Hank went below to get some snacks for everybody while Kevin got sodas for the crew. Why did everything seem so normal? Yet it did, and it was. Nothing had seemed so right to Kevin for a long time.

It was as if all was right with the world.

Sitting on the front deck and looking at the boys basking in the sun, he thought about where he had been and how far he had come. He wasn't the richest man in the world, but comfortable enough to indulge this whim for a motor yacht.

He used to feel guilty about it in the beginning. It was so decadent in many ways. But seeing the boys like this just hanging out, relaxing, and learning to appreciate the ocean and not having to go back to a hotel room made it all worthwhile.

Living on the boat was like camping out in style. It was one of the very few escapes Kevin had from the rat race and the pain of his former marriage. His thoughts drifted back to his glib comment to Pop that "it just didn't work out."

Kevin's ex-wife did not like anything about nature...not a day on the water fishing, a night camping out, an afternoon in the sun, in fact nothing with physical exertion unless it had some practical purpose like making a bed or ironing a shirt.

She was far from lazy. She just did not like to work up a sweat, throw a ball, ski down a slope, hike a trail, paddle a canoe or just about anything Kevin wanted to do for recreation as a couple or as a family.

This was why Kevin felt so alone and cheated. He knew that she probably felt the same way about her plight, having no interests outside of the home or any friends. It was lonely for her, too.

She had a deep rooted jealousy for anything that took Kevin out of the house when he was not working. The only thing that would have made her happy is if he could have gone to work, then home, then back to work, then home again. He tended to stay away more and more until he just hated to go back into the same house with her. Her resentment grew and so did Kevin's attempt to escape it.

Kevin felt she resented his successes in business and his ability to make friends almost on the spot. He realized that life with her over the long haul would be a lonely and alienated existence.

Their relationship wasn't always like that. They had lived together for a year before they tied the knot. The change after marriage was like the difference between night and day, Jekyll and Hyde. Marriage had ruined a completely acceptable love affair.

Friends stopped coming over; one couple actually storming out of the house in anger saying that they never felt more uncomfortable in anyone else's home, ever. That happens when a husband and wife don't get along. How could guests feel comfortable in such a setting?

Friends go to where they are wanted and respected; where their friendship and presence is appreciated and solicited. They go to where their own self-image is nurtured and to where their opinions, accomplishments in life, attention and affections count for something. Her insecurity alienated both of them.

Kevin did not want a divorce. It's doubtful that anyone entering a marriage goes into it with the notion that they will eventually be getting out of it. In large part the boat was purchased as a last resort, in an attempt to keep the family together. It didn't work.

As much as he wanted to put it out of his mind, Kevin couldn't help thinking about this major screw-up in his life. But his unwelcomed ruminating came to an abrupt end when a shriek of excitement broke the silence. Peter had hooked into something big.

Pop came up from the galley with a tray of snacks and slammed them down on the raised part of the bow meant for sitting and sunbathing. In one smooth leaping motion he grabbed the long handled wide fluke net and stood right next to the poor struggling kid.

"Stay with him, boy" Hank urged. "You can do it."

It was obvious, however, that perhaps he couldn't.

"Help me," Peter shrieked. "My arms are getting tired. It's going to pull me in. I can't hold on. Please, take him, take him. Take the pole."

Just when Kevin was about to take the pole, Pop said, "Hey Pete! That's just a little guy you've got there at the end of the pole. You're a big boy. Listen to me! Now, stop yankin' on that darn pole. Just hold it for a minute and let the fish get tired. That's it...rest it on the rail for a second--now, take a deep slow breath and let it out s-l-o-w-l-y while you finish reeling that thing up. Good...you're doing fine."

As Peter did what he was told, Pop reached down with the net and scooped up into the boat the largest "door mat" fluke that they had ever seen. The boys were beside themselves...so was Pop. There was screaming, jumping and scurrying about the likes of which had never been seen on the boat. Peter's face was beaming. He did it...and what a trophy!

Kevin went below into one of the cabins to get a camera and a hand held scale with a hook on the end of it. He didn't know what kind of hormones that thing took, but it looked more like a frigging haddock than a fluke and weighed twelve pounds. No wonder the poor kid nearly passed out.

These fish feel much heavier than they actually are when their flat bodies are forcing against the water. It was beautiful, dark and shiny. There were snow white tiny doughnut spots all over the top of it and its bottom was pure white. The head was large and its jaws were formidable.

Kevin whispered to Pop: "Did your buddies have anything to do with that?" Pop winked. They drifted up the coast, catching smaller, yet nonetheless good size fluke as they went. The snacks were consumed with relish. Barnegat Light loomed in the distance.

-CHAPTER FIVE-

It was time to find an anchorage. The sounds from waves crashing against the mammoth new Barnegat Light jetty grew louder and louder as the **ACT I** drifted closer toward the artificial peninsula. In another five minutes the question of where they would spend the night would be decided for them if they didn't get their buns out of there in a hurry.

"Lines up everybody" Kevin shouted to the motley crew. They were all tired from the fresh air and great fishing action. It was a great day to be alive and out in God's world. The engines responded immediately and they were off.

They rounded the tip of the jetty allowing for a respectable and safe distance margin and started in through the inlet into Barnegat Bay. They got to the lighthouse and made the ninety degree turn necessary to safely navigate the channel with a substantial following sea driven by the increasing off shore breeze.

"Just in time" Kevin said half out loud and half to himself. He hated to come in on a following sea. That was the only thing wrong with the yacht. It was top heavy and a real dog in a following sea. If a giant wave (which was frequently known to build in the inlet) caught them just right from behind, the boat could surf out of control and roll over.

The chances of that happening were pretty slim. However, you always had to maintain respect for and a close eye on that inlet. The yacht would probably right itself immediately, but, who needs the hassle? When the final touches go into the inlet project most of that problem should disappear, he thought.

Pop started cleaning the fluke and threw the heads and fins to the growing entourage of sea gulls escorting the yacht into the bay. As they passed "Old Barney" the water laid right down. It was smooth sailing from there on as Kevin released the extra air in his lungs that he had been holding.

No matter how many times he went in and out of that inlet he maintained the same healthy respect for its ability to claim crafts and, perhaps, lives of unwitting or careless captains.

Kevin was no mariner snob as so many become once they know a little something more than the non-boating or new-boating public. However, every summer it seemed that some new *Victory at Sea* type with no idea of the awesome power of the sea (and the dynamic forces involved in the inlet in particular) would tempt the fates; have a couple of drinks, wait till the last moment to come in during a building sea or just behave in a careless manner while entering the inlet, then...boom, disaster...putting his passengers' lives, his craft and his life in jeopardy.

It happened on a regular basis. Boating is fun when it is done safely. It can spell disaster if mindlessly abused or taken for granted.

Kevin hung a right and started nudging the nose of the boat carefully out of the channel, sniffing for the deep water he knew was there. He wanted to anchor as close as possible to one of the tiny uninhabited New Jersey state owned islands in front of them. They could then swim right off the boat and wade ashore if they wanted to.

The alarm on the depth meter was set to go off at seven feet. "B-e-e-e-e-p" The alarm warned...back off just a hair...feel around that shoal...they continued. There it was. The depth dropped off to fifteen feet. Kevin knew the way from there. He throttled up a bit and confidently steamed toward his favorite spot.

Good, he thought, nobody else was there yet. They had it all to themselves. The boat needed a fairly large area because Kevin had to put out about seventy-five to one hundred feet of anchor line. That meant that with the anchor in the center they could swing in a circle of a hundred and fifty feet or more. Then, the length of the boat had to be included.

"Pop, would you feed out the anchor? We're here." Pop dropped the one hundred pound anchor without even straining. Kevin put the engines into reverse. Pop let the anchor fall to the bottom. He played out about thirty-five feet of rope and wrapped it once around the windlass (power winch) until he could feel and see the tightening anchor line indicating that the anchor was taking hold of the clean sandy bottom.

Suddenly, the rope snapped taught, swinging the yacht to attention; front and center into the wind. The anchor had taken. He unwrapped the line and played out about another forty feet while signaling Kevin to keep backing up.

Hank yelled "Neutral!" The rope was tied off on the windlass' cleat. Now they could relax. The engines were allowed to idle for a few minutes to cool, then turned off.

All you could hear were the sea gulls and the muffled hum of the generator. Other than the small technicality of some space guy back from the dead being on board it just didn't get any better. Strangely, it somehow was all very right.

The reality was starting to sink in and the emotion started to well up inside of Kevin. His chest heaved.

He turned his face toward the water and allowed himself a tear of love and gratitude.

"Thank you God, for this miracle and for the wondrous fantasy which you have allowed to become my life."

"Dad, can we go swimming off the platform?" Andrew entreated.

"Sure guys. You know the rules. The life jackets have to be on and no rough-housing."

The pants came off to reveal bathing suits underneath. These guys were always ready. After all the activity from fishing (not to mention a rather odoriferous air about all of them) a cool swim was welcomed by all of them. Hank found a bathing suit below and over they went.

After about fifteen minutes of what degenerated into horseplay anyway (despite all intentions) an eighteen foot runabout idled up to within fifty feet of the yacht.

"Ahoy, Captain Murdock" a voice called from the boat. At first he didn't recognize her. He looked again. "What is she doing here". Kevin said aloud; as if to say 'Don't look at me, I didn't invite her here'.

It was Adrian Slater and an older woman; a friend or relative, perhaps. The Saturday before, Kevin had met Adrian at Two Bells Restaurant and Tavern located by the Coast Guard station near Barnegat Light. She was with a man at the time. Kevin made a polite gesture of inviting them out to the boat for a drink if they were ever out in the bay and saw him. It was one of those offers that no one ever takes you up on. Guess what?

"Here I am. Where's that drink you promised me?" She said leaning over the side to be heard.

She was beautiful. She was blonde with a statuesque build that would knock any man's socks off.

The two piece bathing suit she was almost wearing revealed legs that had no apparent endings and breasts that cried out to be set free to breathe.

"Huba--huba" Kevin muttered into the water.

The smiling older woman in the driver's seat was pretty good looking herself. She appeared to be about sixty three or so. Her hair looked dyed. No one can have purplish grey hair.

Kevin had recently noticed that more and more older women were either boating by themselves or with other older women. It used to be that when a husband died the boat was sold. Not anymore. So many widowed women who enjoyed boating with their husbands and families were now keeping the boats and using them after their husbands' deaths. Why not? Who said the enjoyment of God's great outdoors is gender related?

If looks could talk hers would have uttered volumes. She had that knowing chesire grin that said 'I know what you're looking at you horny son-of-a-bitch.' Her grin was correct.

Her passenger was about thirty six years old and had the looks of a beauty queen, the bearing of an educated lady and the gentle, feminine, sophisticated charm of a worldly socialite. All of this gleaned from a twenty minute conversation in a night club. However, somehow those charms and attributes were accentuated by that bathing suit.

"Sure, come alongside and tie up" Kevin called as he and Hank scaled the swim platform and ladder.

The boys stayed in the water near the swim platform. Adrian threw a line up to Kevin. He put rubber fenders out and directed both ladies to climb the ladder up from the swim platform.

"This is my mother Gerta Slater", Adrian offered.

"Pleased to meet you Mrs. Slater" Kevin re-

91

sponded as he reciprocated with a similar introduction of Hank.

"Please, no convention or formalities Kevin. Please, call me Gerta" she said in a thick German accent.

"This is a surprise" he continued. "I didn't think that I'd ever see you again. Now, out of the blue...Where is your husband?"

Puzzled, she asked "What husband? I've never been married. I'm married to my writing if anything. Oh! You mean the man you met at the bar while we were waiting for our table. That was my literary agent/publicist. He visits me at our home sometimes when we're here visiting the shore."

They sat on the aft deck of the yacht while Kevin prepared Cuba libres at the bar. What a delight both of these ladies were. Even Pop was getting into it. The boys had waded ashore to explore the island and look for shells. The four adults sat and talked for over an hour. It was one of those impromptu-spontaneous joys that come so infrequently into the lives of those immersed in their work and their own day-to-day living.

Apparently, Adrian and her mother did not inherit their boat (although Adrian's father had died two years earlier), but rather got a wild hair up their noses one day and went halves on the boat that looked more like a convertible sports car than something for the water.

According to Adrian, she and her mother lived together, splitting their time between Manhattan, the Jersey shore and a couple of vacations each year. Adrian wrote self-help and awareness books for single, divorced and or widowed women who have to cope in and with the work-place. By all appearances, she was quite successful at it.

She, also, taught one course in communication skills for business people at Columbia University and owned a company that did the same thing for working professionals in seminar settings. Somehow, she even found time to aid clients in the creation of booths and show marketing for trade shows. Some woman.

No wonder she had no time for a man. But, why should such a goddess be taken out of the running? She was a natural resource. 'Give us poor slobs a chance,' Kevin thought.

It was getting close to dinner. There was still plenty of light left in the summer sky. Kevin turned up the volume on the hailer and called to the boys on the beach to start back. They waved in recognition and waded into the water.

"Stay for dinner ladies," Kevin urged. "We have a mess of fluke and I have a secret beer batter that I'd love to treat you to. How about it?"

The ladies agreed saying that they couldn't stay too late because they didn't want to go back to the marina in darkness.

The boys got back, dried off, said hello to the guests and made their expected pilgrimage to the video games in their quarters before dinner. Hank and Kevin retreated to the galley to cook, leaving the ladies to relax on the aft deck. Kevin turned on the soft music of the yacht's stereo system and the mood was set.

"Kevin, although I know your hormones need a chance to express themselves for a change, you and I have some very important ground to cover very soon. It can't wait. You must be briefed and trained," Hank admonished.

"Pop, you heard them. These ladies will not be staying all night and besides, I haven't had the pleasure of the company of a woman like this for a long long time, if ever. Come on, give me a break here, ok? I feel like I've grabbed the brass ring in life with my successes, yet I have no joy, no companionship, no

93

love, no intimacy. I need it Pop. I need to share my life. I need to love and be loved."

Pop sighed a knowing sigh "I know son, I know. Don't think for one minute I don't know that or what you have been through. But, you have to realize that you have a larger responsibility beyond self. You *KNOW* that. It cannot be denied nor ignored."

They finished preparing the fluke, vegetables and salad and went to the aft deck with food and a bottle of wine in hand. The boys picked at their meals in their cabin between beast attacks and laser blasts.

There were four large glasses of wine in the one bottle brought up. They toasted to each other's health and sipped. Dinner did not take long. Sunset was not far off and all concerned knew that the ladies would have to go soon.

Adrian and Kevin cleared the table, walked through the salon and down the galley steps. She put her pile of dishes into the sink and made way for Kevin to unload his as she gave him a firm squeeze on the right cheek of his ass. He nearly broke the dishes in the sink.

'Whoa...that's pretty damn direct. You think she's trying to tell me something?' he asked himself. What a difference a day makes.

He didn't know whether to piss or go blind. No woman ever came on to him like that before; not even a 'you want to dance' or anything. He wasn't a bad looking guy. He just looked so conservative and, perhaps, not the kind of guy that would respond to that sort of thing. Women don't like to get '*shot down*' either. He liked what had just happened. It excited him.

The end of the world was going to have to wait. Pop would understand. He gathered her into his arms, brushed his lips over her lips, her cheek, her ear, as she let out a barely perceptible purr while her teeth gently danced over his ear lobe. In silence they kissed and touched, exploringly, tenderly...joyfully.

They went back upstairs to join the others. Kevin was flushed. Lingering behind for a moment, he became self-conscious about the rise of Mobey Pickle trying to surface. He had nothing to worry about. Hank and Gerta had climbed the stairs to the flying bridge deck level where they were dancing. Who knew? Maybe they would get lucky. Adrian and Kevin danced in an embrace to the soft music of the stereo.

He knew Adrian had to leave and wanted to say so many things in the short time that they had; at least make plans to see each other again.

As he composed his thoughts the roar of powerful engines abruptly penetrated their solace. Some dumb yahoo trying to get his fishing yacht back to the marina before dark narrowly missed the boat and their anchor line. A huge wake created by the speeding boat's deep "V" hull configuration violently smashed into the **ACT I**. The boat rocked wildly from side to side. Everything loose was thrown to the floor.

"You son-of-a-bitch," Kevin screamed after the boat as it beat a hasty retreat into the twilight.

With a sickening "thud" Adrian's mother fell to the aft deck's floor while trying to negotiate the ladder down from the flying bridge. She fell flat on her back with the right side temple area of her head then striking with an audible squishing noise (like a watermelon being punctured by a baseball bat) against a rounded end of a boat rope cleat.

Hank scurried down after her. Adrian and Kevin bolted out of the salon door to her side. The boys were right behind them. Kevin stopped them at the salon door.

What was initially an obvious indentation in

95

Gerta's skull now became a growing convex orb of sickening purple. Adrian shrieked in an anguished primal scream. Kevin knew it wasn't good. His first thought was 'she's dead. Good God she's dead.'

He looked at Hank. "Pop, you've got to do something. Get your people."

Hank snapped, "Get the Coast Guard. They'll send a helicopter. We can't blow the cover now. Too much is at stake - our mission. I can't do anything for her"

"To hell with the mission," he whispered with a hiss. "Damn it...she's dying."

Turning to the boys he ordered "Boys, go to your cabin...now." The boys, understanding that something was very wrong didn't have to be told twice.

"Pop, if you can do something for her and you don't do it right now, you can forget about my cooperation. It's that simple. I'm lukewarm about this whole thing as it is. Whatever you might have in that bag of tricks of yours, get it out now."

Hank sighed, "OK...God help us" as he turned and knelt next to Gerta's limp body and Adrian's sobbing bent frame. He scooped Gerta up in his arms with Adrian screaming "Don't hurt my mamm...Don't hurt my mamma...What are you doing?" The veneer of sophistication was eroded completely. Adrian reverted in an instant to that primal, protective yet frightened state one finds herself in when something very basic and cherished is threatened.

Hank placed Gerta's lifeless body on one of the salon's couches and put a pillow under her head.

He ordered "Please, get back we don't have much time. The internal bleeding and pressure on her brain has to be relieved right now."

Hank's knowing and commandingly authoritative glance sobered Adrian; forcing her backward in silent compliance.

Hank pulled up one of the hassocks and sat by Gerta's head. "Good, she hasn't aspirated. We don't need that complication; not now" he announced.

Lifting his hands to shoulder level next to his body with his fingers spread apart and canted forward, he drew a long, deep breath; letting the air out ever so slowly.

His body became erect and rigid. His face was oriented directly forward with his eyes riveted in a trans-fixed stare upon some source of strength and assis-tance occupying a place in a realm beyond normal human perception and senses. His entire body devel-oped a scintillating aura of soft pastel pinks, blues and then shocking white. His face relaxed to reveal a calm ... almost saintly visage.

The tips of his fingers developed a faint emerald green glow around them. Then, having built to a cre-scendo of lighted brilliance, an eruptive emerald light discharge pulsed from all of his fingers simultaneously arcing into a single column the circumference of which was that of Gerta's head.

Gerta's head was caressed in this almost fluid, floating and gentle light for what seemed to be about ten seconds or so. Her body gave a convulsive jerk as her chest rose and fell anew with the breath of life. The light faded and reversed back to the junction point of its original union...then back to Hank's fingers, then all light emitting from around Hank's body completely dissipated.

Hank rubbed his face and neck stating "She will rest now. All of us have to talk." He walked back to the table on the aft deck.

Sitting crouched, almost in a fetal position against the cabinet doors of the salon, Adrian sat stunned in a near catatonic stupor. Kevin urgently shook her shoulders.

97

Talking in a hushed...whispered voice Kevin said "Don't worry. She'll be OK. What you saw was real. Sit right here for a moment while I check on the boys. I'll be right back".

Thank God that the boys did not get a clear look at Gerta's injury nor at Hank's demonstration. Kevin was not up for a long winded explanation with one basket case already collapsed on the rug upstairs.

Reaching the boys he calmly asked, "You boys start straightening the boat up down here. I need your help. Everything's OK. The lady is going to be alright, but I have a couple of shaken people upstairs. I have to depend upon you guys to help me by quietly straightening up and keeping yourselves busy while I talk upstairs. I don't want any mention of this in the morning. I don't want to embarrass anybody...deal?"

The boys shook their heads in bewildered yet cooperative acquiescence.

As Murdock climbed the stairs to the wheelhouse he heard the marine radio crackle "Pan...pan, pan...pan, pan...pan, hello all stations, hello all stations, hello all stations and all interested marine traffic. This is The United States Coast Guard Barnegat Light Group...This is the United States Coast Guard Barnegat Light Group with an urgent marine broadcast...Break...! At this time we have reports of a large fishing yacht being operated in a hazardous and reckless manner just inside the Barnegat inlet area. The craft could potentially be out of control. All vessels in the area are advised to avoid this area and or be aware of this hazard.

"Be advised that there may already be destruction as result of this behavior in the area....Confirmation to follow. Be alert and give this vessel a wide berth for passage. Report sightings of subject vessel on frequency...two two alpha...to the attention of this station.

"Coast Guard patrols fourteen and seventeen switch and change to channel twenty three alpha...Coast guard patrols fourteen and seventeen switch and change to channel twenty three alpha. This is the United States Coast Guard Barnegat Light Group...out."

That dangerous bastard was still out there. Kevin changed one of the two radios to channel twenty-three as he passed on his way back to Adrian. She was standing now and walked toward him in the wheelhouse as he instinctively listened for more reports of the danger. With his index finger he shushed Adrian who was about to speak.

The radio again reported "This is United States Coast Guard Station Barnegat Light Group. Patrols fourteen and seventeen are you getting a copy?" Responses were in rapid succession to the affirmative. The patrols acknowledged hearing the last transmission on channel sixteen.

The officer on duty ordered "Proceed...top urgent...to the area between buoys nineteen and twenty five in the Oyster Creek channel. Intercept, board and apprehend perpetrators causing severe hazard to navigation proceeding in a westerly direction. Do you copy?" The patrols responded to the affirmative. "Barnegat station clear...standing by channel one six alpha."

"I hope they nail those son-of-a-bitches to the cross." Kevin said as he signaled for Adrian to follow him aft.

"Just what the hell is going on here? Just who the hell are you two?" she queried with the most righteous indignation that she could muster.

"Pop, we had no choice." Murdock offered.

"I know that Kevin. I know. Sorry I hesitated. I have a conflict here."

Turning to Adrian Hank started, "Well Miss...first off, your mother is going to be fine. She will sleep the night here. When she awakens she will think that she had a little too much to drink tonight with all memory of this event having been wiped away.

"I wish I had more omega-empath force within me to wipe the same recollections from *your* memory. I used it all on your mother and my batteries are kind of low so to speak. I couldn't use it on you anyway even if I wanted to. Life threatening criteria or eminent disaster are the only two circumstances under which the Soclarian counsel will permit us to use this force without prior approval.

"In short, we have to depend upon your silence on faith alone. You saw what we had to do. Don't let us down. No one planned this but, unfortunately, we're forced to take you into the loop and our confidence.

"Your mother will have no brain damage. Oxygen was restored to all parts of her brain fast enough" Hank reassured.

"Are you guys some kind of faith healers or something?" She asked.

"Sit down my dear and believe what I am about to tell you".

"So...I have a choice, maybe?" Adrian sarcastically mocked in a pseudo-yiddish accent with a resigned gesture of her upturned palms; trying to inject a little levity into a very stressful situation. It was obvious that she was relieved by the knowledge that her mother was out of danger.

Through the now completely dark night air came another report over the marine radio. "Securite', securite', securite'...(pronounced say-kur-ee-tay) this is The United States Coast Guard Station Barnegat Light Group...This is The United States Coast Guard Station Barnegat Light Group. Stand by for a marine hazard notice from the commander of this station...all interested parties switch to Channel two two alpha Break!

"All interested marine traffic be advised of hazard to navigation located within the Oyster Creek channel at buoy twenty two. One fish-yacht of approximately forty five feet in length has capsized.

"The captain is in custody aboard patrol boat seventeen. It is believed that there may be one female child and one female adult still missing. The captain of said vessel is too impaired to confirm. Please be on the lookout for flares, life vests or debris in and around said location...Break!.

The voice continued to crackle..."The upturned hull of the subject vessel is drifting with the tide toward the Barnegat Inlet and has not yet been taken into tow. This posses a serious threat and hazard to navigation.

"The utmost caution and alertness is advised at this time. Barnegat station...more to follow...Coast Guard Station Barnegat Light...clear."

"Good God, I hope they're wrong about the woman and child" Adrian whispered. "What bastard would drink and navigate his boat with his family on board?"

"A selfish alcoholic bastard, that's who" Pop answered having re-entered the salon to hear what was going on.

"Just what we need. The tide is going out. That guy's boat is now drifting back toward us. What joy...we might have the privilege of being victimized by the same drunk twice in one evening" Pop quipped sarcastically.

"At least they got him" Kevin added as he turned down the marine band radios and reached for the radar controls. The radar would sound an alarm if the craft got too close. They would be able to repel off of it with their rope poles if the drifting hull came too close to them.

Hank, content that no one would be going anywhere for the remainder of the night, made three more drinks, passed them around and there on the aft deck related to Adrian the crux of what he had previously portrayed to Kevin; letting the chips fall where they may. She had to know and they had to trust her.

-CHAPTER SIX-

The morning sun shown brightly as the **ACT I** plied through the bay waters at the mouth of the marina with the Slater's boat trailing behind on a tow line. Two young boys and a man were on the marina's breakwater waving. It was Winston Tanderoth and his two sons.

The older of the two boys was in Andrew's class in school. It was through the boys that Kevin met him. After a few war stories of shared divorce experiences the two developed an immediate affinity and friendship.

Winston was a very proper Englishman who immigrated to *"The Colonies"* (as he put it). He had inherited a ton of money and wanted to strike out on his own in America. He didn't want to live in the shadow of his father's notoriety in England.

He wanted everyone to think of him as a regular guy. That was a pretty tall order for someone who had the burden of breeding to overcome. However, perseverance was his principle virtue.

Beneath the pomp imposed upon him as a consequence of birth, he really was a regular guy. He was a good man, a good father and a good friend from Kevin's point of view. He was the type of guy who would do anything for you; cheer you up when you were down and simply be just good company.

Winston had a summer house right in the town of Barnegat Light. He was the one who had originally convinced Kevin that Sand Bar Marina was **THE** premier marina to be at if peace and natural surroundings along with just the right nautical touch was what you wanted.

Kevin knew the area and what he was looking for. However, it was Winston who had pointed him to Sand Bar. For that he was grateful.

Kevin navigated the **ACT I** into the slip stern first. The dock boys met the vessel and gave a hand with tying up. The lines were secured and the ramp placed on the dock.

"Pip of a day, old man, what!" came the upbeat greeting they all received from Winston as he and his boys climbed aboard.

No matter how many times Kevin heard him talk he still was amused by this displaced use of the language (displaced at least for an American) and the accent.

Introductions were made all around leaving Winston to wonder what 'the old man' was up to out on the bay all night long with a beautiful woman. Kevin intended to keep him guessing.

As well intended as Winston always was, Kevin could not cope with anymore complications. He did not know what he could say without hurting his feelings. All he knew was that he was going to have to get rid of him; politely if possible, firmly if necessary.

Before he had a chance at either method Winston, in his *'damned the torpedoes'* style, launched onward.

"I saw you meandering back to port from my window. I thought you might be down this week before school...glad I was right. I had a capital idea. I thought I'd pop it on you.

"The boys have not seen each other all summer. All I have been hearing is 'when are we going to see

Andrew and Peter?'

Well, what about your boys staying with us for four days. Anyway, from where I am seeing things it appears that you might appreciate the break, old man. You sly devil."

Winston just turned from a complication into a savior. Kevin did not want to disappoint the boys. But they would be a complication with what was going on with Hank. What a God-send. Now if only mother dearest would cooperate and disappear he might be able to actually socialize a little.

"Commmonn dad...plleeease" came a simultaneous din. He was relieved. They wanted to go. It didn't take much convincing. They knew that when they went to the Tanderoth's house at the shore that meant non-stop miniature golf, water slides in Ship Bottom and soft ice cream stands. To them, Mr. Tanderoth was another name for Santa Claus.

Kevin teased, "Well...I don't know...well, if you're sure that you want these two wildcats on your hands."

Winston gave him this 'You hump. Who in the hell do you think your kidding?' look. They both grinned and told the boys to go and pack four days worth of everything. That meant a bathing suit and four pairs of underwear. After a short call to their mom to let her know about their plans, Andrew and Peter were off like a shot with their friends with Winston close behind to supervise. They lally-gagged and hung around the docks and boats for a time locating some blue claw crabs on the docks' edge. Before you knew it they were back on board scavenging around the boat for crab nets.

Adrian and her mother were feeling a bit uncomfortable and out of place with all this activity, being new guests themselves. Kevin put a stop to that right away.

"Well, now we have the boat all to ourselves. What do you want to do?" he asked the ladies.

Gerta responded for what she thought would be both of them: "I have to be back in Manhattan by 3:00 pm. I'm afraid that we will have to take a rain check. Besides, I think I overdid it a bit last night. I've got a slight case of too much to drink this morning. No more boats for me for a few days. Nothing personal. Thank you anyway. I think that we've already over-stayed our welcome."

Kevin assured her to the contrary and that she didn't do any table dancing the night before. What would have happened if he were alone with them the night before, he thought? The tragedy would have been irreversible.

"You go ahead, Mamma. I'm going to stay at the house for a few days. I don't have any appointments until Thursday. You take the boat back and I'll talk Kevin into driving me back to the house this after-noon."

Somehow, Gerta didn't mind being lied to. Her old-world overly protective mother hen act over the years might have contributed to Adrian's present soli-tary lifestyle. For that, she was feeling a little bit guilty.

Adrian always wanted her mother and father to approve of her. She would never have done anything to disappoint them. She loved them and respected them and their feelings too much; even to the point of rejecting suitors throughout high school, then college then into her working life. No one was ever quite good enough for her according to them. There was always some fault, some misgiving or some short com-ing that they could communicate by word, by deed or by a mere look. They loved her and protected her right into spinster-hood.

The pattern had developed. She had put all of her

energies into pleasing mom and dad, becoming an over achiever, a workaholic, a person driven to be the respectable daughter that mamma always wanted and the achieving, popular, scholarly and successful son that dad never had. A neurotic in the making from the get-go and a no win situation from the start.

She became the casualty of her parents' own neurosis and a vicarious projection and incarnation of themselves and their standards set for themselves. She really could never be right for any man until she was right for herself. Using her parents' unrealistic expectations as a guide, that was and would always be an extremely and ultimately frustrating goal.

She would have to hear from daddy himself...that he was proud of her...that he wanted to let go...to love his daughter without condition...that it's ok...that it wouldn't be a betrayal nor a demonstration of lack of respect if she followed her own drummer.

But it was too late. He was dead. It was up to her mother now. Mom would now have to loosen the reins; realize that her daughter's name wasn't Saint Adrian. She was human with the same needs for intimacy, companionship and personal fulfillment as most other people in the world have. Gerta was trying. She knew that she did not want her daughter to wind up resenting her and hating her.

She loved Adrian and knew that her love must not suffocate her. Her love for Adrian and her husband's love for Adrian had been (in large part) an oppression. They did not see it while it was happening, but she knew now of the unfair effects of it and that it was time to back off and trust their daughter; late as it may be, it is never *too* late. Perhaps, she could start making amends now by starting to trust her daughter's judgements a bit more.

Pop knew this; somehow sensing it both from

Gerta and Adrian. It was as if he could not only read their minds, but read their subconscious'. He said nothing while taking it all in, staring at Adrian intently yet thinking, 'She hurts...She has so much to give, but will not allow herself. She is her own jailer. She smiles yet weeps inside...poor child'.

Kevin, misreading this stare broke Pop's stare whispering: "It's ok, Pop. She's over twenty-one. She's a big girl. I'll be a perfect gentleman."

Pop, a little embarrassed at being caught off guard staring said, "I know...it's not that at all. I was thinking that we have an agenda, Kevin. We are being slowed down.

"I realize you have a life, but please be mindful of the mission. Do what you have to...make a date or something, but let's get on with this."

Winston and the boys said good-bye. Winston's offer to drop Adrian's mother off was accepted. Their boat remained for Adrian's use. The crabbing expidition was ready to leave. Plans were made for Winston to drop the boys off at 5:00 pm in four days. The boys took enough clothing, their toothbrushes and were off.

After walking the boys and Adrian's mother to the parking lot, Kevin and Adrian walked toward the boat stopping midway on the little bridge over the marsh that joined the pontoon sections. They leaned on the rail.

"Now what?" she asked. "I'm along for the duration. Where to from here with the little green men?"

All of a sudden...how did she become part of the equation? She couldn't be. She would get in the way and would tie them all together, perhaps, in a way that Kevin was not ready for.

First off, he wanted Pop alone for this strange reunion; at least for a couple of days. With her he wanted it to be slow and easy...taking in sunsets and sunrises...glasses of wine and good movies...walks on the beach and slow dances on the boat...you know...normal stuff. He wanted to set the pace. He wanted to control...at least to a mutually acceptable degree...a pace they were both comfortable with.

'It's either feast or famine' he thought. 'I get my ass grabbed and my mind blown all in one simple move. Can't there be a little moderation here?' he wondered rhetorically. Can't one thing happen at a time for Christ's sake?...No...not to good old Kevin',...half expecting an answer to bounce back at him from his reflection in the water.

Now, seemingly as a backlash to her parents' influence, Adrian was not to be controlled; seemingly unaware or unaccustomed to the notion of *one step at a time*. She liked to take control of her environment, of her life. She **had** to control. It was her strength, her defense, her style and had gotten her through life to this point...safe...unscathed...emotionally untouched...empty...alone.

Maybe, she would let him in, he thought. Maybe he could fill her emptiness. Maybe they both could dispel the loneliness of the other. This was the place but not the time. Events saw to that. Romance had to wait. This was a long way from the "sock-hop" and they weren't in Kansas anymore.

"Although I might be tempted to spend the next several hundred years with you, this has to be a solo journey for the next few days. I want to see you. I want to get to know you. Let's give it some time and let me work this through with Hank. I'll fill you in with everything later, I promise".

'More than you can imagine' he sophomorically allowed himself. Why not? He was horny and infatuated. That's almost like love at first sight isn't it?

"You're not going to get rid of me that easily" she

playfully protested. "I'm a writer; maybe a business writer, but a writer, nonetheless. I wouldn't give up the chance to tell this story if my life depended upon it. No sir...you're stuck with me.

"My mother's brains get bashed in, I see a miracle happen before my very eyes, I meet a guy I think I could like and I get sprung from my mother for a few days and you expect me to walk off into the sunset? Forget it, Charlie. Now talk to me".

Kevin joked, "You know what your trouble is? You're too shy. You have trouble getting things off your chest, Adrian". From his vantage point, "things" must have been building up over a substantial period of time.

He couldn't get the fantasy of her naked body laying in bed out of his mind. 'Stop it' he told himself. 'You're distracting yourself. It'll be time to play later'.

"I'll talk to Pop. Actually, I'd be thinking about you in your bikini, alone on the beach at the mercy of all those wolves anyway." he conceded, giving in without much of a fight.

"You must agree to be low profile, as quiet and as cooperative as possible if I'm going to sell this to him...OK?" Her quiet?...Fat chance.

"Agreed" she promised with the conviction of someone promising to have a payment for a six month old bill promptly mailed.

"I regret this already" Kevin muttered, putting his arm around Adrian's inviting supple waist as they strolled toward the boat.

Hank was sitting on a deck chair. He was born at night, but not last night. He knew what was coming as he sat shaking his head side to side in his hands...his elbows resting on his knees.

Taking Kevin aside he quipped "Can't you kids wait a couple of days...does it always have to be now...now...now for everything? Forget your hormones...hasn't life taught you anything?".

"Yeah...to listen to your hormones sometimes" Kevin retorted.

The two of them turned back to Adrian and informed her of Pop's mind set and concerns.

"Get your mind out of the gutter...you dirty old man..." Adrian joked. "My interests here are driven purely by academic motivation...pure and simple".

"Yeah...Right!...And Kevin here is a certified eunuch from Siam". Pop was not convinced.

"Either way, I'm not going to argue. We don't have time for that crap. This is not going to be a joy ride. It's a business trip...serious business. We must remember this and not be allowed to be lulled into digression from our purpose at hand during our time together. Lives depend upon our dedication to our task.

"We are human and tend to either deny, laugh off or avoid the unpleasant and difficult in order to cope. You both must be resolute and conscientious in identifying those feelings of either inadequacy, fear or doubt when you are thrown into the new and unknown fray of the days to come and what you will be called upon to deal with psychologically. You must defeat and rise above those obstacles.

"Kevin, you must have the bearing of **command,** you must be in command; command of yourself, your surroundings...and in actuality."

"How your behavior is viewed over the next several days will be crucial to how effective you will ultimately be in your assigned roll prophesied by our own ancestors.

"Yes, prophesied as is the predictable, unspoken message of the drone bee when he is called to duty in building a hive of which he had no prior instruction

111

nor knowledge; to firmly, decisively, without prior knowledge nor instruction instinctively ferret out danger, expose the danger, instill alarm and communicate that danger to the extent that his hive *must* respond, protect and move the queen. So are you that drone. The queen is mankind as a whole. So, too, must you respond without question. So must you, too, accept your destiny."

"You are the essential link. Your niche will be made clearer to you at the proper time. That aside, your credibility will be at issue and must be uncontested and absolute in order for you to be effective in this enterprise.

You, Adrian, must not distract Kevin in your roll as an observer. He is central...the wild card...the link with the pre-recorded message to activate the network essential for the protection of mankind.

"Kevin, I shall not mislead you. You have a definite choice in this. Nor, will I deliberately shame you into this task. However, you will see that the choices will be those of being a coward or of rising to the call of your destiny."

Kevin thought 'Naw, he doesn't want to shame me...too much.'

"The choice will be simple when you realize the mass suffering that is now ongoing and what may be avoided. The choice will be yours. Yet, I know what metal you are of and I am confident of what will spring forth from within you when you are challenged."

Kevin did not object nor joke. Something was churning within him; something primal, something archetypal. The ring of truth hung on every word uttered by his grandfather.

He was becoming overwhelmed, anxious, anticipatory... excited about what he felt was to come. He didn't know yet what it was.

112

He knew that it was real...impending ...undeniable...unavoidable...gentle...nurturing...welcome. The calm was starting...the truth was coming.

Hank had to inform his superiors of what had transpired during the past twenty four hours. They already knew through their selective telepathic group linkage capabilities. However it was an easy mental exercise for them if they wanted privacy.

The great part about this type of 'party line' was there was always someone there to *talk with* if you wanted to or tune out if you wanted to. It was alot like E-Mail without the wires.

Nonetheless, he had to leave. Proper suits would have to be obtained for Adrian and Kevin; custom tuned to their specific body masses, chemistries and electrical capacitances. Instructions would have to be given to Hank. Proper treatment for minimum mental impact on the two visitors would have to be discussed before nightfall...before the three descended beneath the bay...beneath the Earth to EARTH STATION BARNEGAT LIGHT...together.

Hank had donned his silvery suit. He took several long deep breaths, held his breath one last time and slipped the suit's hood over his head. Kevin could see that once the hood was pulled over Hank's head that the front panel of the hood was actually transparent and (a moment after having exhaled into the suit) formed a perfect seal around his face. How could he breathe? He found his answer telepathically. Pop was transmitting...this was wild.

Hank explained that only Kevin could hear him. Normally, Kevin would have to be wearing a suit too, in order to receive. However, they were close enough for transmission and Kevin had an enate receptive ability.

Hank went on to explain that located at the base of the skull in the suit there was, what they called, a

CRANIAL-CORTICAL DEPRESSIVE SYNTHESIZER.
Through the proper combination and use of electrical, ultrasound and electromagnetic impulses, the body's ability to automatically breathe was interrupted in order that the suit could *breathe* for its wearer.

Also, through adjustments, the heart rate could be slowed almost to the point of stopping if this were desired. This became a useful tool when representatives from Soclar found it necessary to travel to the ends of the universe. They were able to achieve suspended animation status while immersed in a circulating seawater bath; a bath that included nutrients that could be absorbed directly through the suit's skin.

Through the environmental functions and the microprocessor nervelike network which actually took on the characteristics of the synapse nervebundle networks of the brain, the wearer became protected against heat, cold, and pressure.

There had to be a thin layer of seawater between the skin of the wearer and the inner skin of the suit. When the suit *sensed* the drop in pressure caused by the taking off of the suit, it automatically absorbed enough of the seawater to allow for an automatic internal release of water, once the suit was put on again.

There were catalytic and enzymatic elements inside the skin of the suit that (through the medium of the thin layer of sea water) had the ability through osmosis and through the dilation of the wearer's pores of causing carbon dioxide to be liberated from the walls of capillaries of the wearer's skin, then, through the skin itself, into the seawater layer.

The suit then in turn liberated the oxygen atoms within the material of the suit and expelled the carbon residue by way of electrolytic and mechanical interactions between the outer skin of the suit and the seawater when its wearer was immersed.

The recovered oxygen then experienced a reverse osmotic cycle back through the skin and into the capillaries of its wearer through a process which primarily utilized the principal of rapidly intermittent electrical field polarity reversals within the body itself.

Even the slightest body motions served as the system's mechanical pump. For extended periods when the body was in a state of suspended animation or near suspended animation, the suit had a mode working in conjunction with the mechanical circulation of the "travel spa" in a spacecraft. The suit utilized a principal much like that of the rotating tourniquet cuffs used on congestive heart failure victims and others in medical crisis, so that the blood supply does not pool. Through the intermittent squeezing of each extremity, this mechanical aid did the pumping of the blood for the heart. The technology was that of a living machine.

In short, even though by definition skin is called "an organ" in this capacity it truly served as one large surrogate lung, liver, kidney, etc.

Body wastes were processed in much the same manner as the gaseous wastes. The wearer could be out of the water for up to two hours without any adverse effects before having to immerse in sea water. Waste products from respiration and other bodily functions were stored in the shell of the suit's skin until that immersion.

Once under water the suit could be worn indefinitely, since nutrients could be assimilated into the suit and then into the body...working much like the root system of a tree. The wearer's skin never even wrinkles.

It was the combination of the wearer's own electrical field, heat generated by the wearer and the chemically induced exothermic and electrolytic interactions between the blood system, the suit, and the outer sea environment that served as the charging and maintenance network for the perpetuation of the suit's usefulness...In other words...ONE HELL OF A WET SUIT. A skin diver's wet dream (so to speak).

Hank quickly took the necessary body profile readings with what he called a "Psycho-medcorder"; a palm sized instrument that glowed turquoise blue when placed against the carotid artery region of the neck of its subject.

"You two try to get some rest. We rendezvous here at zero three hundred hours in the morning" he admonished; giving another one of his 'fat chance' looks.

Good-byes were made. He made his way to the swim platform via the aft deck ladder; scanned the area to see if there were any onlookers, then, stolidly and surreptitiously disappeared below the surface of the bay's steely blue-gray waters.

Looking up from the surface of the water Adrian and Kevin shared an impish 'let's play...we're alone at last' look.

Since they were wearing their bathing suits already they decided to take a quick dip. They climbed down the ladder to the swim platform and jumped in.

The water was refreshingly delightful. They played and splashed each other like kids discovering something for the first time.

Hanging onto the swim platform with one arm and gathering Adrian toward himself...her back facing him, he gently nuzzled her neck behind her ear. She responded with that same contented low groaning purr that excited him so much the night before. While, down behind herself, she felt...explored and found the growing...throbbing bulge in Kevin's bathing suit.

She gently caressed, stroked and fondled her

116

discovery...like a newly found pet...while rubbing her leg against his. Kevin couldn't contain himself much longer.

"You-know-who is probably getting all of this on camera, don't you?" Adrian pointed out; ever so slightly breaking the mood (her not being too far from the truth...He wouldn't put that past the Feds nor the space cadets).

Kevin didn't want to hear about it. He was nearing the automatic pilot...full steam ahead stage; but, managed to snap out of it long enough to suggest they take a warm shower on the swim platform and head up to the top deck to get some sun (and some privacy). She agreed.

Dripping wet from the warm fresh water shower, they scrambled onto the aft deck and up another ladder to the flying bridge sun deck. It was large enough up there to have a party, yet, private enough to do a little naked sun bathing. The front of the boat faced the marina. The front and sides of the top deck were enclosed by a privacy wall and the view from the back facing out into the abandoned channel was obstructed by the Boston Whaler nestled in its cradle. It was private and invited excitingly naughty open air fun.

They sat side by side on the soft sunning mat. Then, as if she were taking off her watch, Adrian nonchalantly removed the top of her bikini revealing full and sensual breasts with nipples that were swelled with anticipation. She then slowly slipped the bottom of her suit down over her legs then off over her feet.

Kevin removed his swim suit to reveal the proper testimonial and rigid salute to such appreciated behavior and natural beauty. They both laid back as if they really *were* going to try to get some sun. Who was kidding whom?

A few minutes was all it took for the intense sun

to add to the moisture on their bodies and to the throbbing warmth of their exposed parts. Kevin sat up and gave a longing and lingering stare at Adrian's legs that were slightly spread apart to reveal the glistening moist hairs of Adrian's gateway to paradise.

He leaned over her, gently kissing her mouth, her neck...then, moving lower, slowly licking her nipples while he stroked her thigh and caressed and probed her now undulating, moist and inviting wonders.

They made love in the sun, taking part in each others' welcoming and inviting pleasures...losing themselves within the rapture of the other's knowing, giving and gentle gifts of love-sharing.

It was only then that they could rest after the flood of their shared experiences encountered over the previous twenty-four hours.

From under one of the seats Kevin pulled out two stored pillows and a light blanket. Pulling the blanket up to protect themselves from the sun, they embraced; falling asleep in each other's arms...comforted...exhausted.

-CHAPTER SEVEN-

The stars above glistened brightly in the peaceful and warm night sky. It was midnight when they were gently jostled from their slumber by the wake of a returning party boat.

Looking up, Kevin couldn't help wondering which cluster of those scintillating diamonds of light pointed the way to Soclar. Adrian and Kevin smiled at each other, briefly tightening their embrace in a "well...hello to you...glad that you are with me" body language squeeze. They had slept for nine and a half hours.

Kevin's rueful wondering became overpowered by his tuneful tummy's hungry demands. They went below and prepared some scrambled eggs, toast and bacon; you know, nothing that would take too long to make...prancing around naked all the while like a couple of cherubs. They took a quick shower and slipped back under the clean sheets of the large bed in the master stateroom; again, trying to wear out or break their newly found toy (or die trying).

After momentarily slipping into a sex induced afterglow slumber, Adrian jerked awake by the rapping noise of someone standing on the swim platform tapping on the stateroom's window. She simultaneously looked up and screamed, seeing a ghostly face illuminated by the room's amber light projecting onto the face of what she now knew was that of Hank's, looming outside of the large port-hole window.

The captain's wheel clock on the wall at the foot of the bed reported that it was already 3:00 am. Hank waived through the window at her with a "get any lately?" chesire grin.

She muttered to herself "It's the voyeur from outer space."

She nudged Kevin saying "Hey, Superman, your peeping Tom grandfather forgot to use the front doorbell, again". She grabbed a terry cloth robe at the foot of the bed and hastened a retreat to the bathroom. Kevin slipped on his underwear and opened the window.

One at a time, Hank started shoving what appeared to be wetsuits through the opened window. Climbing in, Hank said "Don't worry about clothes, you love birds. You won't be needing clothes for these suits. When we get to our final destination you will be provided with the clothing that you need. Travel light. Tonight, that means with nothing.

"Here Kevin, put this on", handing him one of the two silvery suits.

Adrian shyly extend her hand from behind the bathroom door chiding, "Pervert!", as Hank placed the second suit into her out-stretched hand.

"Pervert? Thanks lady. You know, I don't need windows to get my jollies. I do pretty well down under...the bay that is...thank you very much. You make me feel like the old man voyeur in the bakery shop."

Closing the bathroom door behind herself for privacy and with her curiosity piqued, she responded, "OK I'll bite. What bakery shop?"

"Well," he started, "since you asked.

"In a small town in one of the more conservative mid-western states, a beautiful young and well built girl worked in the local bakery. Her personal preference was to never wear underwear. Undergarments bothered her.

"As fate would have it, the white bread was kept on one of the top shelves for which she had to use a ladder.

"Invariably, the young men in town asked her to please get the white bread; during which time they enjoyed immense diversion at her expense by looking up her dress.

"Not appreciating this behavior, she moved the white bread to a lower shelf and the raisin bread to the top shelf. There was no winning for trying for her; the young men switched their preferences to raisin bread that very day.

"While she was on the ladder retrieving the bread for the young men, a man in his early eighties walked into the shop. Exasperated, she guessed 'Well, I suppose that yours is raisin too'.

"With an initial astonished look on his face he finally gathered his wits. Contradicting her, he calmly countered, 'No dearie, but it sure is twitching a might'".

Amused, she quipped, "Hardi...har...sorry I asked."

She emerged from the bathroom garbed in her suit. Now what do I do with this hood?" she asked as she reached for it behind her head.

Hank told her to take three deep breaths and hold the last one as she slipped the hood over her head. He let her know that she probably would try to fight it for the first time much like one fights sticking her finger in her eyes the first time she tries to put her contact lenses into her eyes.

It just isn't natural to stick your fingers into

your eyes. Your eyes know that and they fight you with blinking and other protestations.

"It's not normal to stick your fingers into your eyes and it's not normal to choke yourself. You must listen to my coaching as you exhale into your hood after placing it over your head.

"Do not try to talk. Your suits are equipped with thought transference broadcast transponders. So, be careful of what you think and keep it clean. OK...Put on your hood".

Adrian dutifully put her hood over her face and exhaled her air into the suit. She then inhaled as the transparent film sucked in to form around her face. She immediately panicked and tried to yank the hood from her head, while she gasped and her chest bucked.

"Don't!...Don't!" Pop coached. "Don't fight it...go with it... trust me...look at me! Now just calm yourself."

She stared at him with a wild and crazed look of fear. She grasped Pop's hand with a vice like grip. Pop then stopped her from reaching to pull the hood off as both of her hands went for her head.

Suddenly, Adrian's chest stopped its jerking movements. She was going to be ok. She gathered her composure, smiled and signaled an "I'm ok" high sign to Pop.

Hank, turning to Kevin, said "Well, what are you waiting for...a personal invitation? Put it on."

Not to be outdone, Kevin went through the motions and through the pulmonary cortical transition as if he had been doing it every day of his entire life. If it weren't for his activating the thought transponder his charade would have been complete

"God, don't let me die...help...good...good...that's a little bit better...there..." looking up embarrassed,

122

just realizing that there were no secrets in these suits, he asked attentively, "What's next?" Covering his momentary panic with the quickly manufactured display of bravado and eagerness to continue.

Hank directed them to sit out on the swim platform with him to dangle their feet in the water for about ten minutes so that the suits (which in essence were synthetic life forms) and their bodies may equilibrate and come into the necessary state of harmonic symbiosis.

Naturally, this was all second nature to Pop. After seeing the initial shock for both of the neophytes, Pop wanted them both to feel the biochemical exchanges taking place between their own skin's surfaces, the suit and the seawater entering their suit/life support systems. Before entering the foreboding and darkened depths of the bay, he wanted them to be confident that the damn things were actually working.

To pass the time, Hank explained that the thought transmission transponder only worked when it was turned on. It was programmed to turn on its receiver by the wearer lowering his jaw once. The wearer could transmit and receive by lowering his jaw twice. The entire system turned off by lowering his jaw three times in rapid succession.

If the system were activated in error, there would always be a low frequency tone that the wearer could sense in the cranial auditory discriminator portion of his own brain. It would remain activated for three minutes or until the user initiated his first transmission or exercised one of the feature commands. If the user still did not respond with a command to shut off, then every five minutes thereafter, the tone would repeat itself until the system was consciously deactivated by the wearer.

Hank went on to explain that "The systems have a virtually unlimited range. Each atom serves as a repeater. The signal is never diluted nor weakened. It is sent on its way with exactly the same strength and clarity as it was received. In other words, we can *phone home* whenever we want to. As you can imagine, with the amount of users on the party line at any one time there would be quite a maddening din of discordant babel if hundreds of wearers were trying to transmit all at the same time.

"For business radio users, there normally are assigned tones and frequencies to avoid transmission log jams and to avoid others listening in on conversations not intend for them. In a much more sophisticated way, this is basically how the suit transponder system works," Hank went on.

"Now, you two must activate the frequencies systems yourselves. Each person, each brain has its own frequency for transmission and reception. However, instead of radio waves, we utilize sympathetic vibratory relays from one subatomic particle to the next; a frequency specific to the sender and or receiver. We simply utilize our God given resources made available to us that are as specific and unique to the individual as are our fingerprints.

"In short, the system can operate above water, under water, through mountains and buildings; even into and through the vacuum of space. This is because space is not a perfect vacuum and has large amounts of atomic and subatomic matter dispersed throughout. As opposed to actual radio frequencies and signals, this manner of communication works best in atomically dense environments. It uses mountains, oceans and planets instead of being stopped by them as is the case with radio signals.

124

"Have you ever noticed that very often when you meet someone for the first time you instantly get an impression of that person; a feeling that you are either going to like that person or feel an unexplained repulsion or desire to leave that person's presence? That's called a first impression which is gleaned from several sources and instantly analyzed by you. A general rule and a part of human nature is that we like most and want to associate most with people who are most like ourselves. This is not good or bad, it's just the way it is. You both know the saying 'We're on the same wave length'? Well, there is more to that phrase than most people give conscious thought to.

"When you meet someone for the first time and come within a five foot proximity of that individual, you become enveloped and bathed in that person's frequential aura. That person's specific frequential information is immediately and automatically imprinted into your cortical discriminatory multiplexor without the assistance of any devices. This phenomenon is yet to be researched or discovered by Earth's scientists.

"The druids of England stumbled upon the superficial basics of this natural force. The secret died with them. Either no records were kept or they were destroyed...purposely or otherwise. Many species of animals and insects have developed this sense and make constant use of it. Whales use it. Salmon use it. Elephants use it. Even the bees use it. Things and places have their own specific atomic and subatomic sympathetic vibratory emissions that imprint on animals and on people in much the same way. The difference is the animal kingdom uses it. They don't know any better other **than** to use it.

"They have enhanced and developed this abil-

125

ity by way of compensation in much the same way as a blind person over develops other senses, such as hearing, smell and so on. It is a matter of species' survival and a way to achieve control and independence within their environment.

"However, modern man, on the other hand, refuses to come to the realization that he has this dormant ability; simply because it sounds like superstitious hokum and he can't see it nor touch it. Yet, deep down, most people know there is something to this; something there...something else that they can't quite put their fingers on. They just can't harness it nor direct it, control it, smell it, taste it nor see it...as if in a disturbing, unnerving and frustrating dream; subconsciously trying...as if within that dream being on a seemingly endless journey home to find a loved one...its just being out of one's reach...beyond his view...as with the dream, dissipating into obscurity and oblivion as the confusion of the new day harshly rushes into his consciousness as he opens his eyes and turns off his alarm clock.

"Yet, enough remains...enough survives so that the dreamer intuits and possesses the inner truth and self-assured knowledge that the unreachable is indeed a reality. People who feel that don't have to prove it to anyone. They just feel it and know within the depths of their being that it is a fact of being and may do with it what they wish or may ignore it, also, if they wish.

"You know how sometimes you get a first impression of someone; either you like them or dislike them right away?

Sometimes people listen to that little bird. Other times they dismiss that impression as their own prejudicial painting or shadings superimposed or projected upon that person they are meeting; or they intellectualize the feeling away in some other way.

"That experience represents frequential imprinting, whereby this sense is at work recording basic impressions, feelings, data and or warnings in a primal yet extremely complex sequence. Some people are more attuned to those transmissions and those of their surroundings than others.

"Kevin, do you remember when I used to tell you that your first impression is usually the correct one?" Kevin nodded his acknowledgment of the memory. "Believe it! I know it has helped you. I know that you use it...whether you are aware of it or not." Kevin nodded a concurring nod in agreement.

"Your own uniquely heightened ability to absorb the total biospheric and combined environmentally sympathetic-subatomic emanations from your environment and those around you not only makes you a lightening rod for reception but, also, an antenna for transmission which will manifest itself at the proper time. You will know when that time is. None of us is certain when that might be, yet, that is your value to us and to the scheme of things.

"On a less grand scale, these suits and their transponders take a certain segment of that innate ability and amplify it. To contact an individual you must form an impression of that person in your mind's eye. It's just like turning to that person's channel. If you want a conference call, call upon the images and feeling of the presence of those you wish to communicate with; only, do so in a group setting...as if they were all in the same room with you.

"The catch to it is, they have to be wearing a

suit too. Not everyone has the same potential for being a loud speaker system as you do, Kevin. Even your ability is of little use until the right time. So, before you get all full of yourself and get a big head, you need this gizmo. So, let's try it out".

Adrian, Kevin and Hank took turns practicing communicating with one another. At first it was a strange experience; you know...having someone else inside your head. Kevin thought that his former shrink would have a ball with this thing. It sure could have an application (after the break-up of Kevin's marriage, he needed a few sessions with a shrink). After a few minutes, both Adrian and Kevin had the fundamentals of the thing mastered.

The jaw activating feature was designed and incorporated into the suit in case the wearer's arms became caught or otherwise incapacitated. The remaining controls were located on a cummerbund like band across the midriff area of the suit. There was a yellow bulge located just over the pelvic bone on the right and a red bulge located just over the pelvic bone on the left.

Hank explained that the control on the right was for temperature control. Although the suit had an automatic "safe zone" setting, personal preferences could be easily accommodated by depressing the bulge and stroking to the right for warmer and to the left for cooler.

Used in a similar fashion was the red bulge on the left which controlled buoyancy. Stroking to the left increased buoyancy and the wearer would go up. Stroking to the right would cause the wearer to sink. Striking the bulge with the fist or palm would cause the wearer to stay at his current depth.

Remembering the boys, Kevin confirmed, "I've got to be back before the boys get back, Pop. Are you sure we'll be back in time?"

"Don't worry, we'll be back in time" Hank assured.

For both Adrian's and Kevin's benefit, Hank informed them that the newly constructed jetty projecting outward from Barnegat Lighthouse (almost a quarter of a mile straight out to sea) had sealed the main venting and exit opening of *Earth Base Four.*

The Soclarians could have just vaporized the entombing boulders...but, they would have been found out. Instead, they decided to construct a new egress and venting tunnel under the marina that Kevin was drawn to. An age old smaller vent was improved upon. The Soclarians had previously installed this vent strictly for the use of injecting eggs, fry and nutrients into the bay. Pop explained what they would see and to not be afraid.

"Well trail riders..." Hank transmitted in his inimitable up-beat fashion "We can't stay here all night. It is almost 3:45 in the morning. Keep your eyes on me. Your suits have a night light enhancer, but it still will not be the best possible light. Keep in a tight group. There is nothing to be afraid of down there. Friends are waiting for us below. There are no sharks that we have to be concerned with inside the bay. But, if there were, your suits, although they are flexible, are also tough as steel. So, let's get a wiggle on."

Hank slipped off the swim platform into the glassy calm, darkened and foreboding waters of Barnegat Bay. Adrian followed; then Kevin.

"Adjust your buoyancy controls, folks", Pop transmitted as he pointed to his controls. "I'm signaling ahead to let them know we're on our way down."

They descended toward the depths at a slow

rate; learning their controls and experiencing the sensation of their suits before allowing themselves to feel too comfortable in their new suits, new environment...new roles.

Suddenly, from behind an outcropping of rock and sea growth about two hundred feet away came one, then two...then a total of four mini-sub craft. Their flood lights pointing their way toward the swimmers. The swimmers could clearly see each sub silhouetted against the refracted light projected by the crafts' bright beams.

"Quickly" Hank commanded "adjust your buoyancy controls for rapid decent and swim like hell. Follow me to the door."

Somehow, they had been discovered. Someone or something had given them away. Somehow, the military had made a lucky guess or had been tipped off by someone to surveil the **ACT I**. Either way the jig was up. They had been found out. That didn't matter now. Now, escape was the only thing on the trio's mind.

Their hearts pounded. Their blood pressure rose and pulsed like beating drums in their ears as they struggled to swim downward in a blind panic. Both Kevin and Adrian fought their apparatus because of their immediate and emergent need for more oxygen. The suits adjusted immediately. Oxygen infused and coursed through their blood instantaneously. They again had command of themselves as they streaked toward the bottom aided by the modified small fins built into their suits and by the buoyancy gravitators.

Below, the three could see silhouetted against an increasingly bright blue light a huge, circular, hinged, clamshell like door swinging upward from the depths of the bay's floor. The light was coming

130

from the inside of whatever it was that was opening. The door had to be at least 150 feet in diameter. Two giant pistons were angled to the left and to the right of the opening door...pushing the immense door further and further upward. Tons of sand, rock and other debris cascaded in avalanche proportions off the gargantuan structure.

The subs advanced toward them.

"Kaboooom !!!"...came a crushing...impacting sound wave. The three were temporarily stunned. If it weren't for the super-suits they could have been killed or rendered unconscious.

"Pop...what in the hell was that?" Kevin bellowed as best he could through his synthesizer.

"Keep swimming as fast as you can." Hank responded. "We've been had. They were laying for us. That was a sonic impulse generator" not unlike the internal blasts of air inside the skull structures and chambers of porpoises and whales that are used to disable their pray. The burst had done its job. The occupants of the subs were stunned and rendered temporarily disoriented. Their craft scattered in confused disarray.

Just as the three regained all of their senses, a hot violent burst of water slammed against their bodies, catapulting them backward toward the subs. The four mini-subs again were cast into disarray and were hurtled backward as well...tumbling out of control like minnows in a rough surf.

Almost at the same instant, three red laser like beams shot out at the swimmers. The three were instantly disabled and encapsulated within the grip of a tangible force field; one that almost solidified the water around them. The water did not rush past them. It was being pulled along with them. They were encapsulated in this watery straight jacket

131

as an ancient mosquito would be locked in a tomb of sap turned to amber. They were being pulled against the rushing current as salmon up a stream toward the gaping maw of the brilliantly lighted hole below.

To quell the growing fear rising from deep inside his being, Kevin inappropriately quipped to himself "This must be how Herm-The-Sperm must have felt on his fateful journey up the river of joy " as they continued their downward rush; straight and true...like an arrow toward the center of a target.

As the three descended, Kevin was able to move his head enough to see that the pursuing submarines had stopped their pitching and yawing and were again engaged in the pursuit. However, they were making very little headway against the erupting column of water that rushed past the central column that the three had been imprisoned by.

The group entered the outer rim of the orifice; suspended about twenty feet past the lip by the scintillating beam emanating from the center of the seemingly endless shaft.

The water continued to rocket past them impeding and repulsing the advancing subs.

The subs were almost upon the trio when the door began to rapidly close. The turbulence caused by the slamming door catapulted the submarines anew; this time rocketing them backward. Hank blurted out "Those poor guys can't win for trying." Joking in mock empathy and mimickery he jeered "Scotty, my stomach can't take much more of this."

With about another twenty five feet remaining in the door's avalanche like fall Kevin recognized two of the submarine's occupants through the leading craft's transparent bubble. They were General Edwards and Major Taylor.

Kevin communicated "Damned if they weren't on our case from the start." How could they have been so **on-the-money** with their prediction of the trio's movements? What tipped them off or (more likely) **WHO** tipped them off?

A second resounding sonic blast pounded their bodies. This time the blast came from outside of the clam shell structure. The protective shroud from the beam rendered the blasts completely harmless. Apparently, this was a desperation move by the military to halt their escape. The door slammed shut with a quaking...reverberating *thud* !!! The increase in pressure would have crushed them like bugs if it weren't for their suits.

In his inimitable and prescient manner Hank guessed the forthcoming inquiries and parried them before they were launched.

What might have been a concussion-only bomb at best or a more sinister depth charge at worse had succeeded in unnerving Adrian and Kevin.

"Never mind all that right now" Hank admonished. "We have been found out. It probably makes no difference at this stage of the game anyway. Perhaps, the military will do something uncharacteristic like alerting the media. They are going to find it hard to explain why they have war ships in Barnegat inlet. It's even going to be harder for them to explain trying to bomb **swamp gas**.

"It is getting near the time that we **should** and **must** be discovered. What just happened might be part of the scheme...it must be. We have always been so careful to avoid detection."

Thinking out loud (how could you help it in those suits?) Hank mused "It would take them a lifetime to even come close to getting into that opening. Well, there's no sense in covering it back up with

133

sand now with the sand cannons. Let them ponder, pound, probe and blast the outer covering. It will remain securely fastened".

Sure enough, Edwards had them pegged. Kevin never suspected that they were being watched. Perhaps, it was done through satellite surveillance. He thought that he was being naive to think that Edwards and his gang would just pack up and go home after that full field dress drill the other night. It was done in true marine like fashion; almost like the storming of the beach at Normandy or Tripoli. Except this was an all air assault.

The federal boys did what they always did...almost always anyway. They gave out a crock of a story for public consumption in order to buy themselves a little time to find out the real story before starting a panic. Was that really all that bad in the total spectrum of things? Who knows?

On the one hand a government that claims to be a democracy owes the public it serves the truth. On the other hand it, also, is obligated to initially hedge on the truth at times for either the greater good or in order to protect that same public. It is a damned if you do and a damned if you don't situation at times.

"Situation Barnegat Light to Hawk-Eye Centurion; do you copy?" Clayton Edwards called into his microphone from below the waves.

"Switching to secured scrambled signal designation fox trot- tango-niner-alpha-bravo-zulu-one-zero. Acknowledge!" He barked a second time into the microphone.

At 28,000 feet overhead an airborne command nerve center made wide circles over the area under surveillance.

Almost crushing the mike in his hand the general reported, "Subjects have descended into vortical origin site of electromagnetic flux position."

Continuing in cryptic fashion (militareez) "Observed subjects entering large domed door leading under the bay's floor...Mirrored metallic door approximately 150 feet in diameter...We used minimum ordinance consisting of concussion charges in an attempt to either stop them or slow them down. Strong water current originating from within the vortex facilitated subjects' evading capture.

"Will remain on location for one hour. The fortifications appear to be extremely formidable in construction. Strongly suggest light cruiser now off shore rigged with depth charges and aquatic missiles be routed through Barnegat inlet to these coordinates...ASAP. This unit available to rendezvous with same at zero five thirty hours. Please advise."

Edwards was advised to standby on the frequency while further command decisions were taken into advisement at a higher level.

After a few moments a voice crackled back inside the mini-sub "General Edwards...be advised that at this time naval support is underway for rendezvous at your location at zero five thirty hours.

"Please remain on station at your land base location for reconnoiter in order to provide recognizance information as it may become available to you or your team on site.

"Remain on this frequency. Please acknowledge!"

Acknowledging for the first time that he was speaking with a superior officer he responded "Yes sir!...Acknowledged." The other voice returned "This is theater operations Hawk-Eye Centurion standing by...clear."

The tumultuous waterworks inside the vortex subsided, then ceased to erupt altogether. After being drawn for almost another mile straight downward...then, parallel with the bay's floor...then under and beyond the town of Barnegat Light toward the ocean, the trio was released from their force fields and allowed to swim freely.

Again, the suits did their jobs. The high pressure of the deep water had no effect on their bodies. Adrian and Kevin were no worse for wear as a result of their journey.

They found themselves inside a cavernous room of some type. The walls were constructed of a very thick nearly transparent material. Hank informed them that the material was as strong as the opening's domed lid.

Because of the molecular properties of the material, a very low voltage charge polarized and aligned the material in such a way that rendered the material transparent when necessary. Otherwise, the material was charcoal grey.

Segmented all around them...over and under them were compartmentalized encasements of unfathomable dimensions and proportions. Each contained sand and rocks spread over their bottoms. They contained a vast array of sea creatures and plants of various descriptions and sizes. The water in them was crystal clear.

"Do not be alarmed" Hank admonished. "These walls will never weaken. You are safe. Most of the creatures you see here are breeding stock. Those crabs over there are over seven hundred years old; kept from any harm, nurtured and fortified over the centuries", as he gestured toward a chamber to one side.

The crabs were at least three feet long from

136

point to point. Several hundred feet back in the same compartment, Kevin and Adrian could see eight foot long lobsters.

"These lobsters and crabs have produced billions of eggs for us over the years" Pop explained. "We are the ark; the regenerating source of so many species.   Now, stand here on the center of this black disk. We are about to get dry."

No sooner had Pop given his instruction than the water started receding from the chamber as if someone had broken the walls out of an aquarium and released its water all at once. It drained that quickly. Somehow, they were kept in place through an attraction between the six foot across black disk and the foot pads of their suits.

Both Adrian and Kevin were a bit wobbly when they first tried to stand. With the artificial weight conditions produced by the beam, plus buoyancy adjustments made while they were swimming caused them to not be prepared for the sudden weight of their bodies. Soon they got their sea legs; adjusting to the normal gravity conditions.

Hank peeled back his hood and took several deep breaths. He instructed the others to do the same. Following Hank's instructions and lead the remaining two peeled back their hoods and forced fresh air back into their lungs. Their autonomic reflex for breathing was stimulated back into action by the simple act of peeling back the hood.

He then told them to take their suits off altogether and to remain on the disk. This did not sit well with Adrian.

Decontamination had to take place by use of the hydrogen laser pulse designed to rid their hair, epidermis and mucous membranes that were in contact with the environment of bacteria, fungi and viruses.

The remainder of the unfriendly microbes that might have been present internally were handled by a special liquid concoction that tasted like mango juice which Hank had produced from three small silvery containers that he pulled from compartments in the flush deck's floor. They all drank the contents of their containers and replaced them in their slots in their corresponding cylindrical slots in the floor.

Briefly objecting to her treatment and the cavalier treatment imposed upon her degree of dress and undress, Adrian commented "Get me a robe first. I knew from the start you were a voyeur."

It was a half in jest and a full in earnest statement and tone. She had just about had it with this bare-bones vacation act.

Hank politely turned his back commenting, "You're the one who wanted to come along. This comes with the territory. I tried to warn you. It's not too late for you to go back if it is getting too hot in the kitchen for you" (or chilly in the cellar).

Reluctantly, Adrian restated her resolve to "go for the gusto".

She whispered in a tone audible only to herself "The things I have to put up with for my country."

This was a curious comment. What did her country have to do with her own penchant for curiosity? She wasn't on any other mission that they knew of; or was she?

Only hearing the whisper and not the words Hank demanded in the same half in jest tone "What type of mutiny are you fomenting over there in the peanut gallery?"

He really didn't expect a response. None came. The only sound was that of silent compliance.

Adrian made her point and she could see that

it was taken. She was used to a certain standard of privacy, decorum and propriety. It was a stressful enough situation without having to bare all and totally compromise her dignity with strangers.

The three stripped.

"Now, please do not move for a few moments" came Hank's additional instructions.

A clear cylinder came up around them. A warming bluish glow emanated from the material, keeping them warm. A few seconds later the light went out followed by a soft stream of warm air.

The platform began to descend, revealing levels containing more and more aquatic life. There was a new level every eighth of a mile or so.

Some levels contained land dwelling animals and birds in their practically natural habitats. How strange it was to see an ocelot miles under the sea.

The cylinder stopped its decent in an elevator compartment like room. It was about five feet across. The compartment moved sideways for about twenty seconds. Then, it changed direction and moved sideways again for another fifteen seconds. The movements were very smooth. There were no jolts or jerks, just a fluid transition with only the slightest of perceptible changes in directions. They stopped.

The cylinder lowered around them disappearing down under the floor as one wall slid open to reveal their being positioned to one side of a rather large, well furnished room.

It was furnished with beautiful Earth like furnishings. It had a large bed, dressers, mirrors, red leather seats, oil paintings on the walls and closets. There were two doors; one for the bath area; the other was another way out of the room.

"Damned if this isn't someone's bedroom"

Kevin blurted out. "Wall to wall carpeting and all".

Hank, agreeing, stated "In fact this is a bedroom...for the both of **you** while you are with us. You have an entire apartment that is a detachable pod which can be slid around the perimeter of the **Star Seeker III** or be detached and left here as part of Earth Station Barnegat Light. Why leave home when you can take it with you?"

Turning to Kevin, Adrian interjected "Fine...fine...fine!! Soclarians are the cat's meow. Now...I demand some clothes. Just because we don't have any clothes on let's not go all to hell in a hand basket with ourselves, Kevin. I am not going to parade around this place naked for one more minute. I've cooperated and played this silly nudist bit for as long as I wish to...enough already."

By and large, even though Adrian was probably in the most unusual and stressful situation of her life, she somehow seemed to remain composed, focused, defiant yet funny; like a professional in that when all goes crazy around a professional the true professional's heart rate slows down instead of the other way around.

Adrian seemed to have that quality. Why? What was it about her or her background that gave her that unique quality? She was able to take command of herself; define the here and now and draw others into her frame of reference and time despite the turmoil, unusual surroundings and atypical situation she found herself in.

It helped make an abnormal situation more normal for all of them. Kevin seemed to appreciate it with an acknowledging smile cast in her direction.

In any case she was in the right. It was pretty hard to compromise her sense of decency in one fell swoop. It was a bit much to expect or take for granted. These guys had to bend a little bit Kevin thought.

Pop joked "Don't get your panties all in a bunch...If you had any. Keep your pants on. You'll get clothes."

Her patience was wearing thin judging by the look on her face. Pop had always been a jokester and didn't always know when to stop or to take a hint; even though he was trying to place Adrian at ease with humor.

Kevin knew this because he knew Pop. Pop assumed an awful lot and often took too much for granted. Unfortunately, this situation was not one for someone with a thin skin...good, bad or indifferent. That's the way it was.

They stepped out onto the carpet where a female attendant met them with three robes. Hank told them to make themselves comfortable.

"Take a shower in the adjoining bathroom. As you can see, you have a powdery layer of dead kooties on your skin that you'll probably want to wash off. You will find the clothes you need in the closets."

Proud of what he was about to explain he continued "You know how those airline containers may be slid from their unit loading devices, then pushed along the tubular insides of a cargo plane? Well, in practice that's pretty much how these apartment modules slide on various levels around the perimeter of the **Star Seeker III**; they also may be put directly into place from almost any point on the outside.

"You see? If you want to change your neighbors or your neighborhood, or just have a yearn for a change...**period**, you can move your entire apartment."

Pop was in his glory. He reminded Kevin of Jackie Kennedy showing off the White House. He was pleased as punch with himself and proud to be a part of what he was involved with.

"But wait, there's more. This rig has another great option. When you look at the far window in your living room you will see two things: one will be a convexly curved inner and outer window partition. The outer panel will slide back to allow the entire apartment to jettison free. Both window panels are clear to allow you to see out into the sea's depths.

"The second thing you will see at that window will be a control panel. Each apartment is self propelled and in fact may leave the Earth's atmosphere and gravitational field to meet a mother ship if necessary. Don't touch a thing in there until it is all explained to you.

"We all have the need to get away every now and then. Even though this place sprawls under the ocean floor for miles, we all need to break away now and then or at least realize we can do it if we want to...a psychological safety valve of sorts.

"We do not have a great deal of time. However, I will leave you now so that you may recoup after your jostling trip. You are going to need some sleep. I am going to ask you that after your showers to get into bed, swing that lamp like apparatus over your heads and turn on the switch. You will fall asleep instantly.

"One hour under the impulse sleep rejuvenator provides the equivalent of an eight hour sleep cycle and all its associated benefits.

"Someone will call for you in about two hours...nighty-night." Hank walked out without waiting for a reply leaving Adrian and Kevin to wonder what happens next.

They did as they were asked to do. They took their showers and found loosely fitting sleeping apparel in the closets.

They really weren't very tired. They had just gotten up a little more than an hour ago. However, all things considered they were a bit shaken and the lamp treatment might be just the thing for them. Anyway, they were beginning to really look forward to any excuse to get into bed together.

Adrian smiled at Kevin saying "Well, while in Rome..."

Off came the robes. Naked again. Hard to imagine this was that same old shy Adrian. It was apparent that she would make exceptions for Kevin at every available opportunity.

They got into bed, turned on the apparatus and dropped right off to sleep...well...after a short play break of course.

-CHAPTER EIGHT-

The wake up call came via a low chiming sound at their unit's door. It was a little after 6:00 AM. As Kevin met the visitor, a deep...body shuddering, quaking rumble vibrated through the floor and hull of the level to which their cubicle was attached.

What alarmed Adrian and Kevin was the expression of concern on their visitor's face. They would have thought that it was some kind of pump or other if it were not for the anxious look of the visitor as he looked around himself and upward. A second quaking thud reached them, followed closely by a third. Obviously, it was not something normal.

"You two had better follow me" the visitor suggested. "I have no idea what that was. I am to escort you to the station command center where Captain Senecus, Commander Leotor and Ambassador Feidor await your presence."

"Ambassador?" Kevin commented..."Pop's getting up in the world."

The jolts were increasing in frequency..."pa-boomph--pa--boomph". As a boy, around every July 4th, Kevin used to throw cherry bombs into Barnegat Bay and watch them explode. This noise reminded him of that; like a muffled cherry bomb exploding in the water.

Adrian and Kevin followed their guide to another lift. The command center was located on the upper-most level of this almost county sized wonder of ar-

145

chitecture and engineering.

When the trio arrived they joined an array of individuals as promised by their guide. Hank greeted them and made the introductions.

"Adrian...Kevin...this is Ambassador Justinian Fairborne, representing the Soclarian high counsel. This is Commander Joshua Leotor, Commander of Earth Station Four...(Earth Station Barnegat Light)...Captain Moses Senecus, Captain of **Star Seeker III** of whom you and I have spoken...and Lieutenant Abdul Lasamar, First officer of **Star Seeker III.**"

Amenities were exchanged and they got right down to business.

Hank continued: "Ambassador Fairborne was to speak at the United Nations addressing the general assembly in an attempt to thwart what has now become the inevitable. Saddam has struck. Such an address is now a mute point. The agents of evil have done their dastardly handy work; avoiding our detection and our best efforts.

"The dye is cast. Armageddon is at hand. Even now as we speak, the first signs that the end times are upon this planet are being broadcast to the public...However, as ludicrous or trite as it may sound, they do not know the half of it; not yet."

Captain Senecus proffered, "Your president should have dealt with Saddam Housien while he had the chance. He did not want to go down in history as practicing genocide himself. Nor did he want to defeat an enemy and inherit a populace which would have proven to be intransigent and indomitable. No matter what, you Americans would be the godless infidels in their eyes. Saddam has done a marvelous job in making them believe that the rest of the world is the problem and he is his people's savior. It is next to impossible to recognize poison if it is coated in sugar.

"Now, the madman has sewn the seeds of destruction for this entire planet. He is the great spoiler of all that he cannot possess or rule over. He is like the divorced man or rebuked lover who is insane with jealousy and vows that if he cannot possess his woman, no one else can enjoy her company either. Instead of loving and loosing, he loves and destroys in an orgy like fit of self indulgent, self righteous and simply selfish uncaring psychotic episode of death and destruction.

"Saddam does these deeds in true anti-christ style; doing all of these things in the name of God. I'm telling you, the big boss is ticked."

Ambassador Fairborne went on, "Saddam was a spoiled brat as a child and became a dangerous spoiled brat as an adult. With power and influence, that is a dangerous combination when taken to the extreme.

"As unlikely as it may seem, It appears now, that one man has spoiled this planet. It will be up to one man, with our resources behind him, to try to save the people of this planet. Because of a pre-ordained...genetically engineered throw-back, you, Mr. Murdock, *are* that man."

The concussions grew louder and felt more pronounced on the upper level of the camouflaged one hundred yard diameter observation dome which was telescoped above the sandy bottom. The command dome level was retractable. However, there was no need to drop it below the sand.

Like a gopher laughing at a marauding fox from his exit fifty feet away from where the fox was digging at the gopher's entrance hole, so did the commander flaunt his confidence.

Commander Leotor spoke, "Do not be disturbed by the explosions. They cannot harm us. The U.S. Navy is trying to dislodge our capped dome on the

147

other side of Long Beach Island on the bay side. We are feeling the concussions from the depth charges that they are dropping directly onto the surface of the cap. However, they are succeeding in shaking the entire area and our structure along with it.

"The fools...at the shallow depth the charges are exploding the Navy stands a better chance of blowing up their own hulls than putting a dent in our cap. However, by the end of the day they will be learning of an actual threat far greater than what they must be imagining we represent.

"The jig is up anyway. We have been discovered...which at this time is all part of the pre-ordained plan. The public will be desensitized by degree through the mass media which will actually make the final part of our mission a bit easier.

"Above, they think that they are on a national security mission. It is *our* mission that will protect their security. However, we have little time to loose; let alone trying to debate this issue from the inside of a security stockade.

"Soon, they will increase their bombardment. The populace might be panicked or someone might get himself hurt or killed up there. This cannot be allowed to happen. We are here to help, not to harm.

"Just before the **Star Seeker III** departs, we shall open the bay side dome to allow them to get just inside the first section. We then shall seal off the rest of the access tunnel. This will serve as a diversion. There is so much sensing equipment in that chamber that it will keep them busy tinkering until we can do what we have to do."

Commander Leotor was summoned to a control console to observe the progress of the Naval forces. Kevin started to worry about his children. His look of concern was recognized by Hank.

Hank comforted, "Don't worry Kevin. Your children are fine. You will be back in time to greet them at the marina. Now, you have a job to do.

"While you rested, we had a briefing with the Soclarian counsel. Our Earth's planetary intelligence network was in on the meeting. Push has come to shove. Things don't look too good. Your part in this at this point in history has been made clearer to us and we must now brief you on what is happening in the world and what must be done."

Ambassador Fairborne interrupted, "Mr. Murdock, time is short. You will be briefed in much greater detail while we are in transit. We must make preparations now to take the **Star Seeker III** to Earth Base Station One. Our destination right now is the Persian Gulf."

Ambassador Fairborne excused himself to see how the preparations for the trip were going...a trip toward the destiny of mankind...a destiny located within the cradle of earth's civilization itself.

Lieutenant Lasamar instructed the trio to follow him to the **Star Seeker III** to prepare for departure within the hour. They got onto a ski lift like seat suspended from the ceiling of the hallway they entered. It was like something you would experience on a ride in one of Orlando, Florida's theme parks.

Pop pointed out one of the infirmaries explaining that the little girl and her mother that they saw in there were the two missing victims of the boating accident of two nights before. The seat lift stopped. Pop asked that Adrian and Kevin follow him into one of the rooms of the infirmary.

"Adrian, while I was administering to your mother's injuries the **Star Seeker III** had recovered the bodies of the two you now see in that room. Although it was the father's careless drunken act that could have been avoided had he not been drinking, it is also true that it was our craft that was in the wrong place at the wrong time for them. Under the cover of darkness they were immediately rescued and resuscitated.

"It was their choice to stay with us a little longer than was necessary. We could have cleared their memories of the event. At first the mother really wanted to divorce her jerk husband for putting them in such jeopardy. However, she is going to go back to him with her daughter after he mourns for just a little longer and contemplates his inane and unconscionable behavior.

They have agreed to aid us when it is time to leave the area. They will be carrying a message to the surface for us when the time is right.

"Departure will be in a little over one hour. That will be at 7:30 AM. The two accident survivors will serve as our decoys. There is so much Coast Guard and naval activity out there that we need to draw a little bit of the heat off of us.

"Incidentally Adrian, this is also where you and the rest of us part company" as two rather beefy looking guards appeared through one of the doorways.

"Hey!!! Just what the hell is going on here you guys. I'm not going anywhere...except going with you guys. That's my choice and my decision. I don't care what you say," she vociferously objected.

Kevin was not only confused about Pop's seemingly rude and precipitous behavior but, also, Adrian's sudden "tougher than nails" retort and stance. It was dramatically out of character for her, he thought. It was a much tougher voiced insistence than that made on the connecting bridge at the marina, prior to their descent into the depths of Barnegat Bay.

"Fine, Fine Adrian" Hank responded. "Your objection has been noted and logged. Now, we don't have time for your little sham any longer. I don't believe that Kevin does either."

Adrian flushed beet-red folding her arms in front of herself with her eyes darting from side to side as if she were looking for a place to escape. She also looked like she knew that her hand had been caught in the cookie jar. The guards moved along side of her.

"We knew that when I had first appeared to Kevin that I was being observed by the authorities. It was hoped that I would be observed, but not interfered with. At the time, I didn't even know that. It was kept secret for operational reasons.

"So...you see, how it is...we saw you coming from a long way off. We have known for quite awhile that you are an agent of the Central Intelligence Agency. We tracked you from Langley, to the helicopter transfer, to your landing in Manahawkin, out to your summer home on Long Beach Island where you met your mother right out to where you met us in Barnegat Bay."

Kevin fell back into a chair with his mouth agape...almost catatonic...muttering that he had been "had by a damned CIA agent."

Kevin was used to the deceit of some women...but, no...not now...not again...not now. He cared for Adrian. Wearing his heart on his sleeve set him up for disappointment again.

He wondered why the Soclarians wanted to save such a morally bankrupt race that thrived on deception? Where was the profit in it? It seemed as if there weren't anything worthy of believing in anymore.

That must be the nature of humanity, he thought. It had to be. It was like a never-ending game; gain the confidence, get what you want (money, sex, information, trust, conquest...) deceive and then move

151

on. God didn't mean it to be this way. What was wrong? He wondered what he was doing wrong to deserve this.

As Kevin sat, Adrian let out a shriek and attempted to bolt for the door like a cornered panther. Reacting, the two guards grabbed her arms and wrestled her to keep her standing in one spot.

"Hold on there Mata Hari. No one is going to hurt you" Hank reassured.

"We knew you were a snake before we let you in. There is nothing inherently evil about a snake. You just have to identify it and be careful not to get bitten...you know...keep your hands out of its mouth.

"Now, cut the crap. Calm down and listen for a second. We have used and are going to use you in much the same way in which you have used Kevin here. We wanted to share our intelligence information with you; let you see what we are all about and what our mission is all about. There was no time for us to do that in an interrogation room under a hot lamp in some security prison or bunker. Time is of the essence.

"Very shortly, you are going to be placed along with the two we have rescued into a small shuttle craft. You will have life vests, an EPERB, which is an emergency radio beacon, a five minute oxygen supply and a flare gun with three flares. You will be carried up the coast just off the shoreline of Seaside Heights; out about two miles. Your EPERB will be activated. You will be left in the water at that time. We will then make our move to leave on the **Star Seeker III.** Don't worry you will be safe.

"By the way, your own cylindrical miniature nuclear powered radio beacon device injected into the left cheek of your buttocks has been jammed by our own frequencies right from the time you entered the water. It will broadcast again when you are back on top in the water. In a manner of speaking, your superiors will get wind of your location from that alone.

"I have to tell you though, that was a unique touch. It's nice to see an attractive, firm and active posterior sachet side to side from time to time...but...I never thought I'd see one that was **RADIO-ACTIVE.** You see...*in the end* you were discovered." The guards chuckled.

"Let's call a spade a spade; cut through the sham and work with one another. We need you **right now**...topside, talking to your bosses. Because, in a very short time we will need their cooperation to pull this thing off...the details of which I am currently not at liberty to divulge.

"I can tell you, however, that it is for civil order purposes that we will need their cooperation. Just convince them that we are all on the same side and that they should act accordingly."

Adrian was now calmed and a little more composed. She turned toward Kevin, who looked up at her through confused and watery eyes. He was, after all, an emotionally strong man, but there was only so much he could take. He was reaching his limit of tolerance.

Now, Adrian spoke with a calm measured voice...again in control: "All that he says is true, Kevin...But, I want you to believe in your heart that I truly care for you. As we danced and first embraced, something began to happen to me.

"I know that you don't believe me now; not after this." She looked down with a sorrowfully pensive stare and went on.

"After my mother was saved, I felt a revulsion for my deception toward you...a self hatred. I vowed to make things up to you if I could. I planned to reveal

153

everything to you when this whole thing was over."

She pleaded "Please, don't hate me!" Then, softly sobbing..."I don't want you to hate me. I can't stand the thought of your hating me"...her hands now covering her face.

Hank motioned to the guards to allow her to sit herself next to Kevin. They relaxed their grip and stood by closely, sensing that she no longer felt as threatened. She placed her hand on Kevin's knee and continued.

"It is important to me that you know that I have an abiding devotion and allegiance to this great country, America...and the God inspired truths and goodness that it stands for.

"I come from a family of first generation immigrants, who inspired in me the love of freedom and the gratitude that we all must feel for having the privilege of living in a free society in which we may live without fear of repression for what is in our hearts and minds; a nation of equal opportunity, where individual accomplishment is encouraged and rewarded...a nation which treats its populace with kindness and humanity...a nation guided by what is best in human nature or at least what we aspire to be. That's why I do what I do. I make no excuses for it.

"You know deep down that it is our destiny to be together and to become part of each other's lives in some future meaningful way. It is meant to be. I can't explain it...I **just know** that it is true...and I know that you know it too."

Kevin said nothing as he stared at her then gazed ahead with his arms folded. He wanted to believe her. He felt that something truly worthy of building upon passed between them other than just a little spit.

Yet, the hurt of his past marriage and the specter of renewed deception jaded his perspective. It was stingingly fresh and in the forefront of his consciousness...like salt on a reopened wound. He needed time.

He wanted to believe. He needed deep down in his being...in his heart of hearts...to believe...to trust...to unconditionally let go of his paranoia, so that he could reach for and touch the rapture...the sharing of souls that he knew was possible...somewhere...somewhere out there... somewhere in the chaotic fray of the storm of human interaction...it was out there.

Adrian stood as the guards grasped her upper arms. She gave a defiant shrug of her shoulders to shake off her escorts; allowing herself to be led away unencumbered...under guard...yet free.

Free because she said her piece and said it with dignity and with the assurance that it was rendered with the ring and strength of truth. She was free because she knew in her heart that the truth she spoke would register on Kevin's consciousness. This truth would help to put his mind to rest as he performed the difficult tasks ahead...tasks which she knew would be for the well being of the greater whole; tasks for the greater good...whatever those duties might be.

She now felt and knew that she was an important part of the unfolding mosaic and knew what she must do when she returned to the surface. She must plan well for that time. She was not about to be a mere messenger after coming this far. She was not about to lose Kevin during the upcoming unsettled times either.

She felt a greater calling; a greater duty and was not about to allow an agent from another authority to countermand the directives from her own superiors. Hank was convincing, but Adrian had a boss and as far as she knew, he was still her boss.

She knew that in crucial times she had to *ad lib*

and act in accordance with the situation. However, she knew that if given the chance, she could help to fulfill the needs of both sides. She knew there were no enemies here. What was the worst thing that they could do to her if she constructively rebelled against orders from the Soclarians; orders that she was under no positive obligation to follow?

What could they do, put her in the brig? Place her in chains? She had to take a chance, but how? Where would her opportunity lie?

She stopped in the entrance way to the room and turned back toward Hank as he called after her interrupting her self-initiated and self righteously indignant exit.

Hank directed, "You must get ready now. Your work is cut out for you. I am certain we may rely upon your prowess in your portrayal of this situation and in your ability to convince your superiors regarding their needed and anticipated cooperative role." She again turned to leave.

"Just one more thing. Your mother is bound to rush back to your shore home when she starts hearing the news reports about what is happening in the world. She will be looking for you.

"When you see Gerta, tell her for me that she was a delightful presence the other night; that I hope we will meet again and perhaps, finish that dance. Now...go do your stuff!"

Adrian gave a little smile as she left the room thinking to herself "I'll be damned, she got to him; didn't she?"

Kevin's heart was indeed lifted as he saw Adrian disappear through the passageway. They would see each other again. He knew it. The activity in the room resumed.

Sounding uncharacteristically biblical, Hank

turned to Kevin telling him to "Rise up from your seat and do not be disquieted. All things have a purpose. All events determine an end to which we may not always be privy.

"Be comforted in the knowledge that the benevolence of the Creator smiles upon each of us and that the ultimate rapture is that which occurs when we all are accepted into the arms and the safe keeping of the Almighty.

"Take refuge in the knowledge that, by definition, we are of the flesh and being of the flesh, we are indeed imperfect. We, therefore, must inevitably and despite our best efforts disappoint each other. There is nothing right or wrong about that...nothing good or bad...it just is."

He continued "People have disappointed you, Kevin. You have disappointed people. I will, perhaps, disappoint you and others...I have in the past...You will in the future. You will disappoint the ones you love and they will disappoint you from time to time. That's the way it is.

"Expect the best in people, because it is truly there. It is that God inspired goodness and spark that the Almighty places there just to let you know that he is around. Conversely, if you look for the worst, you will never be disappointed in that quest either...for it, likewise, is there."

"You will never find the complete love, acceptance and rapture you seek in this life. You will come close; which is the best that any of us can reasonably expect. There are moments...just moments...as fleeting as a butterfly's beautiful passage before our eyes. Those fleeting moments are often what we live for.

"However, this supreme perfection, this deepest of all needs will not be found in the imperfection of the flesh, not on a sustained basis.

"That is why it is not possible to come to know our Benefactor and loving Father through man. Some men endeavor to lead mankind in that direction...many of whom you have come to discover to be *Bible* thumping charlatans who ultimately reveal themselves through their own human frailties, iniquities and weaknesses of the flesh.

"On the television they howl, castigate, accuse, warn and conjure the specter of fire, brimstone and the devil himself. They take your faith, your money and let you down...yes...they disappoint you through engaging in what they warn and preach against. It bruises and wounds the spirits of those who so desperately want and need to believe.

"Nonetheless, they, for the most part, are still good people and the children of the Creator. In the main, their hearts are in the right place. Their intentions are good. They are simply of the flesh and are not to be judged too harshly. They are, after all, only human.

"Now, let us continue our mission" Hank instructed as they re-seated themselves on the suspended seat system."

Once they arrived on the bridge of the **Star Seeker III**, Pop instructed Kevin to have a seat next to him directly behind the helm.

Captain Senecus welcomed them to the bridge and explained, "Although the distance we will be traveling today will be very short, it is critical, at least during this phase of our operation, that we remain undetected. Interference might jeopardize our mission.

"Later, we will want to be seen. Now, we must follow a route out to the continental shelf, where we will pick up the trans-Atlantic subterranean transport tunnel system constructed north to south along the African coast...then, continuing underground to the

Straits of Hormuz.

"This link was established in cooperation with other earth stations in order that the tunnels may follow 'hot spots' on the earth...you know...where the continental tectonic plates meet and where there is volcanic activity.

"Even though we might be deep or even subterranean during our trip, the slightest heat given off by our craft might be detected by infrared scanners on satellites in earth orbit. The lava's heat will shield us from that detection".

The captain returned to his duties. Hank began his outline and instruction to Kevin.

"The Straits of Hormuz represent the general area within which the seeds of civilization first sprouted and now the seeds of its destruction ironically lie. They emanate from that region in the persona of Saddam Hussein. He should have been stopped while your president and others had the chance.

"Initially, no one knew the dark intentions of Hussein after he was rebuked and defeated in battle. Soon though, the signs of his remorseless behavior were everywhere. It was clear that he could not be salvaged, reached nor rehabilitated as he raped the environment, tortured the people of Kuwait and hid behind the guise of being the firebrand and spokesman for his people as he killed, tortured and subjugated the vulnerable everywhere he turned.

"However, the concept of fair play, non-interference in the ultimate direction another country takes and the further concept that punishment should not exceed the crime all speak to the basic and inherent goodness of mankind when given the proper circumstances and opportunity.

"It is important that when awesome power is at one's disposal, that prudence, temperance and moderation be the guide and rule. That is what places true humanity above chaos...that is what places your people and your president above the likes of Saddam Hussein.

"In nature, when a wolf lays down and bares his throat, the dominant male wolf backs off. Mankind is one of the very few species on this planet that historically goes for the jugular under such circumstances while at war or (very often) even interpersonally.

"Each of us has a choice when those around us are vulnerable or at our mercy once we have been taken into their hearts or have been given their confidence.

"It has only been recently, with the advent of super-weapons heralding or threatening total annihilation, that mankind at large has been able to take a lesson from the wolf. Wolves know that they must work together to survive; they need each other. A certain respect is evident within their hierarchy. There is a certain nobility in their treatment of one another.

"Their population **is** their extended family. Their showing of superiority does not mean the killing of one another. As ruthless as they are in their hunt for food they demonstrate a kindness, a forbearance and even...yes!!...even a degree of **'HUMANITY'** that man often finds himself at a loss either to attain or maintain.

"Yes...they are dogs...but as we all know...dog spelled backwards spells GOD. Corny, but an appropriate coincidence.

"Consider the silent loyalty; concern when things are not right...when you are sad or sick, the companionship, the perky anticipation, the grateful wagging tail...simply because you are home or pet him on the head; the unwavering household parimeter protector.

"This unconditional noble behavior both on the part of the wild wolf amongst his own, and our household companion...the dog...has been overlooked as instructional, because of man's vanity. To think that man may deign to learn of humanity from an animal.

"It is simply beneath him. Yet, this fellow creature has been placed upon this Earth by the same God that has created man.

"I personally believe that in a way this was God's way of saying that 'Man needs some help. He needs a calm, joyous, warm fuzzy, uncomplaining and non-judgmental presence to help sooth his soul from time to time.'

"Very often, this is something that people just can't. do for each other...it's that simple. Strange but true. Yes, wolves and dogs have a degree of nobility.

"There is nothing noble about Hussein. He is a wolf without restraint nor even the scruples of a jackal. He has gone beyond the *point of no return* and has sown the seeds of irreversible and total planetary destruction in true Jim Jones fashion; taking the ship down with himself and all hands on board.

"Now, instead of being conciliatory at this juncture... instead of admitting the folly of his ways so that his people may not be made to suffer further as a true statesman would do...instead of being humbled by his experience...Hussein is furthering his perverse enterprise, his evil influence and province, renewing and perpetuating the pain, suffering and the deprivation of his own people and now that of the rest of the planet. It's too late!

"His poisons flow into every river of the ecosystem as we speak. The sheer magnitude of this onslaught is beyond our capacity to reverse or suppress. The canisters of nerve gas to be unleashed are too numerous. His evil army of nuclear saboteurs are well hidden and in place...blended with various populations...their criminal intentions and tools

161

shielded and protected by the dark forces and powers of evil and wickedness that Saddam has built around himself.

"The free world made the mistake of defining the phenomenon of Hussein according to its own standards, ethics and moral codes. He *is* Armageddon!!! He **is** the great destroyer of not only mankind but of the environment...plants...animals...the entire planet.

"His people too, like all people everywhere, are the children of our Creator. They should not be made to suffer inordinately for the transgressions of he who places himself in the father figure role of a confused national family and its members.

"The Soclarian counsel realized that this was the mind set of your president and the heads of the other nations involved with OPERATION DESERT STORM. Their mind set was guided by the spirit of the Almighty who dictated, 'Be strong, be courageous, be resolute but be kind and gentle in victory. Exercise forbearance and restraint in victory...for it is not your place nor your right to punish the people of Iraq, but to censor Hussein and encourage his people to vanquish him themselves.

"That never happened. America's intentions were good and honorable. Saddam's evil hold over his people was too strong. Now, Hussein has initiated the irreversible **FINAL STORM** as he mockingly calls it.

"News reports are beginning to panic the world as we speak. He is protected by the forces of evil that shroud his intentions from our scrutiny. Compassion and the milk of human kindness is known to Hussein only as that beverage with which he washes down his meal of conquest, ruin and destruction.

"His charismatic ways, his lies, his calm practiced cliches and mannerisms all manifest themselves in a way that project an apparent deep concern and adoration for his people and his nation.

"He prays on their weaknesses and misplaced loyalties like a clever vulture anticipating a meal of carrion. Selfishly, he turns his nation into fetid rot by degree, by design; uncaring, unfeeling...through the passage of each day.

"His people's crimes are those of love, fear, confusion ignorance and trust. That's called being human. Saddam's crimes are those that emanate from the deepest and darkest recesses of human nature; taking advantage of and strength from the weakness, gullibility and vulnerability of his people to further his own hateful and evil ambitions.

"He has become evil incarnate. Evil works through Hussein at this time in history, as it has done through a single person often throughout history; through a person who becomes a false prophet and justifies all deeds (evil and otherwise) once he has wormed his way into to the hearts and minds of his people.

"He is a false prophet in sheep's clothing veiling his true ugliness, intentions and blood thirsty ambitions behind a shroud of piety, righteousness, beauty or some other seemingly credible or justifiable facade.

"The **EVERLASTING UNIVERSAL NAY**, the great denier, the grand deceiver...evil...YES...**THE DEVIL** practices his craft through those who have come to a high position of trust...a position of strength from which he may manipulate others and events toward evil ends.

"Thank God most leaders have the presence of mind and strength to resist that dark force; to recognize the power and the authority that they wield. They are able to shout **NO !!!** to the GREAT CONSUMING **NO**...to the destroyer...to the great promising deceiver who caters to man's vanity in order to work his will.

"History is froth with such people: Adolph Hitler, Attilla The Hun, Bloody Mary Queen of Scots, Napoleon, Cleopatra...on and on...and now Saddam Hussein. Except now, EVIL wants it all...the end times.

"Evil wants to fulfill the prophesy of the reluctant Soclarians of thirty thousand years ago. They were reluctant to give free reign to Earth's inhabitants. They called humanity *'The human virus.'* This ancient prediction made its way through the ages on earth in the writings of the book of *Revelation*.

"The Soclarians predicted that humans would infect this healthy beautiful cell they called earth. They would multiply and use up its resources. The cell would become fetid with the pollutant by-products of their replication and other activities, ultimately killing and exploding the cell in a fiery and poisoned last gasp; spewing its high-tech encapsulated viral progeny in all directions into the body universe to further infect the universal host.

"That was the nihilistic prediction of those who did not anticipate nor calculate the effect of the Deity in the protection and perpetuity of the body universe; the omni-present God influenced propensity toward acknowledging the benign nature of the universe and God's role in influencing that destiny. Both of these two scenarios are possible.

"The first being the infectious spread of man's selfish headlong plunge toward destruction and extinction (which can be exported throughout the universe), now championed by Saddam Hussein himself...the quintessence and personification of that philosophy.

The second being the scenario which provides a clarion rebuttal and rejection of that nihilistic possibility by insuring that the noble and benign nature of mankind rises above the constantly challenging and

164

beckoning dark forces of evil. This rejection and re-buttal shall survive beyond the corpse and shell of its mistakes...the destroyed planet earth.

"Destruction of this planet is now assured. It is up to us in this assemblage and others just like it, to salvage that which represents what is best in mankind and indeed in the rest of this world."

They sat together in silence, reflecting upon the horrible truths of the situation; upon the plight with which the planet was faced and what that would mean to mankind within the coming hours...within the next few days...through the generations.

As they sat behind the helm they awaited their signal to depart. It came in the voice of a coast guard duty officer's alarm over the radio monitor. It was their cue to leave.

"Pan-pan, pan-pan, pan-pan!!! Hello all stations...Hello all stations...Hello all stations. This is United States Coast Guard Group Barnegat Light. This is United States Coast Guard Group Barnegat Light. Standby for an urgent marine information broadcast...Break!"

Five seconds of silence elapsed then, "All inter-ested marine traffic be advised that an emergency flare has been sighted and an EPERB beacon has been ac-tivated at zero seven twenty hours local time, approxi-mately two miles due east of the Seaside Heights board-walk area.

"Aerial reconnaissance has determined that there are at least two individuals in the water and in stan-dard orange life jackets in that general vicinity. Exact coordinates to follow...Break!"

Three seconds elapsed and the coordinates were given. The voice continued, "Be advised that any and all vessels in that immediate vicinity are requested by the commander of this station to proceed at this time to these coordinates and render aid and assistance as needed...Break!"

"All vessels whose intentions are to respond to this request please respond by switching and answering on channel two-two-alpha regarding your intentions, location and your estimated time of arrival at these coordinates. This is United States Coast Guard Group Barnegat Light standing by on frequencies one-six and two-two alpha...Break!"

The monitor hummed with responding parties...from the Coast Guard patrols themselves, to state police boats inside the inlet, to commercial fishermen, to concerned nearby recreational boaters; the responses poured in.

The duty officer's request from the local Barnegat Light Station's commander was a polite way of saying "You are being ordered, herewith, to respond to this maritime emergency". Maritime law dictates that there is no option other than the nearest vessels' responding in a positive and expeditious manner to an emergent life threatening situation.

Boat owners at that point work for the Coast Guard and **must** respond in order to protect and preserve lives. It comes with the territory of owning a boat. A positive response should go without saying; a matter of common courtesy and a foregone conclusion. It's amazing, however, how many boaters ignore the call for assistance and have to be firmly warned and reminded.

Kevin was reminded by this situation of a party boat captain operating out of Barnegat Light who required just such a firm warning and reminder the season before. The Coast Guard admonished at that time "At this time captain I must remind you of the obligation requiring you to stand by and await either further instructions or the arrival of Coast Guard personnel.

Failure to due so may subject you to either fines, forfeiture of license or other penalties. This is the maritime law of which I am certain you are well aware of."

The party boat captain reluctantly responded with a grumbled acknowledgement and exasperated acquiescence.

It was completely amazing to Kevin to fathom that a man who makes his living from the sea, is vulnerable along with his passengers to the vagaries of an unpredictable sea and or machinery would even consider abandoning a vessel and people in distress if he were in a position to help. An inconvenience to the day in the lives of a few fishermen palls in the face of a situation in which lives are at risk.

"Saelahnse, saelahnse, saelahnse!!!" came the french-like pronunciation command accepted among mariners as the command to clear the frequencies...a command for silence. The Coast Guard personnel struggled to handle one response at a time on the jammed frequencies.

Captain Senecus turned from the monitor and announced "Within ten minutes there will be so much radio and boat activity up there that we could slide Mount Everest out of here without being noticed."

In an instant, Kevin sat up ramrod straight, as if he had been slapped in the face with the inconsistency of the broadcast he had just played back in his mind. Only two people had been sighted in the water. There should have been three; the mother, her daughter and Adrian. What happened to the third person?

Kevin kept his mouth shut. He had decided to trust in Adrian's sincerity and abilities. Somehow he knew that she would be OK. He felt it. It was communicated to him. He had established his own link with Adrian. It was weak, but it was there, without the nifty wet suit. He worried more about the girl and her mother.

They were not talking, but they were communicating... communicating with feelings. He knew that his natural abilities were growing. He was, by degree, experiencing a very positive metamorphosis. It continued. He felt his destiny calling him from the distance. He relaxed and leaned backward into his seat, quietly accepting his developing role; allowing the inevitable to unfold before him.

Captain Senecus barked, "Initiate systems check on my mark...**MARK!**

"Charge the GIEPS on my mark."

This acronym meant the primary gravitational inductive electromagnetic propulsion system.

...**"Mark!"**

Equipment hummed. Multi-colored control panel lights danced in flat sheets of color, causing a strange aurora borealis effect on whatever charged particles were around the dimly lit room. The colors swirled in an unearthly march and cadence of committed intent...helping in the overall mode of projecting an inexplicable professional atmosphere of practiced military competence...of direction...of readiness; like that of having everything 'just so' on opening night at the theater. Everyone had his place...his part.

In a manner akin to a conductor's tapping and raising his wand to command the attention of the pit orchestra, Captain Senecus calmly directed..."Prepare for departure!"

He behaved as if this were just another routine performance. That's the face of a professional. In the face of challenge, knowing that he now journeyed toward, perhaps, a final rendezvous with Earth's destiny, his heart rate dropped.

It was not ice water, but the calm assurance of

knowledge and purpose that coursed through his veins sculpting his presence into that of a hardened (more appropriately a galvanized) military professional.

"This is it...Show time", Kevin whispered to himself; his not feeling very commanding at all. He felt like he felt before his first high school debate, waiting behind the stage curtain...what was out there? How will the message be received? Would he perform to expectations? How did he get there? Was there still time to change his mind. Did he know his material?

That was the problem...what material? Yet he knew the material would be there, the guidance the direction would be there when the time was right. He knew it.

The anticipation he felt was mixed with exhilaration; a feeling much like the one he experienced while sky diving in the military. During his first jump he moved closer to the aircraft's door. The jump master pointed directly at him and then to the door...there was no ladder. He had to have the confidence that his chute was going to open. Faith not withstanding his heart had been in his throat nonetheless. He was exhilarated; just like now facing this new jump of faith.

Kevin silently ruminated; wow...what a difference a day makes. Yesterday...a businessman minding his own business. Today...some kind of indispensable key who must serve as the catalyst to rally...to communicate...to convince and to help preserve or at least salvage something out of the chaos.

His thoughts turned toward the well-being of his children, his failed marriage, how it just didn't seem fair to the boys...and then...he prayed...he prayed for mankind... for his children...for all children...for direction...for comfort...for courage.

"Seal the air locks!" the captain continued.

The hiss of air was barely audible; like that of air

escaping from the conical valve over a passenger's seat in a commercial airliner. In a few seconds the sound faded away.

"Disconnect umbilical companionway from station...on my mark ...**MARK**!"

...Thump!...Sounding like a landing gear coming up, the disconnection took place.

"Activate all water pump impulse thrusters!"

The hum grew louder.

"Take us up ten feet...flat and easy."

The craft gently jerked off the bottom...the sand swirling all about them like a winter snow scene paper weight after having been tipped upside down. The **Star Seeker III** rotated ninety degrees.

"Lieutenant Lasamar, set in a course for the canyon and initiate forward thrust upon your ready mark"

The Lieutenant echoed slowly, "R-e-a-d-y...**Mark!** We are away, sir. Building initial forward speed to 200 knots, sir. Initiating the molecular transponder field...**NOW**!."

Kevin mused; this was not unlike being a passenger on an airplane on his way to an important sales meeting. Being that he was on his way to the Persian Gulf he joked to himself that this one would *be* "The mother of all sales." It would be the sale of his life.

The major difference was that this particular sale would have a profoundly far reaching effect on multitudes. He became resolved and galvanized by that thought. He welcomed his mission. He knew the evil...he knew his adversary. His name was carnage. His name was havoc. His name was Armageddon. His name was Saddam Hussein.

-CHAPTER NINE-

Adrian's second five minute oxygen supply ran out just as the final inches of water were purged from the returning shuttle vehicle's docking bay. Almost as an after thought she was able to finagle a second supply. A minute longer and she would have been a goner. She took a chance; a daring calculated risk. Now what? Where to now?

She was not about to be left out of the main event. In the ready room before she and the two survivors from the boating accident were brought to the surface, she learned that the little girl had a small tape recorder sealed in a plastic bag inside of her waist pouch. Adrian's cunning and imagination had to work fast; putting her survival instincts and her drive to see her mission through into overdrive.

She talked to the mother and little girl about what had happened to them. She learned that the little girl's name was Stacey Harmon and her mother was Susan Harmon. They lived in northern New Jersey in Morristown up in Morris County.

It seems that in a crisis situation, when children are involved, most adults become nurturing and caring toward children; even if the children are not their own. Every child becomes your child. It's probably more the case for women then for men; the maternal instincts kick in.

Men certainly have this instinct too; except the

men tend to face the danger, cope with the threat or try to fix the problem. Then, they attempt damage control and assessment while helping the temporary extended family of the crisis to pick up the pieces. The women become surrogate mothers. This is not a hard and fast rule, just the way the dynamics of a crisis usually seem to unfold. The group becomes a family.

Adrian found herself feeling this way as she instinctively stroked the silky strands of Stacey's flaxen blonde hair; instinctively calming Stacey by her own calmness and human warmth of spirit.

Her own mother was doing her best. However, they both had really been through the wringer. It would be awhile before they were totally out of their shell shock.

The shuttle staging area was pleasantly warm. It was about fifty feet by thirty feet; a large comfortably furnished room with light blue walls. Lush tropical plants were tastefully placed around the room. There were sofas and chairs that could have accommodated at least twenty people. The heat and light in this room radiated from the ceiling, almost sun like. The surroundings, at least in small measure, helped to calm the accident survivors.

Despite the surroundings and Adrian's best efforts, Susan and Stacey Harmon were still frazzled and apprehensive. However, now they were both all for anything that would get them back into familiar surroundings and back into their lives. Adrian needed the little girl's portable tape recorder if she hoped to continue her mission.

"Sweetheart" she softly asked "I have a very important message to give to some friends. I might not be able to see them myself for a little while. Do you think that you could let me use your tape recorder to record a message to them?"

The little girl turned to her mother for permission. Susan nodded her head with a smile. Stacey said "Sure...but you're going to give it back, right?"

"I have to give it back sweetheart, because you and your mommy are going to be giving the message to my friends."

Adrian went off to a bit more private part of the room behind a partition. She recorded what she knew up to that point and the message that the Soclarians wanted her to relate to her superiors. She ended her message hoping and praying that every inch of the room wasn't bugged; then walked over to rejoin Stacey and her mother.

"Thank you Stacey" as she handed the tape recorder back to her already sealed in the zip seal bag. "Let's put this tape recorder back into your pouch now so that we know that it will be there when you and your mommy go home. OK?"

Turning toward Susan, Adrian asked "When you are again out in the open air up top, please follow the instructions at the beginning of the tape. It contains names, locations and phone numbers of whom to contact regarding the information on the rest of the tape.

"Please, don't share the information contained in this tape with anyone other than the intended recipients. Many lives depend upon your getting this tape into the correct hands as soon as you can."

She reminded Susan "We're both Americans here. Our allegiance is to America. The Soclarians are well meaning, but our home is America."

Susan acquiesced with a confused yet compliant "I understand."

Adrian knew by Susan's 'Yea right. Anything you say' demeanor that she would have to explain her

173

working relationship with the government. After briefly filling Susan in on what her vocational affiliations were, she continued "I have to try to get back on board here in a manner that will not be discovered; in a manner that will create the illusion that I went to the surface with you. Your not giving me away is critical in this. Do I have your word that you will keep this between us?"

Impressed and a bit in awe of what Adrian had to say about herself, Susan assured Adrian that her plans would be kept as a secret between them.

The officer who was to take them to the surface came into the room with the rest of the shuttle crew; one of whom carried three life preservers of a conventional nature. The three intended passengers were instructed to put the life preservers on and to follow the officer.

As the group made its way toward one of the sections of wall, the officer in charge pointed a device that looked quite a bit like a garage door opener remote control at the section.

The wall quivered for a split second, like a cohesive drop of water in space that stays together due to mass attraction yet wobbles like jello. Then, in an instant, the wall dropped to the floor like a sheet of ice that just realized it really was just a sheet of water after all. The residue seemed to just evaporate.

An expansive room was revealed behind the collapsed wall. Valves, piping, instruments and several pulsating instrumentation lights were situated around the room. A large and imposing airplane hangar like door was located to one side of the room.

Before them was the shuttle craft that had all the appearances of one of those tourist exploration submarines that seemed to be cropping up all over the warm vacation islands these days. However, this one was a bit wider at the beam; about eighteen feet across. It was about seventy feet long and had a greenish blue hue to its outer surface. It sure would blend with the ocean water Adrian thought.

It was beefy. It looked like it should have weighed over 100,000 pounds. Yet, it was suspended by some type of force over the room's floor by about eight inches. There were no propellers. There were, however, small wings on either side and a tail assembly that looked like that of a small jet's. There was a jet engine like opening in the bow of the craft and a series of clustered nozzles at the stern of the craft that looked like nozzles for a rocket.

The group entered the vessel through a side opening. There appeared to be a conventional submarine topside opening twenty feet before the stern of the vessel. This opening was level with the top of the tail assembly. The three were given instructions of what to do when they got to the surface.

The plan was to advance to the prearranged point off the Jersey Shore coast. They were then to surface to the level of the topside opening in an attempt to discharge the passengers without being discovered and captured. If for whatever reason the three might find themselves temporarily underwater, they received breif instruction on how to use their five minute air supply canister.

The crew and passengers found seats and strapped themselves in. In the front of the vessel the officer in charge sat at an instrument console behind a large bubble like dome. It reminded Adrian of something she had seen as a child in a movie about a submarine that had been attacked by a giant squid.

The movie frightened her then and the reality petrified her now. The gamble she now planned might be the last gamble of her life. She felt duty bound to take it. But was that all there was to it?

Could it be that now that she felt the stirring of love within her that, like the lemming, she was willing to take a headlong plunge of faith off of the precipice of reason into a watery unknown, hoping and depending upon her God, her ability, her just cause and her developing love for Kevin to save her?

The lead officer declared "Secure for chamber flooding!" His co-pilot retorted "check!"

Water rushed in like an avalanche...all at once. One moment the shuttle bay was dry. In the next instant the chamber was completely full with water swirling all around them. Yet, the vessel did not budge an inch. It barely vibrated at all from the water that crushed all around them. The force that suspended the craft above the chamber's floor held the craft fast against the cascading water's rush.

Then Adrian felt the sensation of being elevated. She had no way of knowing how far she was traveling upward, but the chamber was indeed going up. The sensation of movement stopped. The two sections of the chamber's door simultaneously parted to the left and right revealing the open ocean before them.

As the shuttle made its exit into the open ocean, a large school of blue fish darted in all directions around them; formed again into a singly moving formation and sped away.

The shuttle performed a 180 degree turning maneuver and faced the closing giant door sections. Sand bubbled all around the chamber as it descended and disappeared; like a giant horseshoe crab with sand flying all about it. Soon there was no hint that it had ever been there at all; leaving a smooth sandy bottom that blended with everything around it.

The vessel moved along the coast for only seven minutes or so, about fifteen feet below the water's surface. The shuttle came to a stop and surfaced in just seconds. The topside hatch was just a few inches above the relatively calm surface of the ocean.

Adrian and Susan exchanged knowing glances as the three of them were directed toward the slowly opening hatch. The officer in charge had the radio beacon in his hand. He handed it to Adrian after activating it and extending its antenna into an upright position. He then tied it to her life jacket. He checked to see if all three passengers had their emergency air supplies; then ushered the trio out of the hatch while following the last one, Stacey, so that he could lift her into her mother's arms.

Becoming emersed in the chilly ocean water, Stacey began to realize what was happening. She started to shriek in panic. Her mother said "Shhh...Remember what I told you. A boat is going to pick us up and take us to daddy. It will be OK."

"Ma'am, we must leave right now before we are discovered." The lead office advised. He reassured "You will be in good hands very shortly. God be with you." He disappeared into the shuttle with the door starting to close behind him.

"Susan, there is no time to explain. Give me your air canister and keep the one Stacey has! There is no danger of drowning now" Adrian urgently requested. "I'm going back down with them" she added.

Understanding, Susan rapidly complied as Adrian slipped her own life jacket off so the emergency beacon would stay with Susan and Stacey. Also, she would not have been able to hang onto the descending sub if she kept her life jacket on.

Susan promised, "I'll get your message through" and continued half in prayer, "God speed and good luck to you Adrian".

"And to you both" Adrian reciprocated as she

latched her hands and feet onto the ladder like structure behind the exit hatch tower. She activated her air supply and disappeared beneath the waves, towed by the waterborne chariot of her destiny.

The **Star Seeker III** made its approach to the Hormuz Station (Earth Base One) via the tunnel access under Saudi Arabia, then under Kuwait. This station extended two miles beneath the ocean's floor and covered half the linear area than did its newer counterpart under Barnegat Light.

The **Star Seeker III** glided toward the tunnel's terminus located underneath the Persian Gulf station. The station's umbilical companionway for receiving this type craft was located directly in the middle of the station's underside. By all appearances, the area excavated under the station was like a mini-ocean in its own right.

Kevin and Hank remained seated as the **Star Seeker III** made its connection; this time from the top of the craft. The jolt registered more softly than that of an aircraft landing. No one applauded...sort of an anticlimax.

As the hum of the primary thrusters and other related machinery began to subside, Kevin began to feel a strange sense of exhilaration, vibrant, an overpowering sense of awareness...of self...of his surroundings...an awakening...an innervating...invigorating bristling of every molecule in his being...like a fish that had just been thrown back into the water just before expiring.

He was home. He was in his element. He couldn't explain it...but he knew. It was something triggered by his proximity to this place...to his destiny.

"Joint regional conference will commence immediately in conference room one...alpha deck" the voice announced over the speaker system.

"That includes us, trail riders" Hank explained to Kevin.

Kevin was still between the states of newly experienced euphoria and **TECHNO-SHOCK**. That's the shock experienced by one in a manner similar to a fish's being born and raised in an aquarium and then as a middle aged adult fish being dumped into the Amazon River. New dimensions of experience and onslaughts to his psyche were being hurled at him now in waves.

He told himself 'be calm! Breath in and out slowly! You are in charge of yourself. God's not going to give you anything that you can't handle.' He took comfort in that thought. After his marital difficulties that is how he coped.

Yes, not being able to see the children whenever he wanted to hurt him dramatically. What hurt even more was knowing that his children probably hurt at least as much as he did in not being able to see daddy whenever they had the need to...on the spot when the feeling arose...the frustration...the unfairness of it all. Nobody was a winner in that fallout.

Yet...God holds all of his cherished children in the palm of his hand and provides comfort through the unvoiced yet omnipresent knowledge and reality that He will never give any of us anything that we can't handle. Kevin's ex-wife told him that.

In the face of a cruel occurrence, that was a kind thought to impart. He thought how thankful he was that at least there was something worthy of redemption out of the whole mess...a short phrase. It actually was a very significant truth and credo. Thank God the breakup did not degenerate into a miasma of bitter hatred.

Neither of them could ever really hate the other. There was never hatred, just a profound sadness and feeling of loss...a mourning...like a loved one had died.

He ruminated that Pop had come back...like a gentle wind that had merely become misdirected for awhile. Maybe lost love might be like that too...just misdirected for a while, but never really lost forever...just out there...lost in its wanderings ...searching...waiting.

Snapping Kevin out of his daydreaming, Hank admonished, "Get with the program trooper. Hustle, hustle...Huba-huba! We've got a world to save."

The floor section that their seats were on backed up on an angle to the right, so they could step directly onto a moving walkway. That's what Kevin thought it was. Previously, he had assumed in error that the floor moved...like at an airport's conveyor transporter. Yet, now when he looked down, nothing was moving.

Captain Senecus, seeing the look of confusion on Kevin's face enlightened him. "We are riding on a compressed gas about one sixteenth of an inch above the deck's floor. The compression takes place because of the particular polar orientation and properties of this gas. We call it **argonitane.**

"The gas is so compressed that you would not be able to penetrate it with your pen, a knife or even a bullet. It creates a diamond hard surface that is always uniform. The quantity of the gas determines the platform's height above the floor.

It is compressed and channeled through the use of a magnotherial regulating device in the floor. It might be difficult for you to comprehend, but this state of the gas is still considered to be liquid. It is not solid according to your standard because it remains fluid to the extent that it can be channeled, bent and moved through the utilization of the regulators without the mass' cracking.

"The particular properties of this elemental gas

180

allow a simple regulator under the deck to define the boundaries that the gas is able to fill. By passing the magnotherial impulse through the mass, the particular properties and geometric idiosyncrasies of this element's atoms allow us to form walls as high as we wish. Indeed, some of the containment walls of certain earth stations are constructed with this gas.

"If the force is interrupted, the gas collapses like a wave upon a beach. It dissipates evenly over the particular surface upon which it finds itself and becomes harmless.

"Even still, we may retrieve the gas if it is not too far away from the regulator, by simply turning the force back on. The wall snaps back to attention within seconds. Not bad, huh?

"By angling the force to 165 degrees on plane and by making a continuous loop of the gas cascading down into a reservoir under the deck (the flow of which is not obstructed nor interrupted in any way) we are able to set the gaseous mass into motion. That's what we find ourselves moving on right now."

They were in a corridor on the earth station. It had the same gas transport system on the deck that they were on while in the **Star Seeker III**.

"Gentlemen this way, please" prompted the ambassador, Justinian Fairborne.

They were guided into a large conference room. The walls were magnificently adorned with artwork depicting nature. Sculptures of many types of animals; some of which Kevin had never seen before, were situated throughout the room. Hank told him that many of the sculptures represented extinct earth species.

The five of them, Ambassador Fairborne along with Captain Senecus, Kevin Murdock, Commander Leotor and Ambassador Feidor (Hank) walked around the rather expansive table in the middle of the room.

Fairborne introduced his group to each member of the conference standing around the table. The group buzzed and murmured in a concerned and collective monotone.

"...and finally Mr. Murdock" Ambassador Fairborne went on, "This is Daramer Mostrale. Once you are on land she will be your guide and translator. She is a direct descendent of the original colonization of this area and was recruited in much the same manner as you were."

Kevin's jaw dropped. He greeted Daramer as a robot might mechanically respond to a command. This woman commanded awe through her raw beauty and by her mere presence alone.

Intelligence, womanliness, passion, vibrance, "Joie le vive", sex appeal, savvy and friendliness seemed to flow from her every pore.

Kevin was both thunderstruck and speechless. That five foot frequential aura of hers was working overtime, communicating all kinds of neat stuff.

Her hair was jet black with the luster of polished onyx. Her supple butter-soft skin had the combined beauty of golden honey and a browned cognac. Her green and mysteriously haunting eyes saw beyond the skin and seemed to search his very soul. There was an understanding calmness behind that stare; non-threatening...kind.

Daramer was about twenty eight years old give or take. He estimated that she was about five feet eight inches tall.

She was strong, yet very feminine. Her form fitting outfit demonstrated the gently curvaceous musculature of a well exercised body.

Pop, seeing that he'd better break Kevin's disquieting stare whispered to Kevin's back, "Down boy...calm down sailor. True, you're in a foreign port, but I'd think you could be a little more subtle...you know what I mean?"

Momentarily turning from Daramer he sheepishly whispered "Sorry, Pop, I couldn't help myself" as he unconsciously maintained his grasp around her hand.

She had the beauty of a sunset and the alluring freshness of an oasis' breeze. It really wasn't love at first sight...but he sure wanted more sights.

Her shy, yet not quite coquettish demeanor and her self-imposed...slightly subordinative deportment while casting her eyes downward, revealed her conditioning in a "men come first" middle eastern/Bedouin milieu from which she sprang.

Yet, he could tell that she was her own person and would not take any guff from anyone. All this from a gaze and a touch of their hands.

Realizing her non-verbal communication and a bit embarrassed that she allowed herself to be caught somewhat offguard, she withdrew her hand, straightened and reoriented her bearing...front and center...to the "here and now" business at hand.

"Please find your seats ladies and gentlemen. Our work is certainly cut out for us today and we must be expeditious and deliberate during our proceedings today. Our normal banter and pleasantries must be kept to minimum today" Ambassador Fairborne suggested as he presided over the assemblage.

There were several earth agents and other consultants present. The other Earth Base commanders were in attendance along with the captains of their attendant **Star Seeker** class craft.

The ambassador informed "This shall be our last earth base summit conference. The murmur heightened in the room.

Suddenly and unexpectedly, the chamber's doors hurtled open. All heads turned toward the interruption to witness a squad of guards escorting Adrian, who had somehow appropriated a work uniform. Standing there with a blanket draped loosely around her shoulders she looked horrible, bedraggled and tired.

The first to speak was the escort squad's leader. "Sir, we found Miss Slater asleep on the floor of the laundry area. She was behind one of the sanitizers. What do you wish we do with her?"

Kevin thought he was looking at a ghost (again) as he sat with his mouth agape.

Hank said under his breath "This broad's got brass ones. How'd she pull this one off?" Not really expecting an answer, (especially since Kevin was somewhere between catatonic and comatose with bewilderment).

Ambassador Fairborne erupted. "Commander Leotor what incompetence has permitted this outrage? Our information had to be in the proper hands hours ago."

The commander was flabbergasted and caught at a loss. Starting to formulate an excuse for the inexcusable, Commander Leotor apologetically blurted "Sir she was placed on the surface by one of my most trusted officers. I have no idea what..."

"Sir, let me speak!" Adrian barked out interrupting the commander and silencing the growing murmur.

The guards grasped her firmly shaking her in the process in an effort to still her voice. Kevin leapt onto and across the table, springing into the air, propelling himself like an arrow catapulted from a cross bow. He was on the guard before he knew what had hit him.

The surprised guard holding Adrian on her left went down under the cascading weight of Kevin's hurtling body. "You son of a bitch!" Kevin screamed as he landed his fists again and again into the offending guard's face.

184

The other guards regrouped and tried to pull Kevin off as Ambassador Fairborne commanded "Enough!".

Steeled with anger, the rivetting volume and tone of his voice stopped all action in its tracks.

"Take that man to the infirmary the ambassador ordered.

"Mr. Murdock, your behavior is heinous and unconscionable. There was no need for that display. You are not exempt from our laws and codes of conduct. This is a disappointment. If it were not for your role in our enterprise we would immediately rid ourselves of your presence. Do you understand sir?"

Kevin had just about had enough. "You go straight to hell." Then pointing to Adrian while looking toward the ambassador Kevin retorted "She is weak, she is tired and is at an extreme disadvantage here. She certainly does not need to be nor does she deserve to be manhandled.

"She is obviously meant to be here for some purpose unknown to any of us, to have overcome such odds and obstacles to be here now and at this time. Did you ever consider that? So you can take your threats and your pompous selfrighteous indignation and place them securely in any orifice you so see fit. You take care of your goon. I'll take care of **her**; this **obvious** threat to us all. Do I make **myself** clear? Do **you** understand **me**?"

Ambassador Fairborne reflected then gave a flipping wave of his hand and said "Well, she's here now. We can't very well send her back. Let her go. Let her talk. Thank you gentlemen for bringing her here. You may leave her with us."

Understanding, the guards withdrew from the room; the doors closing behind them.

Walking over to Adrian he asked in a rather fatherly, subdued almost apologetic tone "Are you ok my dear? Have you been harmed?"

"No, I'm ok" Adrian offered. "I'm just a bit cold and worn out, but I'll be fine." Kevin picked up the fallen blanket from the floor and wrapped it again around Adrian's shoulders.

Kevin had seen Adrian held, pushed and shoved once too many times. His reaction to her treatment even surprised himself. However, at least he was certain of where he stood with her. He believed now that something more than a few oral germs had passed between them. His faith had been shaken by this secret agent thing, but something real existed between them. Now, he was very certain.

He gave Adrian a gentle kiss on the forehead and led her to a chair. She smiled and looked up at him as her eyes began to water.

Choking back her emotion, she started anew "Sir, your information did get to my superiors. I was able to tape record the information and send it along with the crash survivors. I took one of their extra air packs and rode the outside of the shuttle vehicle back to the Barnegat Light base.

"I was driven by something to follow, to come here. I knew I was risking my life. I can't explain it. I just had to be with Kevin on this one. I had to be with all of you."

Looking at her with an understanding eye, the Ambassador activated a control on the small instrument panel at the end of the conference table.

"Unicom central, this is Ambassador Fairborne."

"Yes Ambassador" came the response.

"Open a direct link with the United States government and with the United Nations on the pre-prescribed frequencies. Find if they have received our information and what actions they have taken. Also, keep all links open and initiate the EVACU-COM network now. Do you understand?"

"Yes Ambassador" came the acknowledgement.

"Miss Slater, come what may, you are with **us** now. You will accompany Kevin and Miss Mostrale ashore along with other designated members of the team. Since none of us really knows why you are here, you are to be an observer and requested to do as you are asked as the situation dictates. Agreed?"

Adrian nodded her head in acquiescence. She sat back and listened next to Kevin as the Ambassador again brought order to the gathering.

He continued on as if little if anything had happened in the room. "Yes my friends, indeed this shall be our last joint conference. This should not come as a surprise to any of you. Everyone here knows the severity of the situation with which we are faced. People are dying from the poisoned water systems and the biological warfare releases as we speak. Next, the gas will come and then finally the nuclear weapons. Saddam knows his business. We do not have a moment to spare.

As Kevin listened, his finger tips rubbed in tiny side to side strokes over the table's surface. Still listening, Kevin thought that the surface of the oblong table was unusually clean and shiny. The material was strangely textured, like rubberized glass. However, it did not become depressed when pressure was exerted against it with his thumb.

Hank explained earlier to Kevin that when the table got dirty, they would simply turn the magnotherial force to ten percent power. The atoms of the argonitane gas would move apart and rise; just moving up slightly and contained within the rim of the table's rimmed perimeter. Any dirt, debris, fingerprints (or even a charging renegade's footprints) would fall to the bottom.

After the procedure, the field would then be turned up to full power. When the gas again became rock hard a sixteenth of an inch room air gap could be created to allow a laser field to vaporize the accumulated debris. The dust powder then would be blown into a small filter...a self cleaning table, floor, counter top, etc. On Soclar, it was used on household surfaces instead of wax.

"Ladies and gentlemen" the ambassador continued, "much will be expected of you all today. Today **is** the beginning of the end and the start of a new beginning. I am not talking in riddles. By late tomorrow afternoon, Station Barnegat Light time, we all will be on our way to Gariedon.

"For many of you, this is your first time on this earth base. Unfortunately, it will also be your last. I am going to ask that for the sake of expedience, you keep your technical questions for another time...unless you feel that the group would benefit from such questions of course.

"There will be much that you will see here and not be able to understand. Just bear with us and realize that time is now our enemy along with Saddam.

"However, during this logistics conference your direct and succinct input regarding the situation at hand will be both solicited and welcome."

As the ambassador continued his presentation the room became darkened. The conference table became a changing, churning, undulating, three dimensional, tangible model of the areas surrounding the six earth base stations. Each came up separately as that particular area was discussed.

The argonitane gas responded to the mapped and programmed force variations within the table. Peaks, valleys, forests, waterways, roadways, and man-made structures took on striking depictions of reality as if viewed from the air.

Matching the actual geography of the territories being discussed, the gaseous constructs took on appropriate colors and hues through filtered and directed lighting.

As the meeting progressed the plan emerged along with the code name **"Operation Noah's Ark."**

The ambassador outlined the plan for each earth base and how the logistics would work for the evacuation. One of the largest concerns regarding the scale of such an evacuation and eventual journey is that of communicable diseases and sanitation.

Most of those present knew the procedure. However, for the benefit of the rest, it was explained that other than benign intestinal organisms needed for digestion, all parasites, bacteria and viruses would be purged from each individual as they crossed the threshold into the earth stations. There would be no cancer causing viruses, no AIDS. Man's plagues would be left behind.

Fairborne went on, "As planned, the CIA has now gotten the real picture and believes what they are hearing and seeing. They have agreed to mobilize the U S and help coordinate other international resources in order that bedding materials and other vital supplies would be the first consignments taken aboard.

"I have just been informed that even now as we speak, other supplies that we just don't have enough of are being gathered by the cooperating nations."

Kevin interrupted the ambassador by bending his elbow on the table and pointing his index finger upward, gesturing to be recognized.

"Yes Mr. Murdock?"

"How is this great multitude going to be fed? What provisions have been made regarding the enormous sanitation needs; not only in transit, but once we arrive at our destination? Of equal importance, what will the social order be like?"

The Ambassador responded. "Valid questions Mr. Murdock. "In-transit, needs have been anticipated and provided for. Some advance preparations have been provided for on Gariedon. However, in many ways, accommodations will be fairly Spartan at first.

"People will first learn to live in a real community again. This system will be much like the Israeli's kibbutz system. Social interaction and interdependence will be of paramount importance. Learning to live without destroying the environment will, also, be the hallmark of the society.

"The American Indians had a good grasp on this concept. Western Civilization could have learned much from their concepts of spirituality, social interaction, love and respect for that nurturing source of sustenance and naturally achieved sense of tranquility called MOTHER NATURE.

"On Gariedon, people's propensity toward identifying with things and the technology of things instead of each other and real life will be a practice of the past.

"Certainly, technology and academic achievement will be revered and have a place. However, earth's inhabitants, especially those in western civilizations, have lost sight of the fact that technology is a lot like cocktail music. It should be in the background. It should not overwhelm the moment . It should enhance the moment, be a part of your existence. It should not be the overpowering focus of your existence.

"This is a major contributing factor as to why people find it so hard to relate to one another. They spend so little time trying. So much gets in the way. The unbridled quest toward *having* the physical manifestations of technology and toward *seeming* to be something greater than God's glorious creation called *man* eventually translates to endless posturing.

"So, instead of *being* in the world and interacting harmoniously in a manner in which all might benefit, this unrelenting posturing puts more and more distance between people.

"Sadly, that is the principal reason why mankind finds it more and more difficult to stay with his spouse, to stay happy and to stay loyal.

"Striving toward perpetual physical youth, seeming instead of being, living up to the unrealistic expectations and standards set by marketing interests, equating coexistence and cohabitation in the same context as **having** and **possessing** frustrates both parties in a marriage.

"This invariably leads to disappointment and dissatisfaction with the other. It results in damage to self esteem and most often ultimately results in irreversible feelings of resentment...resentment caused by artificial sources...outside sources...sources that neither of them can control...a universal standard that negates, countermands, ignores, discredits and dehumanizes the human condition and the natural order of things...the intent and resource provided to man as a gift by our mutual Benefactor."

The group contemplated and assimilated what they had just heard. Kevin caught himself agreeing with the ambassador...secretly saying to himself 'Yea...that's right. Boy I wish I could have written that down and could send it to my ex-wife along with a note saying,..."See it wasn't all because of us. It was a little bit you, a little bit me and a lot of *IT*...The kind of *IT* preceded by BULLSH...."

A wave of overwhelming emotion gripped Kevin. The ambassador's words rang so true that an archetypal...primal cord was struck within his heart. Unbeckoned, tears started quietly streaming down his cheeks.

For the first time, he began to understand the forces involved in the collapse of his marriage. For the first time he was able to comprehend why his wife did some of the things she did either to him, in spite of him or with no concern for his feelings.

In his heart he was able to begin to forgive her. The hurt would always be there. The horrific memories might crop up from time to time regarding the split...but, he knew that he could begin going on with his life...by degree...freeing himself from feelings of animosity, hatred or anger concerning the stinging realities involved.

Certainly, she was responsible for her own behavior during the marriage. However, she was also a victim. Her basic nature was not evil.

All too often under certain stresses, under the pressures such as the ambassador had portrayed, people who would be otherwise predisposed to be good or good intentioned, benign or generally kind in nature toward a spouse, would succumb to the temptations established by the artificial standards...the temptation and standard promising something else...greener grass...a pie-in-the-sky non-existent Utopia; instead of realizing or acknowledging their own personal responsibility in achieving their own self-fulfillment...their own personal Nirvana or heaven on Earth.

A person must first **BE** happy, be responsible for his own life and responsible for the achievement of happiness. To expect someone to **MAKE** you happy is an unfair burden and expectation placed upon a partner. You can be happy together, but to expect

192

someone to **MAKE** you happy is unrealistic, unfair and bound to result in disastrous frustration, resentment and probably divorce.

Whoever promised a clear, unobstructed or lighted path? No on*e* **OWES** that free ride to anybody and shouldn't be faulted for not providing it. A spouse or "significant other" can only offer company along the way.

This oversight, this mistake...this transgression should never be perpetrated at the expense of another human being. It is irresponsible.

"Making it work" within the covenant and context of a marriage includes two ends being held up. It is this failure, this carelessness, this recklessness, this cavalier lack of responsibility to the marriage, this frailty and susceptibility to this social virus that Kevin could never forgive. He could understand it, but could not forgive it.

He was beginning to forgive the person. It was this disease...this virus of the heart that he knew he could not forgive nor live with.

He thought 'Physician, heal thyself' must be her clarion motto if she hoped to find true happiness with another man in the future. It was neither Kevin's job nor intention to rehabilitate her. He knew that she bit deeply. He was not going to put his head into the lion's mouth again.

He thought that mostly everyone is at least vulnerable to the self-deceptive lie catered to by the everlasting NAY...the great deceiver...the perennial liar...the great evil...the quintessential definition of what society had become.

This is how Kevin began to reconcile himself with life, with his wife...with humanity. He thought that ultimately we all must answer to ourselves and the dictates of our own consciences. We cannot be responsible for the behavior of others, no matter who they are.

Kevin had composed himself before his facial expression became too noticeable. The ambassador began addressing the other concerns Kevin had raised.

"Sanitation is of minor consequence in the total scheme of things. Not that it is not important, it's just that we have it covered with very little logistical impact.

"Urine and feces are vaporized along with other refuse by abundant refuse units intended for that purpose. During your stay with us you might not have realized that this is how things worked...no fuss...no bother...just gone.

"Water supplies will be provided through units that look like large water coolers. A reverse electrolysis process combines free floating atmospheric oxygen and hydrogen to supply fresh, pure water whenever and wherever needed.

"Livestock, crop seeds and of the like will be supplied from Earth and Soclar. However, the dietary mainstays will be technologically provided.

"Nano-polymer molecular processing units will be available for each communal unit. As towns are developed and free enterprise once again becomes a part of the society, homes will be made available for all, along with individual molecular processing units.

"These gizmos can make anything with the proper programming and substrate simply by entering a program code number. The larger units have the ability to duplicate smaller versions of themselves. They can also make building materials.

"For instance, if you wanted a fourteen ounce beef filet, you would enter on the programming panel the code for the exact meat you wanted and the exact weight and thickness. Through the top you would

194

place the prescribed amount of greenery from the local flora push start and...presto! You have a raw steak
complete with fat, blood cells and just the right amount
of sinew for authenticity's sake.

"You may then grill it, broil it, rub it on your
navel or otherwise do anything with it that you would
ordinarily do with a natural steak.

No one was amused...Kevin whispered "tough
audience". Timing...the secret behind a good line.

Fairborne went on, "No animal dies for your meal
and everybody's happy. We do not discourage killing
livestock, but why do it needlessly?

"These units even have the ability to convert wood
chips, top soil, mulch, seaweed and a multitude of other
organic substrates into food products. It is not necessary that everyone knows the chemistry, physiology
and other particulars involved with the engineering
aspects of these units. However, for those who truly
want to know, there will be instruction available.

"Mr. Murdock has been briefed on his critically
unique role in this operation. Even though the high
counsel command on Soclar has informed us of his
role, there are variables and other specifics that are
known only to the deepest inner workings and recesses
of the cosmos.

"I suppose that's the Deity's way of saying 'The
best kept secret is the one that is never told.' In the
final phase of the global alert even **we** will be in the
dark and will be forced to **go with the flow**. This will
be in everyone's best interests.

"Kevin, Adrian and Daramer will be met by friends
at Al-Faw-Bubiayan, where the Tigris River flows into
the Persian Gulf. They will stay in the town for a short
time and mingle until discovered and captured by the
Republican Guard. As with all suspected spies, they
will immediately be taken to Baghdad where they will

personally meet with Saddam. He's like a sadistic cat that likes to play with his food before slaughtering it."

Fairborne added, "The world press has already been alerted that something of an apocalyptic nature or of global importance is about to occur in this area of the world. They know there is to be a showdown. No nation now doubts the source of the current disaster nor doubts the evil design of Saddam Hussein.

"The onsite American and United Nations forces will make certain that global press coverage via satellite will be able to get through. They're just going to do it.

"They realize that any further attempts at diplomacy with Hussein are futile. The communication plan in this theater of operation is code named *FINAL ALARM*. This communication operation and what has made it necessary is being treated as a *fait accompli*...a done deal. Nothing will stop it.

"No one is going to be asking Saddam for any permission in order to operate within his country's borders. He gave up that right the minute he became a marauding international outlaw and invader. However, at that juncture he will in fact be demanding media and world attention.

"He is proud of his handiwork. He is now like Caesar at the Rubicon. The die is cast. His orders have been given. His evil has been or is now being carried out by his henchmen. He is now a non-participant within the new reality in which we find ourselves.

"Yet, he knows that at the end his destiny driven by his insane and out of control ego and vanity will force him to place himself right in the middle of the public's eye. That is, also, part of the plan.

"You see...evil must be a visible and tangible entity in order for people to focus in their hearts...in order to decide in the deepest recesses of their beings

196

where they stand. They won't have to shout it out. Yet, their mind set on where they stand regarding good verses evil must be made clear within their souls; like at the foot of Mount Sinai when Moses asked his people to choose between good and evil. It must show in their hearts.

"Saddam is evil incarnate. Those with evil intent...those who live for evil...who revel in evil...who respect evil...who depend upon evil for their way of life...for their sport in order to satiate their perverse and corrupt need to victimize, subordinate or humiliate others by and through their quest of foul and unholy pleasure at the expense of others and or rely upon that evil for their own profit, will find Saddam to be a kindred spirit through this last drama.

"In them, during those last moments of truth and revelation, he will elicit their worst and true selves. It too, will show in their hearts.

"Conversely, the good at heart will be repulsed, finding no redeeming qualities in Hussein whatsoever. Their focus will be completely different and I may add, identifiable. This, too, will be made manifest through this final drama.

"By this time everyone in this room realizes or should realize that we do not only perceive and experience the cosmos as a whole but, indeed, are perceived and experienced by the cosmos at large. Each vibrating subatomic particle in the cosmos registers and is impacted by the existence of other proximal matter.

"This impact is perceived on the particular level that has been ordained and prescribed by the universal order itself. The great mason himself concocted that. It ties everything together. It helps the **body universe** to monitor and take care of itself.

"Don't get paranoid. The moon doesn't care if you masturbate or pick your nose. But, we are all linked with everything and everything is linked with us.

"Saddam represents counter-universal flux flowing contrary to the best interests of the universal good and the universal long term best interests of the whole.

"Saddam's is a self-fulfilling prophesy whose course has but one final destination. His insatiable, insecure and evil ego will drive him to the center of the stage that he has created. This must be. This has been preordained.

"Indeed, this convergence of the forces of good and evil will play itself out before a world audience. However, much of that audience is now and by that time will be in transit. That is where the mass media will be playing its part.

"This aside, the entire planet will ring with sympathetic frequential transmitted emanations as a result of the cosmic enormity of the ongoing events over here.

"Be that as it may ladies and gentlemen, we cannot turn this into a symposium on the specific mechanics of the inner workings of the universe's most interesting and thought provoking secrets. Just know that they exist and have faith.

Looking upward he continued, "Suffice it to say that the *HE WHO KNOWS* knows what HIS job is."

The group allowed itself a nervously subdued chuckle. His timing was getting better.

After some additional discussion, questions and answers the meeting was about to be adjourned.

Suddenly, defying explanation, the room swirled with a warm wind...a wind from an undetectable source. It tossed Daramer's hair around her face. It was a sweet purging...cleansing wind that had the invigorating freshness akin to that experienced after a summer thunderstorm.

Kevin felt euphoric. Almost like the feeling of anticipation while waiting for a loved one to get off of an airplane that had just landed...but why?

At the head of the table, Ambassador Fairborne stood silently...peacefully smiling while approvingly inspecting the attendees. A fiery golden yellow aura began to erratically pulse from his body.

His features and clothing began to metamorphose before their very eyes. Everyone in the room gasped at this unexpected sequence of events...yet remained transfixed by what was unfolding before them.

Fairborne's face became etched and somewhat elongated. Flaxen white hair reached down to his shoulders. A long beard of similar lustrous white hair formed on his face laying over what had now become a crimson garment.

The crimson garment was a robe of unparalleled beauty. It glistened in the undulating light coming from the emanating rays of golden light the source of which could not be detected.

The garment was trimmed with pristine white embroidery that appeared on the cuffs and all outer edge seams of the garment. On his feet appeared scant leather strapped sandals. In his left hand he clasped a wooden staff. On his right shoulder stood a jet black falcon.

Whoever he was, he certainly knew how to make an entrance and right now, He had the floor.

"Do not be disquieted my children. To those of you to whom I have never appeared I say unto you KNOW THAT I AM AND HAVE ALWAYS BEEN. I am not here to alarm you at this dangerous time.

"Be comforted and be calmed. The end of your fears is at hand. The end of man's injustice to man is neigh. The end of man-made strife and inhumanity to his fellow man is upon us. Lift up your hearts...may your countenances reflect the peace and knowledge of this truth so that all may know these things to be truth through your personal presence and existence.

"Justinian will be the flesh through which I shall perform my tasks through this turmoil. When the multitude hear my word from all of you they will know it as truth and know what to do.

"For those who do not allow righteousness into their hearts, for those who harden their hearts to the truth and continue the mind set of evil design, lifestyle or intent...they will be excluded from the continuance of further fellowship within the family of man. How that exclusion will be made manifest will be both swift and terrible.

"It has come to this. Vile debasement of my intended direction for mankind now is defiling the face of this jewel called *Earth* that I have given mankind the privilege of habitating.

"Vileness begets vileness. There is now a perpetual, evil and sordid headlong rush toward pandering to the lowest...basest instincts of man. There has always been a lowest standard of behavior. There has always been another boundary to explore and cross; another temptation.

"Now, however, at this point in human history, mankind is choosing to avail himself of these opportunities in wholesale fashion. Transgressions upon transgressions are visiting upon the souls of man. Lower and lower the downward spiral is now progressing in a hatefully gleeful race to cross each new line for the lowest possible standard of human decency and decorum.

"Certainly, there are so...so many exceptions to this...so many of those who resist the popular tide. It is those exceptions who must work to re-root the tree of life...to nurture it back to health for the safety and happiness of all.

"However, now society at large has become the serpent in the garden. Now nothing separates mankind from the animals. There are indeed certain things a rat or a snake will not do. We can no longer say that about the society of man.

"Harken and know these words to be truth: There is to be a reckoning the likes of which the eyes of man have never witnessed.

"Know also my children, you are my disciples. In your new home, no matter where that new world may be, my word must live and be law. I know your hearts as I know the hearts of all men. Your goód hearts are the vessels within which my words will dwell and flourish.

"Be of good cheer and comfort to one another, for I will be with you during your labors. My command and your task is that of the rescue of the righteous. Take solace and comfort in that thought."

The falcon loosed a punctuating scream as **HE** departed the body of Justinian. The same warm wind brushed past the assemblage. The ambassador regained his own appearance.

Fairborne slumped forward, reaching his hands out to grab the edge of the table. The staff fell to the floor...pulsating briefly with a lingering remnant of the golden aura. The robes remained in place...these objects remaining, perhaps, as a physical mandate; as a reminder to the group of their charge and the ambassador's authority during the execution of their duties.

The falcon remained present on Fairborne's shoulder darting his head from side to side...as a stolid obedient sentinel.

The room became deathly quiet. Everyone was assimilating what they had just witnessed and heard. After stooping to pick up his staff the silence was broken by Ambassador Fairborne's command.

"We know what we must do. Let's get to it." No one responded. Not a word was uttered. They all filed from the room... pensive, humbled, inspired, charged, and confident. They made their way to the dining area.

Adrian, Daramer, Hank, Kevin and Captain Senecus solemnly grouped together as they were transported along the invisible moving walkway. They sat together in silence eating their meal.

After eating, the ambassador briskly strode over to their table, staff in hand...falcon still at his post. He gave instructions to Daramer and Kevin, wished them good fortune and walked off.

They had been properly snapped out of their mesmerized mental states. They had their final marching orders. The five were escorted by members of the crew to their quarters for a short time of being alone with their thoughts and to allow the sleep inducing apparatus to provide them with some much needed concentrated...deep sleep.

-CHAPTER TEN-

The morning light filtered through Winston Tanderoth's bedroom window as did a fragrant ocean breeze laced with honeysuckle and roses. Outside, the warble and twitter of a mixed group of birds proclaimed to the world that they were filled with the joy of being alive.

He linked the fingers of his hands together behind his head and settled back to his pillow thinking that it *was* a good day to be alive.

He gazed quietly at his second wife Jenifer resting quietly next to him...her breathing slow and rhythmic...her eyes closed, telling him she was still asleep. As if in response to his stare, she rustled and stretched under the cool white satin sheets.

Winston and Jenifer had met while she worked for an American company that had an office in London. She was an investment consultant and also a fund raiser for new companies needing start-up capital.

The two of them found they had much in common. After a couple of ski getaways to the Alps the rest was history.

She showed such tolerance and love for his children from his previous marriage. Winston always believed that this was a bonus. He loved her deeply.

However, he understood deep down that if she considered the children as an inconvenience he would not have been able to sustain the relationship with her. If she were such a person, he knew that he never would have fallen in love with her.

The children were an inconvenience to his first wife, Harriet. Her initial intentions were good. Harriet simply changed her mind about wanting the responsibility.

Her social schedule, her friends, her life style, her jet setting ways were incompatible with child rearing. It impacted the children greatly...especially the older of the two boys, Brendon.

Harriet acted out her rebellion toward her situation as a mother by taking on multiple lovers. She wanted to be single. That was the whole magilla in a nutshell. She wanted to be free from having to devote herself full time to the rearing of children.

She just didn't get it...that her freedom wasn't something that a baby could take away from her. There's always vacations for two, baby sitters, nannies (which they could well have afforded and did employ), dinners, mutual friends, weekend hotels... on and on.

Freedom is what *you* make it, how **you** define it and how **you** live it. It is a state of mind, not what is imposed upon you by the introduction of new life...a new baby. A baby is a gift from God and is placed into your safekeeping.

Winston saw the children as a blessing. Harriet convinced herself that they were a life sentence that condemned her to an unanticipated and unwanted servitude. She believed that they somehow made her less attractive...less desirable to her friends and potential male friends. She wanted to be eternally alluring and the object of never ending male attentions. Her ego needed that.

She was so used to being fawned over from childhood right through her relationship with an adoring husband...so used to being catered to, waited upon and served, that she could not make the transition to care giver or love giver. It cramped her style.

The concept of mutual dependency and interdependency never set in. Transcending **self** for the benefit of another never caught on.

She had the fantasy that children would be like pets...like the cute little angora rabbits that she had as a child. When she was tired of *them* someone else had to take care of them for her.

She forgot about that part...the part about when the novelty wore off, innocent vulnerable lives still had to be provided for. Blame her parents for that one. It carried over to her adult life.

Winston did not have an inkling about the lovers. He ignored the warning signs...her frequent late nights out with the girls, men who were just "jolly good pals" calling the house, the frequently cold turned back in bed when he tried to make romantic overtures, or even ignoring her insistence that he go on vacations to the summer house at the Essex seaside without her so *he* could have "quality time alone with the children" as she put it.

What a crock. What a blind jerk, Winston often mused in retrospect and self recrimination.

He was blinded by his love for her. She was charming, a beauty, a tireless hostess and simply stated...a regal lady of impeccable and obvious breeding. It was those virtues and her coquettish demeanor that served as the bait that Winston took hook line and sinker.

It was on one of those vacations to the summer house with the boys that Winston received his reality therapy...his wake up call...the cold resignation from his wife without even two weeks notice...with no nothing.

He had sent his house staff home a few hours ahead of himself to London in order to make certain the house was ready for his return with the boys and to give Harriet some advanced notice. He was met at his London's house door by a somber housekeeper who looked downward avoiding his eyes.

"What's wrong Mary?" he queried.

She said nothing as she broke into tears, grasping her uniform's apron and burying her face into it.

He learned that while he was on vacation, Harriet had left London and had flown to Argentina with a dance troupe flamenco dancer named Rahul...abandoning him, his two year old son Donald and his six year old son Brendon.

Winston asked himself when he had a little more perspective on the matter...'Couldn't she have done something a bit more original?' The scenario had the hackneyed and melodramatic tinge of a cheap, droll and plebeian dime store novel.

Wives really don't do that sort of thing in the real world he insisted to himself. It's old hat...its been done...the gardener and the wife, the butler and the wife, the milkman and the wife and all that sort.

The blow was crushing to all three of them. They never saw Harriet again with the exception of her popping in long enough to collect a divorce settlement and to sign some papers about custody of the children.

Winston vowed to himself to insulate the children's emotions to the greatest extent possible within the capabilities of his resources and abilities. He vowed to cherish his children...taking on another life partner again only if he were absolutely certain of her...only if she could make a commitment to all of them as a package deal.

He mulled over all these past commitments to his children and to himself as he now found himself lying next to Jenifer three years down the pike having again found love.

He was a lucky man he thought...lucky to have found Jenifer...a precious pearl and more than he could have ever hoped for.

Yes, intimacy and his own happiness was crucial to him. Jenifer's happiness was crucial to him. But he was very devoted to his children. They were his first responsibility...past, present and future. He was responsible for bringing them into the world and was perpetually cognizant of the awesome responsibility that this reality represented.

It was his concern and helping them heal from *their* hurt that helped pull him through his own.

He smiled appreciatively and lovingly at Jenifer's peaceful face as her features began showing signs of animation. She reached for the border of the satin sheets and drew them up toward her neck.

When the mood struck them they would reach down into the bottom of their linen closet and break out the *kinky* sheets (as they liked to call them). Every now and then they enjoyed playing under the satin sheets. It made them feel wickedly naughty.

They slipped and slid under the sheets enjoying the sensation of almost frictionless movement. It was like sledding in bed.

On the downside of things, Winston could never quite get an adequate toe hold when it was most critical.

His nickname for his bride was Jenny (or Wild Thing when they were alone). She was wearing the red silk naughty nighty that drove Winston wild. It tucked in at all the right places up and down her five foot nine inch frame, complementing her soft curvaceous body. It revealed her soft ample cleavage unapologetically. The outline of her nipples protruded with assertion, tempting invitingly.

Jenifer had long jet black hair, smooth light skin, high cheek bones and full inviting lips. Her eyes were unexpectedly deep blue; a piercing deep blue that you would expect to see in a blonde. The contrast in colors on her already beautiful face enchanted men.

She was just as beautiful on the inside, too. She was kind, intelligent, feminine, a friend, a good mother, a considerate mate, hell in bed...all the things a man could want in a wife. She was a find and Winston knew it and appreciated her, every minute of his life.

He could read her mind like a book when she was in the mood for romance. She made sure of that. This day, body language was probably more responsible for the transmissions he was receiving. To expose the alluring and subtle temptations of the game would ruin the mystique of the whole thing.

She would teasingly tilt her eyes upward toward him with her face still angled downward. Classic bedroom eyes Winston always thought to himself; innocent...but yet not so innocent. She would part her lips slightly, occasionally curling and twisting her tongue in and out of the corners of her mouth, then along the bottom of her upper lip, then her bottom lip, making her mouth's skin glisten with moisture.

On this morning she was transmitting hot and heavy. Fears concerning what was going on in the world and the looming dangers talked about on the news seemed far away.

Winston slid his hand under her silky nighty, along the inside of her thigh, stroking softly across her stomach, then over her hip finding the creamy soft round mound of her buttocks. He nuzzled behind her ear then down into the curve of her neck, evoking a soft purr of appreciation.

She reached between his well muscled loins and gently caressed his anxiously throbbing manhood. He was always gentle with her. He built her up slowly; priding himself on his control. He stroked and played her body's surfaces like a harp, building a crescendo of desire within her.

Today though, his control was at an all time low. He knew she was ready for him and he was more than ready for her. After she threw the handle on his emergency brake he reacted like a coiled spring...like a locomotive careening downhill...in one fluid motion catapulting himself between her opened legs and pinning her arms down by the wrists...pumping like a well greased piston...faster and faster.

They undulated and rolled on the cool sheets to music and choreography conducted by the hand of joyous rapture...losing themselves in each other...oblivious to all else...the way they wanted it to be...the way it should be.

Their honeymoon never ended. Maybe it did for some couples, but not for them. Jenifer and Winston kept their marriage fresh.

She was thirty six...he forty one. Yet, they were like a couple of kids together. Together, they shared a passion that many couples only dream about.

Jenny and Winston had collapsed into each other's arms enjoying the afterglow of total release, when a cacophony of alarmed noise erupted from the town.

All four boys were sleeping on two beds and

209

two cots in a large loft like bedroom that had been converted from an attic. Andrew Murdock leapt out of bed running to the window to see what the commotion was all about.

Sirens pierced the cool early morning silence with urgent and unrelenting shrieks. The fire whistle from Barnegat Light Township's fire and first aid department had first started, joined by distant sirens droning from townships further away.

Soon, emergency and military vehicles began whisking by the main road about a block from the Tanderoth's beach front home on Second Street.

It was starting. Whatever last night's deliberately vague warnings from the authorities were about, things were now certainly underway.

A major event had taken place during the night in the mideast, somewhere in the vicinity of the Persian Gulf. The household did not take particular notice of the rather vague report on the news. So many major events and crisis broadcasts were streaming in...one was like another.

However, there was mention of alien intervention. Was that alien as in foreign or alien as in from out there? It ended with the deliberate put off "Reports are sketchy. More will follow tomorrow morning as additional reports come in."

It was late. The family had taken the vague report as just more of the same.

But, what was happening this particular morning?

Everyone knew that it had something to do with Saddam Hussein. His followers were victimizing the free world in a hellish misdirected orgy of self-righteously justified and self-indulgent cowardly slaughter...striking from hiding like snakes or packs of rats; having been taken in, protected and nurtured by the kindness of their host countries...spreading

210

their venom and doctrine of hatred.

Saddam defined God for them. Obviously not able to think for themselves, his frightened followers believed **him** and followed **him** believing that he was sent by God...an archangel of avenging death and destruction.

They were Saddam's dark angels, his lieutenants from hell. To Saddam they were children...children to be bent to his will.

The population of the United States had been warned by the media to remain close to a radio or television; that important and urgent news of global significance would be forthcoming at any moment.

This was that moment. Winston rocketed from his bed, abandoning his bewildered wife. She took a moment...then slipped out of bed unsteadily. Reality snapped back into sharp focus for Winston.

Jenny wondered, when will such a moment occur again? Will we ever make love in our own bed again? What will this day bring? Will our family be safe? What is happening to our world?

These thoughts raced through Jenifer's mind all at once as she moved through the bedroom without direction; temporarily stunned by the switch in gears.

"Get dressed Jenny." Winston gently instructed, seeing her glazed and vacant stare.

"Make certain the boys are dressed. I'm going to turn on the teli downstairs. Bugger it all! No rest for the weary I suppose."

He threw on his clothing and shoes and rushed downstairs to the living room.

He turned on the television and started going through the channels. All stations had on the exact same thing . The emergency broadcast system had been set into operation.

The printed message on the screen instructed

"Please stand by for an urgent broadcast from the White House." A single tone sounded as background to the message.

He felt an ominous feeling hanging in the room. From stories that his father had told him he imagined that this must have been how his father, mother and their family felt while waiting next to their radios to hear the American president's speech to the joint house of representatives and to the nation following the attack by the Japanese on Pearl Harbor.

Winston knew that he had to take charge of the group, not only giving them direction, but comfort at the same time. At least his children had him and Jenny. Peter and Andrew Murdock did not have the same luxury of that solace. Winston was fully aware of that unsettling reality as he heard everyone descending the stairs.

Where was Kevin? He wondered how in the hell come he had not contacted them. That wasn't like Kevin. By now he must have heard something on the news about what was going on. Was he that deep in lustful pursuits to ignore a radio or television for so long? He supposed that it could happen, but it was not likely. What was wrong?

Early in the evening the day before, he had gone to the marina to see if Kevin and Adrian had come up for air yet. The **ACT I** was there.

He called into the boat and knocked on its side. Nothing...not a sign of occupancy. He thought that they might have gone with others or, perhaps, to a hotel.

He was about to leave when he heard the squawk of Kevin's parrot, Matey.

"Strange," he thought out loud. "That's not your form at all old man; leaving your feathered shipmate unprovided for and all."

212

He climbed aboard and slid open the port side door leading into the wheelhouse. The boat rocked gently, almost unperceptively, under his weight. Spying over the wheelhouse's observation sofa bench he found poor old Matey languishing in over-heated abandoned solitude.

The bird was panting from the heat. Without cooler air and enough water the bird would over-heat, dehydrate and die.

Walking over and peering into Matey's seed dish he sympathized with the now bewildered psit-tacine.

"You jolly well are out of victuals my seedy friend. You need immediate resupplying."

Winston reached into the bird's cage, took out the bird's water and food dishes and loaded them up with seed, water and some vegetables and fruit that he found in the crisper of the galley's refrigera-tor.

Kevin had explained to Winston a bit about the care and feeding of parrots when Winston first saw the bird. At least he realized that parrots do not live by seed alone. He remembered something about fat and cholesterol reducing the life span of parrots and how just seeds and nuts alone raised those levels.

"There now my fine feathered friend. That should keep you for a couple of days anyway. I'll pop back in if your master doesn't show up...Cheerio!"

Winston opened a couple of vents and win-dows just a crack to keep the bird from suffocating from the heat. It should be ok he thought. The evenings are temperate enough.

"Tell your master to ring me up when he pops in, will you? There's a fine fellow" as if he really expected comprehension from Matey.

Worried as he left, he stepped unto the dock and strode toward his car, admonishing himself to call the police by mid-afternoon the next day if his old chum did not make an appearance or claim his children.

Some small navy boats and coast guard boats were still in the area. Even with the reduction of military craft, Winston could feel mobilization all around him...like a gearing up for war. Where was Kevin?

Before he could reach his car he was accosted by none other than the marina's irritating manager, Ted Painedast.

He whispered to himself "Damned! Can't I avoid this character just once?"

"Is there some reason just **why** you were on that boat while the owner is away?" Ted demanded sarcastically.

He knew damned well that Kevin and Winston were best of friends. Winston spent almost as much time on the boat as Kevin did. However, this irritating pain in the derriere had to constantly exercise what little authority he had in the most excessive and self aggrandizing manner possible.

The main malfunction with this petty and sanctimonious inconvenience was that he had to embarrass people and subordinate them in order to somehow make himself more important. He could not conduct his business nicely. There always had to be a challenge or an edge to his approach.

He just didn't realize that if he were a bit more like a regular guy he **would be** important in the eyes of the people he associated with.

Instead, he was someone to be avoided. He treated the clientele in a manner that suggested that

214

he expected them to behave in cookie cutter fashion; that everyone should stay around their own boat slips and behave like neat good little boys and girls, so that his would be a quiet class in which not much was expected of him.

This contradiction in what he wanted, in how he saw himself and in the way things actually were, often erupted in his violent verbal and or physical acting out (especially when he had been drinking). People constantly complained about his behavior. Yet, he was allowed to keep his job. What a mistake.

Kevin often commented "Should trying to have some fun be this difficult?" when having to deal with this obstacle.

Kevin, Winston and the rest of the marina always thought of this individual as being like a toll booth. You had to pay homage in some way, either through direct comment or through the default of having to be the recipient of his abuse in order for you to be allowed to pass along the docks.

Winston had reached the end of his tolerance with this man. "Well, quite frankly old chap, this time I decided to pee on the carpeting. Mr. Murdock is sure to understand. Cheerio old man! as he continued toward his car whispering under his breath "Blimey that felt good."

As everyone joined Winston in the living room, the telephone ringing behind the sofa made him jump straight out of his seat. His gaze and attentions had been riveted to the television. After daydreaming about the evening before, he became painfully attentive to the screen when he was startled from behind.

He said "Who on God's earth could be calling us now at a time like this?"

After he recovered from the startle he hoped that at last it might be Kevin, as he reached for the phone.

"Hello---Yes. Who is this? This is Winston Tanderoth. How may I help you. Yes I will accept the charges."

He listened in silence for what seemed to be ages. Everyone watched him as he occasionally nodded or closed his dropped jaw only long enough to say "uh-huh--uh huh---yes--right---no, you're kidding--I'll be damned--is that so?" etc.

"Is that my daddy?" Peter Murdock chimed from the sofa.

Winston flagged him silent with his hand so that he could pay attention to the caller. Winston asked his caller to hold while he asked Jenny to take the children into the kitchen to get them some cereal and juice.

Jenifer's curiosity and frustration were overwhelming as she urgently whispered with her hands beseechingly outstretched "Who is it?"

Winston excused himself again and pleaded "Please Jenny, everything is alright. I'll explain it in awhile. Please, just give me a moment."

She was neither satisfied nor mollified by his put-off. However, she did as he asked, taking the children into the kitchen, acknowledging Winston's lead in trying to make the situation as normal as possible.

The group disappeared into the kitchen, not knowing what was being said on the other end of the phone.

What Winston was hearing on the other end of the phone was a rather surreptitious low toned woman's voice saying "I'm a friend of Adrian's and Kevin's." She then softly demanded, "Who is this?"

216

When she realized she had the right person she identified herself. "My name is Susan Harmon. My daughter Stacey and I are the ones who were missing from that boating accident and then found near Seaside. Did you hear about that accident?"

After she knew Winston understood who she was, she began telling of her experiences with the Soclarians, Adrian, Kevin and eventually the military.

After about ten minutes she continued in a whisper, "I wanted to try to contact you earlier. This is the first that I have been able to break away from the government and military people. They think that I am calling my family. They're keeping me right here at the Barnegat Light Coast Guard station.

"While Adrian was giving me her instructions and making her tape recording she told me about Kevin and that his children were with you. She knew that you had a summer place in Barnegat Light. I hoped that you had a listed number. I'm lucky you did. It was right here in the phone book.

"I'll be so happy when this whole nightmare is over. It's like my whole life has been stolen from me. I'm trying to be patient with these guys, but they're treating me like a prisoner. I don't deserve this. I've done nothing wrong."

Who could blame her. Here she was giving vital information and assistance and then became a prisoner for her troubles.

Her voice quivered as she continued; "I know what I'm telling them and what I'm doing is very important. It's just getting to me. I think they just want to keep some of the particulars under wraps for as long as they can.

Winston asked no questions. He just listened, dumbfounded.

She went on "Adrian said that she would tell

217

Kevin to look for you and his kids at your summer house here in Barnegat Light if the situation permits" her voice calming a bit.

"I can't talk much longer. I see that the goon squad is looking at me through the glass of the door to the room here.

I feel like just walking out the door or just refusing to cooperate any longer. If I could, I would. I've really had enough of this nonsense.

"But, they have my family under house arrest at home in Morristown. They're calling it protective observation. I want to try to call them now before they hear me on with you. If I can't get back to you, take my home phone number down. When things get back to normal, if they ever do, maybe we can exchange war stories. The number is 201-555-2769."

He wrote the number down. In the background over the line Winston could hear "Ma'am, you were supposed to be on the phone with your family. Ma'am please hand me the phone."

"But...but...I just..."

"Click..." the phone became silent.

The television flashed blank, then immediately displayed the seal for the President of the United States.

Reeling from what he had just heard on the phone, Winston said to himself "Why not? With everything that's going on here it could happen. This could make sense. Why not?"

Focusing on the screen, he saw the changed frame.

"Jenny, would you and the children please come in here? There's going to be an announcement."

Jenny and the kids were just finishing their breakfasts. They filed back into the living room.

Peter Murdock asked again "Was that my daddy?"

Winston lied "Yes it was. He said that he was in a real hurry and had to get off the phone. Everything's alright. All this confusion is holding him up a bit. He sends his love and asks that you be good chaps and be patient while he is away for a bit longer...Right !?"

Andrew knew that this was a lie. He saw how agitated Mr. Tanderoth was and how uncomfortable he appeared to be. Anyway, why would Mr. Tanderoth identify himself on the phone to Andrew's dad? They had been friends for years dating back to Mr. Tanderoth's first marriage.

It could not have been a collect call because Andrew knew that his dad had a credit card for calls.

He kept quiet. He was very mature for his age. Almost instinctively Andrew knew that the lie had a good reason. His dad always said that Mr. Tanderoth was a good and honest man both in business and personally. There was a real friendship and trust between the two men.

Andrew knew that whatever was going on, he and his brother were in good hands. He had no problem accepting the temporary surrogacy of the Tanderoths. He knew that if the shoe were on the other foot, his dad would have been right there for the Tandertoth's children.

"Everyone please find a seat. Donald...Brendon you sit together with Peter and Andrew over there" as Winston gestured toward the long curving section of the couch.

Winston surreptitiously pointed to Jenny, to himself then the kitchen announcing "Mumm and I will be right back. Please behave"...as he took

Jenny's hand and retreated to the kitchen with her in tow.

"That was a lady on the phone who had the damnedest story to tell about Kevin. He is alright. I cannot tell you everything right now because we don't have enough time. It's all tied in with what's going on with the Navy and with what's been on the news.

"We are going to be watching his children a bit longer. Kevin will be OK but he will be delayed. Let's go back to the kids."

"Hold on there hot shot." Jenny demanded while pulling Winston's shoulder back around to face her before he could make tracks back to the living room.

"Not so fast. I deserve a bit more than this. Do you think that you're going to just make this pronouncement and walk away? What gives? I can handle it. Remember, I'm your partner? What's going on here?"

Winston knew she was right. There just wasn't enough time.

He was emphatic as he firmly placed his hands around her shoulders and pleadingly yet sternly looked into her eyes.

"Jenny, I know this is queer. Please just trust me in this. Believe me, you will know everything soon. There will be time later for me to explain everything. But not now, please!"

He never held anything back from Jenny. Their relationship was honest and open. She sensed the urgency of his pleading request and relented "This had better be good."

As they entered the living room, Winston pointed out to the children "We need to be quiet now. The president is going to come on the teli and explain something very important to us. So, we have to be very quite...alright?"

As they waited, Winston thought to himself half in sympathy with the president, that the president bloody well couldn't announce that the world was coming to an end, that the population could perish at any moment, that everyone had to evacuate their homes and planet and or that we were being invaded by aliens, all in the same emergency speech. It just wouldn't be cricket, pulling that on an entire population all at once. Yet, the hither to this point ineffective twit had to do just that.

The president was caught between a rock and a hard place. Survival of the people he was elected to protect was now the paramount concern. A white lie was a better alternative than certain death if he could not otherwise motivate the populace.

Politicians historically have had a pretty good hold on the half truth market he thought. It's not that half truths or withholding information is inherently bad. But, it sure doesn't do much for faith in government when it is discovered.

There is a saying that "Figures lie and liars figure." Sneering at the picture tube Winston thought all one had to do was listen to the current president talk about the national debt, taxes and promised reform to figure that one out.

However, this time the president had to cut to the quick and motivate the public without panicking them. It is a bit machiavellian, but the end justifies the means in such a situation, Winston reasoned. No matter what, there would be some panic. It's just a matter of how much and how to cut the losses...damage control.

Withholding the whole truth would just have to suffice. The president could take the flack later if flack came. Winston did not care too much for this new american president. But he still sympathized with what the man had to face.

That's what being the boss is all about...total responsibility. Let the chips fall where they may. Winston had been there many times before on a much smaller scale in his manufacturing business...making tough decisions.

In Winston's opinion, there is nothing in the Harvard School of Business that prepares you for it, try as they may. Very often, there is nothing romantic, enviable nor nice about it. But, that's the price to be paid for position. It comes with the territory.

Winston, Jenifer and the boys were jolted from their own particular musings by a man's crisp voice stating "Ladies and gentlemen, the president of the United States."

President Hilliard Klenston appeared on the screen sitting behind his desk in the oval office.

Partially as a manifestation of his revulsion for this particular president, Winston could not help to look at Klenston's face and joke to himself about how much the president's nose resembled a male part; complete with a narrow vertical dimple down the middle.

Not a very altruistic thought Winston chuckled guiltily to himself. Yet, it often was a source of innocent joviality when he and Kevin would reflect upon how appropriate this observation was in view of what Klenston was doing to the american public and in the face of his campaign promises and subsequent performance record.

His favorite quote by the president was "I didn't know that the deficit was that bad before the election." when Klenston commented two weeks after taking office about raising taxes and breaking campaign promises from the get-go, right out of the starting gate.

During his relatively short tenure as a U.S. citizen, Winston had come to learn that poking fun at politicians was as American as baseball and apple pie.

How great that was; being able to voice opinion, even if it were unflattering. It is that right and many more like it that filled Winston with appreciation that he chose the USA to establish his roots. However, he wasn't kidding anybody. He knew in his heart of hearts that wherever Jenifer was, is where he wanted to be. Her being from America was a bonus.

The president began, "My fellow Americans, I am speaking to you today not only as your president, but as an appointed spokesman for all this planet's nations as a whole.

"As of midnight last night, a state of marshal law has been in effect for every state in the union. This state of marshal law is likewise in effect for any and all United States' territories and or civilian areas controlled by this government.

"Under marshal law, many of the constitutional rights that exist under normal circumstances are temporarily suspended. You will be compelled under this law to obey the directives initiated by my office. These directives will be executed by the military.

"Marshal law is designed to maintain civil order during an acute national crisis; to prevent looting and or other criminal behavior while the nation is distracted or otherwise preoccupied by a particular threat.

"In this particular case, for example, when an evacuation order is given, reluctant citizens will be evacuated involuntarily and by force if necessary.

Civil disobedience will be met with appropriate force...armed force if necessary.

"Personal travel will be severely limited. In fact, only specific travel on specific roadways proceeding in specific directions will be permitted at all. More in this regard will be explained to you later.

"Above all else, remain calm. Do what is required of you during this immediate crisis, remain orderly and we will all get through this period together.

"However, I must reiterate and emphasize that the military will be authorized to use deadly force in maintaining order. Your cooperation is not only respectfully urged, it is an absolute requirement.

"So that the same message may be received by as many individuals as possible, it has been agreed by all nations concerned that we put our differences aside for this circumstance.

"This announcement and my other comments will be transmitted simultaneously around the world by satellite. So, if I speak slowly it is for two reasons. First, you must understand everything that I will be telling you. Second, sufficient time must be allowed for translators to translate my comments for their own nations' populations.

"Each nation's leader is speaking to his or her nation now as I speak to you so that they may believe and not be suspect of any motivations other than what my urgent message contains.

"There will be a fifteen minute break so that all regional television systems may connect with the satellite feed. I shall continue my message in exactly fifteen minutes.

"I implore you, the message is of the gravest nature and requires every citizen's attention. If you suspect that a friend or relative is not already near a radio or television, please call them on the telephone and inform them of this broadcast.

"Additional civilian and military microwave and satellite capacity has been allocated to handle the increase in phone traffic...so please make your calls during the break.

"I ask that everyone set your most reliable watch, wind up or battery powered clock to coincide exactly with the time that will be displayed on the screen for the next fifteen minutes. Any future communications or directives may rely heavily upon everyone having the accurate time.

"I shall return in fifteen minutes from now."

The camera refocused from a closeup of the president and panned backward, revealing more and more of the oval office... then faded to a blank screen. Immediately following, a digital time display appeared along with a header that stated "The current time is:..." Under that a smaller message read "Time remaining to broadcast:..." with another digital display counting the minutes and seconds backward from fifteen minutes.

Everyone turned toward Winston. His tongue could not concoct any answers. He wished he could say something that would allay the apprehension that everyone in the room must have been feeling. The apprehension was vividly inscribed across all faces, including his own. He knew what was coming.

Jenifer recognized that Winston was at a loss for words and that he felt helpless. During the time that she had known him, she realized that he always wanted to be the strength for those he loved or cared for. This was part of his constitution. He wanted to have all the answers, to make everything right...to be in control...to have control.

Now, he was floundering. She saw his pleading look that begged...help me out here. This one I can't sustain by myself. I have no control of this.

"OK kids, everyone onto the beach for a fifteen minute breath of fresh air. Here's the soccer ball. Go knock yourselves out!" she ordered handing the ball to Brendon as the kids all made a subdued yet relieved progression toward the door.

The kitchen's screened door slammed shut behind them. In a matter of seconds the ball was in play and the children were screeching happily in contrast and in defiance of the looming danger.

Jenifer and Winston followed the children as far as the kitchen and watched them through the window. Winston poured himself a cup of coffee and nibbled on a cold toasted bagel.

Simple pleasures...a cup of coffee, a cold toasted bagel, beholding the innocence of children playing or just standing in the kitchen talking to your spouse, all took on new significance for Jenifer and Winston.

All that they took for granted, all that was familiar would change and they knew it as they watched the children through the window.

"They don't really have a clue" Winston noted. "Andrew has a bit of a handle on it, but he is sensible enough to trust us and not alarm the other children."

"What...what exactly *is* the clue they should be getting?" Honey, you seem to know a bit more about all of this than the rest of us. Do you mind sharing this with the rest of the class young man? Or is this going to be your private or personal province?" She cryptically quipped.

She continued "OK, OK, something dramatic is going to happen. We have a few minutes. Fill me in."

"Alright sweetheart. You're just going to have to take all of this on face value. When the president makes his comments you will realize this is all the truth and factual and that Kevin is right in the middle of it."

He spent the next ten minutes telling Jenifer all that he had learned from the phone call with Mrs. Harmon and answering Jenny's questions to the best of his ability.

"Be strong Jenny. The kids need to see that we are keeping our wits about us. We must act calmly and as normally as possible."

Jenifer agreed. She did accept the information on face value. This information, her love for her family and faith in her husband plus her fear for their collective futures galvanized her resolve to be strong. Or at least it galvanized her intentions to resolve to be strong. She hoped that she could be.

In the distance they could hear the sounds of deuce-and-a half military trucks and the clanking of tank tracks beating an urgent cadence against the pavement. The National Guard had been mobilized. This was a certainty. But why put so much oomph and muscle into the Barnegat Light area Jenifer wondered?

Again, a long tone sounded on the television.

As Jenifer swiftly moved toward the kitchen's door she said "Let's get the kids inside. It's time."

The group reassembled in the living room. The digital timer display showed thirty four seconds and was counting down. Winston set his watch as did Jenny.

As the children settled down, without any introduction this time, the President began to speak slowly, deliberately and with frequent pauses.

"Citizens of the world, as you are all well aware,

227

terroristic activities have reached a level within our nation and indeed throughout the world, the likes and proportions of which defy comparison with anything mankind has ever been required to cope with.

"Our fresh water supplies have been poisoned on a large scale. There is very little potable water left anywhere. The aquifers of this nation are rapidly being infiltrated both by chemical and biological toxins.

"Nerve gas and other toxic airborne killers have been released on a grand scale throughout the world. The clouds from these releases seem to dissipate relatively quickly. However, before dissipating, they have taken a horrifying and cataclysmicly high toll on human life.

"We know for a certainty that the ones doing these acts are agents directly answerable to, loyal to and directed by Saddam Hussein, leader of the Iraqi people. Let there be no mistake, these acts have been laid directly on his doorstep.

"Many of you might think, as I have thought, that we should have removed this pariah...this cancer...from the face of the earth while we had the opportunity. This is all academic now.

"Yes, we knew what he was. However, we either underestimated his charismatic abilities or over estimated the resolve or ability of the Iraqi people to recognize this outlaw for what he is and do something about it themselves...*without* involvement from the rest of the world. Normally, when someone has an irritating splinter that becomes the source of discomfort and infection they dig it out. This did not happen as expected with Saddam.

"Our government leaders truly believed at that time that he would be cast out by his own people for the horror and suffering he brought down upon their heads.

"We all thought and believed that they would dispatch him from his position of power and prominence in their government and in their lives. We all thought...'How could the Iraqi people tolerate this obvious central cause for their suffering and their depravation?'

"This is because we as Americans, British, Australians, Canadians and many others view things through rose colored glasses, tinted with our own experiences, our own standards and our own Judeo-Christian heritages and perspectives.

"We just did not have a proper understanding of their culture and the hold that their leaders have on them. Saddam can do no wrong in their eyes. Or the wrong he does is part of a grand correct scheme that they somehow have faith in.

"This scenario has turned out to be a tragic mistake on the part of the Kuaiti liberation forces and a flawed judgement call that has cost us our homes and millions of lives with many more lives to follow, I'm afraid.

"Even as I speak, our military and investigative branches of our government are discovering or identifying more and more agents of this lunatic, Saddam Hussein.

"We are discovering that these agents are indifferent to the pain, suffering and death that they are causing. They are, themselves, unafraid by the prospect that they are in fact creating their own deaths.

"They are fanatics of the most dangerous kind. Their loyalty to this evil maniac defies reason or anything that we as a people might believe to be normal or rational.

This vessel from which such evil emanates, Saddam Hussein, has a hypnotic effect on his followers, almost akin to that of an addictive hallucinatory drug.

"Our worst nightmare has now been discovered to be a reality. The main event has yet to unfold. Within the last two days, we have discovered six atomic devices assembled within the boundaries of our nation. Two were discovered in California, one in Texas, one in Colorado, one in Florida and one in Maryland."

Behind Klenston, pictures of captured nuclear bomb apparatus were displayed on an easel. He swung around and pointed to the pictures with a long wooden stick.

"Scores more are out there still. We were able to obtain this particular information from three of the saboteurs who had come to their senses and realized that such a *jihad* would leave nothing to conquer...that there is no victory in the slaughtering of the inhabitants of this world and in the poisoning of the planet's atmosphere in such a way as to alter the course of all of humanity for ever.

"We are presented with a **checkmate** and a **stalemate**. We are defeated at this point. However, in their victory they are defeating themselves and the human race. No one now is going to win anything. Our days are numbered by the whim of Saddam. It's just a matter of time before the other shoe falls.

"He is in hiding. No one knows where he is.

"We know from our intelligence network that in total there are literally hundreds of nuclear devices placed by his agents, not only all around our nation but in many other nations as well.

"These devices and materials for additional devices were purchased from the fractionated Soviet Union's new independent nations and states. Saddam offered big money. The starving nations needed the money and elected to turn a blind eye to Saddam's need for such weapons.

"We do not know when these devices will be detonated. We do know that he has instructed his agents to remain within a maximum of a ten minute walk from the bombs that they are responsible for.

"He has trained an army of fanatic specialists to assemble and eventually detonate these devices. There is no defense against this tactic.

"We might encounter a defector here and there if we give it enough time. However, we do not have that luxury. We know that we do not have enough time to gamble with. We, also, know that Saddam realizes that it will be difficult to maintain control and discipline of his agents for a protracted period of time if they are not near him.

"He will act soon. We must not misjudge this reality. The man will do it. He will play this final hand. His trump card is about to hit the table. Of this you may be absolutely assured. Let there be no doubt, whatsoever. Remember, this is a man who gases and poisons the children of his own nation.

"It is for this reason that we must act without hesitation nor without delay. We must calmly act decisively and with a degree of cooperation unparalleled in the known history of human civilization or experience.

"It is too late to build bomb shelters in your back yards. Even if there were time, there would not be a world to emerge into when you finally opened the door to that shelter. Our only course of action is that we must leave this world in mass and without delay.

"Thank God we have been given the means to do so. We have established contacts and an alliance with an extraordinary civilization that will aid us in this flight.

"I will outline this alliance, the exact mechanics of our exodus and to where we are going and how life will be there, later in this statement."

Upon hearing this revelation, Jenifer shrieked hysterically. She went ballistic. Her resolve to try to remain strong had left her...at least temporarily.

The president paused at this juncture; almost as if he heard a collective gasp from the nation or heard Jenifer's scream all the way to Washington, DC.

Winston leapt from his seat and gathered Jenifer into his arms.

"Shhh...Jenny---shhh. Let's hear his plan. There is nothing new in what he just said. This is what I have been telling you about" as he thought of the millions of people that didn't even have the least bit of an inkling as she had.

She gulped and shrieked at the same time "We're going to die. We're all going to die. Oh God! Oh God! Please help us! I can't take it! Oh God."

She collapsed into quaking sobs. The children started to sob in reaction to Jenifer's outburst.

"Jenny," Winston whispered, "the children. For God's sake please...try to calm yourself and listen."

Only a few seconds had gone by. Yet, the hammer blow delivered by the president's proclamation stopped time dead in its tracks within the room.

The president deliberately maintained his pause; looking downward and adjusting his notes, rubbing his face, giving a sigh to emphasize his own awareness of the gravity of what he had just announced

232

to the nation and to the world.

Within seconds, from outside, the sounds reached their ears of automobile engines starting and tires screeching on the pavement as some neighbors raced down the street in panic.

...-Boom!!! The sound of the first car ramming a road block was heard. Machine gun fire erupted. Then silence.

"Everyone be calm. There is a plan and we must hear it" Winston entreated calmly yet firmly.

The children were silently whimpering as they trembled on the couch. Jenifer's reaction did not help. Winston knew if they just followed the plan being laid out by the president they all had a chance. Fear now was their worst enemy, then Saddam.

Jenifer was beyond consoling at this point. She was near fainting and collapse. Winston just hugged her. The younger children did not realize the full implications of what was being said and what was happening, but were calmed to a degree by Winston's own self control. Brendon and Andrew were riveted to the set. They were now all too aware...the fear etched in their faces.

The president continued, "I realize this and all that I am about to tell you will seem surreal to all of you. There is no need to panic.

"The only hope any of us has for survival is to not panic, follow the instructions I am about to give you and those of the military once evacuation is under way."

Jenifer and the children were beginning to calm down once they started hearing these words; that there was hope.

Jenifer collected herself, rose and reseated herself between the children, placing her arms over the shoulders of two of them like a mother hen. The kids soon cuddled in closer to her and to each other...all listening intently. A scene certainly being repeated in millions of households across the nation.

The sounds of cars nearby returning to their driveways could be heard through the open screen windows. Where could they have been going? We're all going to have to get there together, Winston thought...where ever *there* was. Attempts at individual escape would be pointless and counterproductive.

They continued listening to the president, understood him, believed him but...for some reason...they made a brief psychological attempt to try to deny that it had anything to do with them. How could it? It was too bizarre. It was too foreign. It was too final. It was their order to evacuate their homes and their planet.

The president continued "Again, please remember, only take one bag of personal belongings such as clothing with you. Food will be provided, sanitation will be provided and eventually, all that you will need in your new homes will be provided for.

"Financial institutions will be guarded by military personnel until the last civilians are evacuated. As we speak, the world's gold reserves and currencies are being stockpiled and being placed safely away. We will be leaving a ghost world behind. What is of value to you are your families and your lives.

"We shall come out of this crisis together, as a united population under God. Living according to the universal code intended by the Creator and universal consciousness of which I spoke.

"At the crucial time He will let his presence be known to us all in an undeniable manner by which we may all be assured that this divinely inspired code of living is not something concocted by man nor subject to man's interpretations.

"One half hour after this broadcast ends, it will be repeated in its entirety."

President Klenston delivered the specifics of the evacuation plan with the help of generals and two officer representatives of the Soclarians whom he artfully introduced in a matter of fact way that somehow made all this seem acceptable and credible.

The Tanderoth household became one of millions, resigning themselves to their fates as they listened to the outline of their destinies.

-CHAPTER 11-

The predawn hours in the mountains of Iraq were so peaceful and beautiful that Daramer felt inspired to share her feelings that "Truly God is in this place and with us today."

The group of five plus their two guards were dropped off by helicopter just north of Irbil. To the side of the mountain flowed a tributary of the Tigris River; the mountain being equidistant from the Turkish, Syrian and Iranian borders. Each border was approximately eighty miles away to the northwest, the north and the south from where they stood.

The large military helicopter had settled upon a reinforced concrete landing pad, that had been constructed within a giant carved niche having been scooped out of the side of the mountain near the top. An elevator took the group to the summit of the mountain where they were allowed to enter and leave a rather large guest-like cabin.

The mountain was Saddam's hideaway and his personal fortress, replete with full military staffing, an array of armaments and sophisticated communications. What a contrast to the serenity within which it was nestled. The only construction that looked like it belonged was the cabin at the top.

The light of the stars splashed and dazzled across the onyx sky above and across the eyes of the witnesses present. It seemed only moments later that the dimmest of azure lights started blending into the darkness of the eastern horizon.

The moist, flowered, sweet smell of the summer's predawn air rose from the lush valley and the flowing waters below.

"How could such evil, such cataclysm or such horror find a place in a world that includes such splendor as this; let alone spawn from within it?" Adrian asked rhetorically.

Daramer, Kevin, Adrian, Hank and Justinian Fairborne were all prisoners of Saddam Hussein. Saddam always seemed to have the same sick euphemism for such detainees. They were "guests of the state."

As predicted by Fairborne, like the alley cat that Saddam was, he enjoyed taunting and playing with his catch before the kill. It helped quell his sense of inadequacy. Kevin thought this could be due to the fact that perhaps Saddam had an unusually small wanker. Maybe that was it.

What happened to him to cause such a hatred toward his fellow man? No one was safe from him. Not even his own people. The insanity of evil itself ran through his veins.

The five had to be captured. It was part of the plan. It was preordained. Yet it could not be made to look too easy. The drama had to be played out on a world stage configured by Saddam. He had to be the master of ceremonies in order that his rebuke of the infidels be more poignant in the eyes of his followers and the world at large...so he could somehow justify his vile and evil deeds. But how...how on this peaceful stage in the middle of nowhere could this be done?

Hours before, Captain Sencecus personally navigated a shuttle craft through the darkness only a few feet above the calm waters of the Persian Gulf. The group had grown by one.

Ambassador Fairborne added himself to the shore excursion team at the last minute. He knew that he was going all along. He just never shared that with anyone until the last possible moment. He wanted the group to be resolute and galvanized, proceeding toward their collective and common destiny; proceeding into the fray alone...with confidence.

He had to be concretely certain. He had to test the metal and resolve of the unit's individual components. There was no margin for cowardice nor uncertainty. The bees had to go straight to the nest despite all obstacles...straight to the hornet's nest.

He informed the surprised group that "I'm just going to tag along for advise and for my own observations. Anyway, as you all may recall, apparently I have connections you may need"...robes, staff and falcon still in place. How incongruous he looked amidst his surroundings. Yet, his presence brought relief, comfort and bolstered strength to the group.

True as that was, no one admitted it out loud. Yet, Justinian received the message loud and clear as a warm smile of recognition crossed his face. They all settled in for the ride, alone with their own thoughts.

After leaving the earth base station and having ascended to the surface, the shuttle craft glided quietly past the Kuwaiti shoreline, past Abadan on Iran's southern border, past Basrah and delivered them to the marshy shoreline adjacent to the city of Al-Qurnah at the confluence of the Tigris and Euphrates rivers. The nearest town where their

239

allies would be coming from was Al-Faw-Bubiayan...their first planned destination.

Soldiers from the local Republican Guard outpost observed the shuttle craft docking. This was not part of the plan. The darkness of night and the reeds were not quite enough to shroud the craft's arrival. They could not believe their eyes...seeing this strange craft silently hovering several feet over the water.

A set of steps unfolded from the side of the craft revealing the first of the passengers. Obviously, this was some kind of secret weapon sent by the American infidels. After the gulf war, they took no western weaponry nor technology for granted.

The passengers were discharged onto the old and rotting dock. Practically in unison, several of the guard members shrieked "American commandos!!! There they are! Kill them! Kill them!"

How could recent intelligence information be that far off base. These guys were waiting for them. They were expected, that was obvious. The group had somehow been found out...or worse...betrayed.

Saddam was certainly expecting something. He had to be. He moved his forces around. Yet, this was taken into consideration. The soldiers were supposed to be five miles up river. Saddam, also, had a force...a dark force on his side.

Shots rang out. Machine gun fire sprayed all around the discharged passengers, splintering rocks from the shoreline. Mushy chunks of wood from the rotting dock and pilings exploded as the hot metal indiscriminately struck.

"Hit the deck!" Hank ordered. He was designated as tactical leader of the team. Even though he was outranked, the tactical leader had the authority in the field.

Fairborne knew the soclarian military protocol and abided by it. Anyway, he had already told the group that he was just along for the ride.

The group followed Hank, diving behind a cluster of large rocks adjacent to the dock in an attempt to shield themselves against the attack. The falcon accompanying Fairborne thundered into the sky after Fairborne made his plunge toward the rocks. They were pinned down.

"Isn't God supposed to be on our side here?" Kevin whispered to Hank.

"Friends were supposed to meet us here. What about this wonderful plan. We're supposed to mingle and then get caught...you know, nice and easy like."

"Where's your faith my boy? Very little is ever easy, even **with** divine intervention" Hank said, smiling back at him.

Kevin thought to himself that this cowboy grandfather of his was actually enjoying this. Yet, he knew that they did not come all this way to be made into swiss cheese by the Iraqi army. Everything would be OK.

"Connections...connections. Remember, we have connections. We need connections **and we need guns**. How come we went into to this without guns?" he sarcastically muttered.

Hank reminded "Guns will get us killed here. Our weapon is the commission with which we have been charged. Our shield is the virtue in our hearts among other sources", as he glanced toward the unseen black falcon circling above...almost completely obscured by the darkness.

The falcon stayed aloft, circling alertly above...watching, knowing.

The shuttle craft was turning to make its trip back to the base when a shower of gunfire echoed and ricochetted off its hull. "Plink-ping-plink--pang--pang."

Senecus knew or at least was reasonably assured the group would be safe when he heard through the vessel's outside listening device "Cease fire!...Wait!...Cease fire!" The Iraqis were giving them a chance to surrender.

Daramer had brought along a simple white flag, pretty certain that she would be using it. She waved it with vigorous conviction over her head. Yes, she was protected by those in higher places, but she wasn't taking any foolish chances.

She muttered "Don't tempt the fates. God helps those who help themselves...Just in case he's looking the other way right now" as she continued waving the flag.

The Soclarian agents at work in the area knew that this particular contingent of battle seasoned guard members had been in the Gulf War. That's why this location was selected for infiltration...just in case the soldiers got to the group first. Almost every guard member had experienced the kindness and forbearance of their American adversaries once they had been captured.

They had been told by their leaders that if they were captured, the Americans would rip off their genitals and barbecue them for breakfast right in front of them. Then, as they were tied to stakes on the hot desert sands, the enemy would rub camel dung on the open wounds and watch them die from infection and searing pain.

The military leaders knew that this was the

worst image they could possibly conjure and inscribe into the minds of their soldiers, so that they would fight hard and avoid defeat and capture.

The British, Saudi, and American forces were struck with awe by the degree of fear these soldiers had once they found it necessary to surrender. The depth of this fear was far beyond anything that they had expected or had been prepared for. They soon learned the reasons from their prisoners...the specter of mutilation, emasculation and slow death.

Also, the Iraqis knew of their own atrocities that they visited upon the Kuwaiti people. They were barbaric, showing no mercy. They expected the same treatment in return. This just did not happen.

Prisoners were given water. They were cleaned and fed. Their wounds were treated. They were treated with dignity and humanity. Their confinement ended in repatriation and in their bewilderment, wondering why they were allowed to leave with their lives, let alone with full bellies.

They apparently thought that the Geneva Convention was something that podiatrists did in Miami Beach once a year. It was certainly nothing that pertained to them...nor did they expect any protection from it.

This was one of the primary motivating factors at play with the welcoming committee's leader. The additional factor was he believed that this would be a great moment in his career...if he could present these infiltrators...these infidels alive to Saddam. He ordered his men "Give them a chance to surrender."

He shouted toward the rocks in broken english "You come with hands behind head and you live. You not do this things or run, you die fast now."

"That was clear enough for me" Adrian noted, "Now what?"

Daramer responded back to the soldiers in perfect Arabic "We have come in peace. We wish you no harm. We have a message for Saddam Hussein. We must take the message to him ourselves, in person."

The soldier spoke again, "Let me see you. You will not be harmed if you keep your hands behind your heads" the leader repeated in Arabic to Daramer, just in case he was not understood the first time in English. "Come forward now."

"OK everyone, this is the moment of truth. If we can keep these gentlemen calm for the next few moments we will be over the hurdle.

"Follow me!" Daramer declared as she led the group out from behind the rocks...hands clasped behind their heads...a subordination and a homage to Saddam and his henchmen that the group nor anyone else would ever have to perform again.

Hank did not play on ceremony and deferred to Daramer since he did not speak Arabic.

"Your assassin ally dogs have been captured. They will soon pay the ultimate price for their treasons against Saddam and Allah" the guard's commander proudly reported.

Little did the commander know that the small group of Iraqi collaborators were much less likely to pay the ultimate price than were Hussein's own partners in crime. The hours ahead of them all would reveal that distinction.

Events followed quickly after that. The ego of Saddam Hussein dictated that he must personally take charge of the fates of all infidels who deign to either challenge him or violate the borders of his country.

If there were anything that one could rely upon with this ego maniac, it was that his dangerous paranoia was predictable. On this day, the traveling messengers relied upon that fact.

A few radio transmissions were exchanged between their captors and some unknown location. Soon a helicopter was spiriting them away. They knew without being told that they were going directly to Baghdad.

Predictably, the group was not disappointed. However, they didn't even have the time for the grand tour. Saddam met the helicopter at the army air base in Baghdad. He inspected the group in the helicopter, smiled a twisted evil smile and extended his hand in a sweeping motion... urging the passengers to exit the aircraft and to follow him.

They were ushered directly into an army barrack rousing bewildered guards and their cadre, as the group of five passed through the building into a soldiers' lounge. Saddam gestured toward two leather couches configured in an "L" in the corner of the room, indicating that he wanted them to be seated. Naturally, on the opposite wall was a large framed picture of their host.

Standing next to his own picture with his left hand intermittently placed on his chest then waving it into the air in front of himself (much like a mustached Napoleon) he spoke in Arabic to the group with Daramer translating.

"So...you infidel spies want to see me. Sinful yankee spies will never receive mercy within these borders. What did you hope to accomplish? You who are less than the dirt under my feet? What do you have to say for yourselves?" he blustered as he gesticulated and punctuated his intimidating phrases with wild hand gestures.

Kevin couldn't help think to himself that this guy is always on stage. As he ranted and raved he looked beyond the five... glaring over their heads in his own dream world reality. He was acting as if he were delivering his life's most important speech before millions of adoring trembling constituents.

Perhaps, he **was** delivering an important speech... or at least one of his last. This meeting was the beginning of his end... the end of his reign of terror.

Hank and Daramer laid out the soclarian mission. Justinian gave a few clarifications. Adrian and Kevin simply sat and listened to the translations. Saddam had his own translator, who remained in silent acquiescence, signifying that the translations were legitimate.

Kevin knew that this was not the moment for his particular contribution... his ultimate contribution. Yet he felt the need to further close this sale. He was not convinced that Saddam would jump at the bait. Challenging Saddam, he took a dangerous chance. It was a calculated chance, sensing that Saddam needed them alive more than he wanted them dead.

"You have to kill us" Kevin blurted out. An audible collective gasp sounded from the group. Giving Kevin an elbow in the ribs Adrian chastised "Shut up! Are you trying to get us all killed?"

Unswayed, Kevin continued. "You wouldn't dare take the chance of pitting your will against that of our people. You know that you would lose.

You know you would lose face."

That was all Saddam had to hear. The losing face part did the trick.

To put it mildly, Saddam was not tough to figure out. Some people could be read like a book. Saddam could be read like a bull horn.

This preliminary advisory meeting was more to put Saddam on notice so that he could focus his forces and energies for the world to see... so that he could bring the putrefaction of his presence on Earth to a head for lancing.

Until that point, no one in the group really believed they were going to persuade Saddam to do anything... to change anything. They, too, were playing their parts. That is, no one except Kevin believed.

Everything that he had read about Hussein, everything he had heard and now everything he sensed while in Saddam's presence shouted "VANITY, EGO, INSECURITY AND CHAUVINISM." It was all like a built up charge within Hussein. Kevin knew he had the key. He floated it up on a kite into Saddam's cloud; knowing that, like electricity, it could be channeled, given the proper path and outlet.

The astringent was applied. The infection was being brought to the surface. After Kevin's little pitch, the first part of the group's task was over.

Saddam never let the deep emotions of anger nor happiness be seen by others; not real happiness... the kind that shows ultimate satisfaction in either deed or the deeds and joys of others. This occasion, however, released the flood gates.

First he turned beet red. He looked like a steaming tea kettle. Just as quickly as his initial response, he roared with laughter and delight.

247

Then, like the slamming of a cold steel prison cell door, his face hardened.

"You Americans expect me to believe this load of camel dung? You insult me. Do you take me for a fool? Do you think I am stupid? Do you believe that I now have the world by the neck because I am a gullible idiot to be led by a ring through my nose like a contented prized pig?

"You are the pigs and I am your butcher. You have given me what I need to show the infidels for what they are. You will be slaughtered in the abattoir of Iraqi justice before a world audience, after I use you to my ends.

"Now, begone from my sight slugs of the swamp!" he ordered with a flip of his hand. The guards herded the five out of the room.

The rest of the group looked toward Kevin with a 'thank you kiddo...you sure know how to impress a guy' type look. However, Kevin's knowing just how and where to play the ace card probably saved their lives or at least saved them from permanent exile to one of Iraq's hell hole dungeons until the end came (which was to be very soon).

The guards led them to an area where they could use the facilities and splash a little water on their faces. That was it. After a few minutes they were back in the air on their way to Saddam's mountain fortress.

After a spartan and tasteless meal of a boiled grain mixture unceremoniously doled out by the guards, the group reflected upon the rapid fire progression of events they had encountered. Resting back on the lush green grass looking up at the stars, they discussed what they might expect next. Now all they could do was wait.

Kevin looked at the ambassador, then looked toward the sky thinking about the soclarian's home and their conquest of space. He whimsically commented, "For centuries mankind has looked to the stars, searching for truth or for some meaning to his own significance in the universe... if there is any to be found. Why do you suppose that we have been so compelled to do this and so preoccupied with this? What inspired the soclarians in the beginning in your own quest for knowledge of the universe?

"Is it that we humans are so innately dissatisfied with ourselves or human existence in general? Is it a quest for something nobler or maybe a nobler side of ourselves?"

Fairborne realized that Kevin was understandably nervous and frazzled; his having a need for some small talk and company. Justinian took in a deep breath and released a sigh relaxing back into the grass. "Well Kevin, it's quite simple really and at the same time quite normal behavior given man's nature.

"The various space programs on earth, the quest by humans to explore space, to plumb its depths and to seek truths on a universal level are all simply manifestations of the children of God... of the children of the universal spirit... of children crawling around to find themselves, to find their origins, their creator... *their father*.

"The answers that we all seek... the truths that we all yearn for may be found within our own spirits. The spirit that we do not give enough credit to, or sometimes ignore **is** the intangible quantity... the intangible and invisible substance which conjoins and flows with creation and all there is, has been and will be. "The eager space

249

explorer is a lot like the single vacationer who knows that he is not happy or feels fed-up with his life or his life's seeming lack of fulfillment or purpose. He goes to a far away exotic tropical island to find happiness, to find what he is missing, to find a purer or uncomplicated love and acceptance, romance, companionship, peace, rest, relief from his problems, relief from his own self doubts or self hatred for what he has made or not made of himself or his life.

"Often, what the traveler finds when he gets there, is disappointment and frustration. He is the same person in *paradise* that he was before he left home. He exports all that he is and simply transplants to a new location that condition and vessel filled with the same enigmatic baggage and needs.

"He then returns home in despair to find that nothing in his life nor within himself has changed. Most often, a changed life must start with a changed self.

"Man would have soon learned to travel many times faster than the speed of light on his own, without the help of an advanced civilization. He eventually would have learned the techniques of projecting his consciousness to any place in the universe through the development of his spiritual self and his intelligence, working in harmony with the universal consciousness.

"However, in the end, after seeing all there was to see, after collecting rock samples from far away galaxies or after encountering new life forms throughout the universe, he would find out two things: One...he would find that the universe was as described in your biblical scriptures. We exist in a universe...a *world without beginning and*

250

without end. Two...he would also feel a bit like the little girl in the story we all know of who tries to get home after defeating evil... in that she realized ***there's no place like her own home***. After acknowledging this revelation and truth, she was sent home by virtue of her own strength of will and conviction.

"She confronted evil and defeated it. She dreamed her dreams, discovered new knowledge and found her shining city. Her repeating that truth, saying it over and over again was really her faith and her finding abundant strength within herself and her own spirit.

All she really needed, she already possessed. It was all around her and within her all the time, right under her nose... inculcated as standard operating equipment within her... as it is within each of us.

"All there is to see, all the expanses of space and all there is to discover within the physical universe, is wholly and totally the manifestation of the universal spirit... the universal consciousness... the Lord our God.

"These **things**...their every pulsating atom... are physical constructs created by the concrete reality of the universal spirit... of the Creator and creation itself...unlimited energy transformed into physical reality.

"A portion of that spirit flows within each of us and we may call it our own. It is that part of us that will join back and coexist with and within all things when our physical missions have ended.

"It is at that point and only at that point we will know total knowledge, truth, love and acceptance. Until that point, your people must try to take greater heed of their spiritual selves and what is being communicated to their minds through its link with the Deity... the universal consciousness... as it touches their spirits."

Daramer was listening intently, nodding her head in agreement. She turned to Kevin and added "It is this quest, also,... this void... this emptiness that especially western man tries to fill with **things** or with unrealistic or media generated concepts of beauty or perpetually lustful love that runs so contrary to basic arabic beliefs.

"It is little wonder why such a homicidal maniac as Saddam Hussein was able to conjure and rally such resentment against the west.

"Over here, inner beauty has its rightful place. Here perfume is replaced by the sweet radiance of the soul. A man is inspired by the softness and smell of clean hair when he places his face against his woman's head. It is not EROTICA SURPRISE hair spray or NAKED ON THE BEACH hair shampoo.

"To us, making love is a joy reserved for the gratification and soothing of each other's souls... a quenching of one's most intimate thirst... an oasis in the hot desert of human transgression against fellow man or our day to day tribulations.

"Sex is not a pseudo art form to be perfected and practiced for one's venal satisfaction for a moment's pleasure. Nor is it a numbers game to see who can bed down the most partners. It is a comfort and pillow for the soul, provided so that both man and woman may take solace and rest beside the refreshing waters of God's own healing shores.

"It is this ocean of peace that God has provided us access to. Western man even pollutes these waters with his abuses... taking for granted the sanctity of this joyful resource and gift that God has built into the existence of mankind.

"Remember... Love is like water.
It seeks its own level
without being forced.
If boiled, it burns what it touches
and then evaporates.
If diligently conserved,
it nourishes the thirsting fields
of the soul
to yield the fruit of joy.

"That is what intimate love means to us here. That is what is revered. I believe that we are closer to God and his treasured values here in this land. Here, we do not have false gods masquerading in the forms of new cars, bigger homes, bigger boats and all that technology has to provide.

"It is not that these things should not be obtained and enjoyed; they should not be allowed to rule us nor become greater than simply just **things**.

"What I am saying is that instead of these things bringing you closer to God and to each other, they most often force you further apart.

"Your children watch television when they are not in school. If they are not doing that, they are playing video games. If they are not doing that, they are in a corner somewhere with a pair of stereo headphones on.

"Manifestations of technology are your children's surrogate parents. These **THINGS** are their surrogate friends. Adult concepts are foisted upon them too early, forcing them to cope with things that they were not intended to cope with at an early and innocent age.

"Children see that emotional adult interaction is trivialized by what the technocratic society wants them to see. **THINGS** are their new gods... and so it continues with the adult population as well, once the precocious little darlings grow up. This is what they become... the sum total of that which their childhoods have made them. What else could be expected?

"There are a few enlightened people who fight this trend in the western nations. However, their voices are overpowered by the din of the technocratic cravings of the populace at large.

"In America, you have a nation of happy sheep... sheep that follow the false prophets of the new god; the god of technology, the god of alienation... a god that accentuates and plays upon your differences through technological interactions, instead of drawing you closer and emphasizing your similarities through fellowship and spiritual interaction made possible through an emphasis on caring for one another and caring for something beyond **SELF**.

"Sorry about the soap box Kevin. Sometimes, I get carried away. I used to feel like taking out a full page newspaper ad asking...**Don't You Get It?**."

Understanding her intentions, yet feeling a bit outgunned and unable to defend the indefensible (nor really wanting to), Kevin remained silent, soaking in the lesson, the predawn beauty, the odors of the good earth and the peaceful feeling generated by his surroundings and company. He was calming himself... gearing down before the curtain went up.

Atop this peaceful mountain he was unaffected by and could have almost forgotten about the furious worldwide preparations. **Operation Noah's Ark** was well under way in anticipation of the signal for **Final Alarm**.

-CHAPTER TWELVE-

As was the case around the other earth base stations, things were bustling in and around the township of Barnegat Light. The National Guard was now fully deployed. War ships patrolled the coastline and flanked the inlet. Fighter planes, cargo planes, radar and communication planes crisscrossed the ski... overhead. Most of them were dispatched from McGuire Air Force Base. Mobilization was at hand gearing toward the largest exodus ever known.

Land bridges between the mainland and Barnegat Light had been created. As Moses parted the Red Sea, in true biblical fashion, solid rock land bridges were caused to rise from the bottom of Barnegat Bay...complete with arches that had about a thirty foot clearance from the water's surface.

Decades before, with the knowledge that such an exodus could become a reality, the soclarians prepared underground chambers that housed plates of gravitational concentrators. During this night, the concentrators were pressed into service.

The noise and commotion caused by the earth's upheaval caused people to think at first that Saddam had set off his nuclear devices. Then, after not seeing a flash, the radio and televisions reported that there had been an earthquake. Things settled down.

It would be some time before the real source could be ascertained and then reported accurately. By then, the highways of exodus would be complete...no time for a permit.

As the **Star Seeker III** hovered over Barnegat Bay under the cover of night one by one, each section rose. The **Star Seeker III** surgically applied a barely visible fusion beam of intense heat to the mass of rock and sand, causing the materials to liquify, fuse then solidify flat as they cooled.

With the same fusion beam, the **Star Seeker III** then formed archways underneath the bridges to allow tidal flow, to prevent stagnation, to facilitate the free passage of sea life...just in case...just in case this bay might be used again in some distant time...in case some life survived the coming holocaust. This scene and this activity were mirrored around the globe at all earth base stations.

In less than an hour, an eight lane land bridge had been fabricated, complete with on ramps. It extended from Pennsylvania...directly east over the New Jersey Turnpike...straight across the Garden State Parkway and Route 9...right across Barnegat Bay...directly down the middle and out of the inlet, past the end of the jetties...ending at the 400 foot gaping maw of the reception orifice one quarter of a mile out from the end of Barnegat Light's jetty.

Similar configurations are visible on the planet Mars. When evil had its way there one half million years ago, the same scenario was played out with the same equipment. The planet was turned into a cold, dusty and lifeless sphere, having been knocked out of its original orbit that had been closer to the life giving warmth of the sun.

Most of its atmosphere and water were blown off the surface of the planet at the same time. The water that was left, froze and became covered with the planet's blowing dust.

Super weapons in the hands of evil's disciples wreaked havoc on that planet as well. All that remained was a crisscross network of elevated roadways that earth's inhabitants had later labeled as canals.

At the inlet, disintegration chambers of immense size were located to the left and right for the last quarter mile of the roadway. Anything and everything that could be found on wheels and could move under its own power began streaming onto the causeway. Buses, trucks, cars...a flood of vehicles began inundating the roadway at the lighthouse.

As quickly as the vehicles arrived, the passengers exited. The vehicles were disposed of down into the disintegration chambers. What had not been turned into sub-atomic particles was reduced to microscopic residue, then purged and sluiced out to sea by the constant wash of the vast pumps in conjunction with the rapidly flowing tide.

The current in the inlet was always rapid. However, now with the inlet's being constricted even further by the highway, the inlet became a seething white water spectacular during peak tidal activity.

It was only during slack tide that government vessels could negotiate the inlet at all. If it were not for the boulders forming the jetties on either side, the land would have simply just washed away.

However, the Soclarians did manage to rise and harden those barriers, fusing the boulders and other materials to a smooth gleaming surface to further assist the sluicing out of the inlet.

If a boat got caught up against one of the jagged rocks, it would have been ripped apart in an instant. Loss of life would have been certain. The sides had to be smooth.

Regular army troops and national guard troops policed the roadways, facilitating the continuous rapid flow of refugees. They were authorized to utilize deadly force if necessary.

However, that threat was not necessary. Everyone wanted the same thing...to escape...to live. Everyone helped everyone else. Cooperation could not have been better, nor was it expected to this degree.

No matter the hour, pedestrians streamed into the reception area, where they were triaged by an army of military personnel and Soclarians.

On the other side of the world, the Iraqi morning bloomed all around Saddam's deceptively peaceful fortress in the mountains. As the sun made its first appearance over the horizon, so did helicopters filled with equipment and personnel from the news media. Saddam had sent his invitations. A desperate world wanted something to grasp...some information or news.

There were several landing areas in the valleys, plains and plateaus. They landed in and around a natural amphitheater, the stage of which was a rock outcropping one hundred feet above the base of Saddam's mountain.

Representatives from the UN came. Helicopters from surrounding neighboring countries came, private helicopters flew overhead. They swarmed in from all directions. The hive was coming alive.

Now Saddam believed that he could deal with the western infidels once and for all, before dispatching them and the world into oblivion.

The roadways were already clogged with the traffic of those who were loyal to Saddam. Mislead and brainwashed subjects of the realm treated Saddam's invitation to attend as a mandate, as their own call to salvation...a call to arms...their call to glory. They trusted no other truth...not even the **real truth**.

Saddam had called his invitation to attend "The final confrontation and mother of all battles in our righteous Jihad...the solemn right and duty of all countrymen of Iraq." How could anyone resist such an eloquent invitation?

Over the next five hours the acreage below began to darken with masses of humanity that streamed in by air, land and water. As the heat of the day went up and as the sun rose to its zenith, so did the crowd rise and so did Kevin's state of awareness.

As Hank had told him from the start...as Hank had coached him, his destiny was at hand. Now came near the time of his ultimate challenge. Every atom of his being shook with that realization. Justice would have its day and the most vile of all evils...a world killing evil...would be vanquished.

He trembled; not with the tremble of fear, but rather with the tremble of a well prepared athlete at the peak of condition, just itching for the start of the game. He would soon know that as prophesied, his unwitting role as the world's champion and gladiator would come full circle...would come to light.

Now he knew how. Below his feet he felt the way, as the forces of justice strengthened and reverberated within every atom of earth upon which he stood...within every atom around him...within every atom of his being. He felt it...he could reach out and touch it. To him, it was as thick as honey.

The drone had his inbred and instinctive blue print. He really never did have a choice. He was born to this. It simply was his time to come out...to metamorphose...to evolve. His genetic awakening was dawning.

From their grassy knoll, the group of five watched with an eerie sense of detachment. They were lost in their own thoughts and had reached a peaceful understanding within themselves that "what will be will be."

The die was cast. They knew their parts. Although they were walking in the valley of the shadow of death, they would fear no evil, for they knew God was with them. His mercy would follow and protect them, their being cast into the midst of the fray not withstanding.

The two guards stood impassively behind them. The falcon had found them. It circled overhead, screeching in protest...scanning for a clear line of site...looking for a target to focus upon...to overwhelm his prey with swift dispatch.

Kevin asked "Pop...I know it's coming. I know it will be soon; but how will it come? What is our Lord and Creator looking for? How will he choose? Whom shall he choose to escape his wrath?"

The ambassador answered for Hank. "I know that you know. But, it is all so new and unexpected for you that I realize that it is difficult for you to put these sensations into words.

"It shall come much like the angel of death during the first Passover. Pharaoh was our Saddam back then. This is our second Passover. However, the stakes are much higher this time.

"Pharaoh and Hitler after him did not have the tools to end all life. Evil incarnate and its loyal following now have that ability. However, he knows that he is losing ground and has resorted to desperation before his moment is gone. He is grasping the opportunity and playing all cards.

"At the time of Pharaoh's and Hitler's reign, as in large part during Saddam's, the souls of man were jeopardized. God's laws were being violated on a wholesale scale. Just and righteous followers of the laws and word of God were victimized, slaughtered and enslaved. But, this gift...this pearl we call Earth and all life on it was not in peril. That is the one major difference this time.

"God's will shall be made manifest differently this time. It shall not be lambs' blood being painted on

261

door posts that will lead to spiritual and physical salvation. It's not going to be that easy this time. Rather what will be sought are stains of the soul that cannot be painted over nor washed away at will from the soul's door posts."

Hank, putting it a little more into the vernacular added, "The force and being of HE WHO IS...THE DEITY knows who truly has been naughty or nice. A person is not a deed. Most people do something evil in their lives for which they have repented or have felt guilty about later."

This had the sound of truth to it. Kevin knew in his heart that the force sought a pattern...a mind set...a soul set.

Hank went on..."However, a mere physical act of placing lambs' blood on the door post won't appease the Old Man this time. We are not talking about something as nebulous nor as eternal as heavenly life after death...going to one's glory...going to one's salvation nor singing with the angels.

"This is a bit more practical, you know...like you are going to be alive tomorrow. We're not just talking about saving your mortal souls...we're talking about saving your **here and now** butts as well...the physical survival of your existence as the type of human specimen that will be allowed out there in the universe to perpetuate the species."

Daramer contributed "Wholesale abandonment in the belief of the Almighty, hatred and disdain for the works of the Creator, hatred of their fellow man...crimes against the environment and crimes against God's creatures...barely anyone is free from guilt in this regard.

"However, some men have become pariahs in the sight of God and the universe...Our God is outraged by what has been made of His creation. He has decreed that this scenario and all which has contributed toward it...contributed toward marring His gifts of life and creation, be rebuked."

Fairborne followed the point, "Ours is a busy God. He does not want to have to do these things time after time. Let's face it, He takes pride in His work and wants to see it appreciated, not abused.

"All within the realm of His creation He loves and He jealously protects as would any parent. And like any parent, He has limits to His tolerance; limits to what He will allow to happen to the whole of His earthly creations...His **CHILD**.

Kevin turned to Hank who continued "He teaches to turn the other cheek. However, He never figured that mankind would mess with mother earth so completely. He's clean out of cheeks to turn.

"You know all of that end of the world stuff the bible has been warning about over the millennium? Well, time's up. Our Benefactor is pulling the plug. God will vanquish iniquity before it destroys all in its path. It is that simple and the time is upon us."

Kevin asked "How could He cause so many to die. Is there no hope for the wicked? Can't the almighty make them come to their senses? Since He is all powerful isn't this possible?"

Fairborne tried to put things in perspective and to put the conversation to bed "Through us, the Soclarians, He is salvaging the seed if his creation of human existence. He is not causing deaths. He has merely made the alternatives available. Man is free to choose his own course...his own destiny. God has given his children above all else, that right to choose.

"However, when those choices interfere with the rights of others to live at all, or causes their home (the earth) to be permanently uninhabitable...or causes the beasts of the earth to cease to exist, He must act decisively and openly. **Causing** so many deaths as you put it?...No!

"This earth has nourished and suckled these evil hearted people. They must now be sanctioned as would be the murderer who seeks to assassinate his own mother. No less justice should be afforded to them.

"Yet in the final moments they will, again, have a choice. Their hearts must be rid of such hatred and treachery, free from plotting an Armageddon...They will have but an instant.

"Causing?...He is **allowing** this agent from hell, Saddam, to serve His purpose...His wrath...His intent to cleanse through the focus of evil through Hussein.

"Again, remember our God is not **CAUSING** anything to happen, He is **ALLOWING** it to happen. We, the Soclarians, are simply the stop-gap...the seed saver...the life boat for the **MOSTLY** pure at heart."

The sun became hotter and less bearable. Salty perspiration ran into the corners of Kevin's mouth, his tasting the brine as it found its way over his tongue. The solution stung his eyes as it seeped into their corners. Rivulets of sweat trickled down his spine and soaked into his pant's waist band.

The buzzing and droning chatter of locusts sang in a chorus of alarm...a chorus that mirrored the sense of impending doom in the air. The unseen forces and energies surged and flowed all around them...almost tangibly, but not quite...not yet...but tangible they would be.

From the east came the ominous drone of yet more helicopters. Over the horizon, close to the mountain tops, appeared a squadron of helicopters flying in a formation that made them look like a flock of geese. The confrontation grew closer.

Kevin could feel the presence of overwhelming

evil growing closer...piercing the envelope of peace and serenity that he and the others had felt surrounding this natural sanctuary. A place like this had to be the setting in order for such glaring opposites to be experienced and observed...to be felt.

The hand held radio that one of the guards wore slung around his shoulder crackled with urgency and with a loud impatient voice. The group was unceremoniously and abruptly ushered toward the fortress.

The group was led to the elevator that went through the middle of the mountain. They were delivered out onto the rock outcropping\stage of the amphitheater. They walked past workers assembling a public address system and faced a crowd that, in an instant, went from a meandering murmuring rabble to a hateful murderous throng, as they spied the group.

The crowd rushed forward and compacted itself at the base of the mountain...screaming for the death of the infidels...death to the west...death to the American president...death to just about anyone or anything that was not Saddam Hussein.

The world press had located itself at strategic positions designed to achieve the best vantage point. They moved about with obvious impunity.

A strange thing about the press...all sides want their stories told, their demonstrations covered and, therefore, tend to always play up to and protect (or at least ignore) the press.

The lead helicopter from the "V" formation settled closer toward the earth in the middle of the field in front of the outcropping. People scattered as the chopper touched down.

Soldiers unfurled a wide red carpet to form a walkway in front of the chopper leading toward the fortress. A cordon of soldiers lined the walkway on either side, forming a wall against the crowd.

First, aids emerged from the helicopter. Then, the sullen and stoically impassive figure of Saddam Hussein stepped to the opened door...hand extended, with the back of his hand leading his papal like wave of acknowledgement.

The capricious crowd changed its previous focus, clamoring with adulatory adoration for their leader...pressing frenziedly against the parallel walls of soldiers.

The din created a whirlpool of sound that slammed with tornadic fury into the group of five waiting under guard in the shadows of the mountain fortress.

After collecting hugs, bows and the standard demonstrations of submission from his fawning advisors and generals, Hussein made his way toward the concrete bunker entrance to the fortress at the base of the mountain. When the elevator door opened onto the outcropping, the crowd erupted with renewed fervor.

Saddam did not acknowledge the group of five. He strutted past them...parading back and forth, gesturing with his standard hand gestures...grandstanding...playing to the crowd...working them into a frenzy.

Hussein spoke for fifteen minutes, extolling the virtues of his evil intent, slandering the west and the rest of the world at large. This was his day; his day of glory. This was his crowning achievement; what he thought was to be the public downfall of and his humiliating subjugation of the infidels. This was the pinnacle of all that he stood for and strived for.

Not once did he give any credence to the position or to the mission of the group. How could he? It would mean his demise. However, down deep in what was his innermost being, the forces that controlled him, the forces of Armageddon...the forces of the very devil himself knew that "sink or swim" time had come..."put up or shut up."

It was high noon. The poker game had started. The stakes were the highest and all cards were on the table. This was the ultimate showdown and somebody had to leave town. Soon there would be no town left to leave.

Saddam ranted and raved "You see the great Satans here before you. See them for what they are."

He hesitated, then faced the crowd with one hand on his hip and the other sweeping high in front of him and continued "Now behold the forces that are on our side, the forces for justice, the forces of revenge, **the forces of Jihad!!!"**

Slowly, Saddam levitated himself three feet above the rock outcropping. Without moving his body whatsoever, he moved out over the ledge of the natural stage and remained motionless about fifteen feet past the ledge and about one hundred feet over the crowd.

The forces of evil were strong within him...but just strong enough to pull off a few parlor tricks...just strong enough to give credibility to an evil sham.

As he turned, he wavered and sank down just a bit, almost imperceptibly. Kevin could sense and could see in Saddam's face, that moment at which his strength and that of his shadowy backers could not be sustained. Yet, Hussein pulled it off long enough, as he glided back to the outcropping.

The crowd was awe stricken. They fell to their knees and prostrated themselves before Saddam, convinced that this false prophet was Allah himself.

Yet, he was the wolf, the predator, the pariah cloaking himself in the trappings of the sheep...the gentle yet strong...the believable ram that would lead the flock.

The crowd was now on its feet screaming and praising their deliverer when the first hint came that

267

something was lurking nearby...something powerful...something unknown.

The air pounded with the concussions of something unseen. It was a disturbing unharmonious pounding that struck discordantly; picking up the downbeat in syncopation with Kevin's own heartbeat...pressing against his eardrums "drub-boom-drub-boom-drub-boom!"

Adrian had reached her emotional limits. She quaked as Kevin slid his arm around her waist and pulled her toward him. "Just a little longer, kiddo. Hang in there. We're going to be just fine" he reassured.

Just beginning to show itself over the peeks of the mountain range was the gargantuan form of the **Star Seeker III**. It approached the gathering and hung over the amphitheater as it eclipsed the sun, placing the crowd in its shadow. The air around it pounded in sympathetic rhythm with its engines.

The crowd screamed in terror as they scrambled for any cover they could find.

Adrian pressed her back firmly against the rock in a frenzied, panicked, fantasy inspired attempt to become one with the rock, so that she might not be seen.

Kevin placed himself between Adrian and the commotion. He placed his hands on either side of her head and tilted her face, forcing her eyes to meet his.

"Hey, baby...these guys are on our side. The troops have arrived. You're a big time government operative. You know how this stuff works. The good guys come and the bad guys get creamed. Lighten up!" he comforted as he placed one hand against the rock and gently kissed Adrian's quivering cheek.

"ZZwartzzsskratsss..." came the blinding blast with a sizzling eruption from the Star Seeker, punctuating its arrival. The blast struck the peek of a nearby mountain top...not vaporizing it, but exploding and pulverizing it into millions of bits of debris that showered out in all directions. Thousands of tons of debris rocketed into the air and fell to earth as an avalanche cascaded down the face of the mountain toward the valley below.

This was the only warning Saddam was going to get. Either he got with the program, called off his dogs and capitulated or no fortress in the middle of a mountain would be large enough nor any hole in the ground would be deep enough to protect this mole's tail. Yet, no one expected his ego to allow for this eventuality.

As long as he kept digging holes in his own garden, he was of no real threat. The US figured "Let his own people deal with him". He went way beyond that point and his garden became the world. He had the time and the opportunity to plant the seeds of destruction and death. He now was reaping his dark harvest.

The iraqi leader knew that the media was broadcasting every second of this event to every corner of the globe. Thinking on his feet, like an expert debater, Hussein took the negative and the moment to make it work for himself.

This interruption was unexpected. Yet, he seized the moment...grasping at straws...grasping for anything to redirect the momentum. After briefly losing his composure, he took the offensive. He had to make this visitation seem planned.

The **Star Seeker III** flew off to a distance of about five miles and hovered in the distance, its engines pounding the air with muted defiance and challenge...not unleashing its full fury...straining against the air, as a snorting bull backs away and scrapes at the earth before making another charge at the matador.

The falcon circled and screeched high over the outcropping.

Speaking into the microphones Saddam loudly

269

sputtered "See what forces we have at our disposal?"...his not knowing (or not wanting to know) either way what the craft was going to do next. If it did nothing else and disappeared, credibility and victory would be his.

"At this momentous time my allies have come to stand beside me."

Hank whispered to Daramer and Adrian "Can you believe this guy's brass?"

The crowd reformed with confidence and cheered wildly.

As if on cue, Kevin lurched forward as if jerked by a rope. Hank and Daramer restrained Adrian as she tried to stop him. He stood next to Saddam on his left hand side. The guards were still riveted in place with fear and confusion. They did not interfere.

Fairborne walked forward and stood to Saddam's right. Justinian remained there holding his staff in his right hand, pointing it toward the heavens. It was now Kevin's and the ambassador's turn. Their script and stage directions had been written and preordained.

Kevin knew at that moment how all was to be. He had no questions nor reservations. He extended his hands downward on an angle toward the earth...his fingers joined and extended, pressing together as if ready to salute.

He had come out of his cocoon. The metamorphosis was complete. The prophesy had come to pass as his genetic timing coincided with the events and forces around him.

As salmon are called back to the streams of their birth, as geese find their way to their winter grounds flying in the dead of night, as the butterfly emerges after its metamorphosis, so too was Kevin summoned to this place at this time...transformed, he emerged.

He trembled with the forces surging through the

earth, focusing themselves through his genetically engineered awakening. He stared resolutely forward.

"You see..." Saddam continued extemporaneously screaming "Now, even my enemies come to my side in submission and in solidarity."

With his lies still fresh upon his lips, Saddam brought the wrath of justice down upon his own head. Justinian and Kevin turned to face Saddam. The falcon dove from the skies. "Skreee" echoed the piercing cry from its throat, as it plummeted toward Saddam's skull, landing with a "thump"...digging its needle sharp talons into Saddam's scalp.

Saddam could not move his feet. His boots became part of the rock upon which he stood. He screamed in pain and swatted at the falcon that pecked with deadly accuracy at his eyes.

From deep within his throat came a roar akin to some monster from another age, from some dark place. He wreathed and wildly flailed his arms. The falcon holding fast all the while...being tossed to and fro, back and forth.

Saddam's face transformed into that of something vile...something evil. Evil was etched in deep wrinkles around his growing head. His eyes grew wider and darker. His eyebrows became small hairy bushes. His neck thickened and large purple veins bulged up and down his throat. Small horns grew out of his skull. It was his time, as well, to metamorphose...to completely evolve...to be seen.

They had him. He was trapped between them. They had him at his worst. He was discovered and unmasked for all to see...squeezed in justice's vice to be treated...to be cauterized.

Bolts of lightening like energy crackled from the rock upward into the receptor's extended hands...into Kevin's hands...the coil...the step-up transformer...the lightening rod...the conductive catalystic key. The force

271

crackled all over his body. It arced and snapped from Kevin's head over Saddam's head connecting, with Fairborne's outreached staff. Justinian, too, became enveloped in the crackling force.

The glowing, crackling, undulating energy formed a framed archway around Saddam's gyrating body. There they stood for a good thirty seconds. Justinian and Kevin remained motionless and unharmed, appearing as gatepost guardian statues.

Saddam's guards cowered toward the recesses, nooks and crannies of the mountain's face along the outcropping's inner perimeter.

Suddenly, the falcon flew from Saddam's head and landed on the rounded knob at the top of Fairborne's staff. It pointed its head directly toward the head of Hussein.

The energy surged through the bird, crackled and overflowed toward Hussein, surrounding him in a glowing, fiery shroud of death. Smoke and searing flames erupted from his body. The dark billowing smoke flowed downward toward the crowd. In less than a minute, Hussein was reduced to a pile of white ash that blew away with the wind...following behind the smoke.

Then, the flowing energy burst forth from Justinian and Murdock, and dissipated into the air. Fairborne stepped forward as if to speak. He stopped and stood in front of the stunned crowd, looking from side to side; the falcon now on his left shoulder, the staff in his right hand.

A hush came over the amphitheater. He said nothing, for nothing had to be said. He just stood there, transfixed with the calming visage of one who represented the truth-...a mirror for all present to reflect and look deeply into their own souls.

What had just happened needed no explanation.

It needed no clarification. Good and evil, justice and treachery...right and wrong were focused and confronted one another on this singular worldwide common arena.

This *was* the moment; the moment when lies were to be separated from the truth; when choices were to be made...when hearts would be known and made manifest to and in the light of the universal consciousness. There would be no hiding, no equivocation, no deals...no more time. The truth was before all and could not be denied.

Kevin and Justinian stood together. They held the staff between them as the gap was bridged. The connecting switch for the forces of universal truth and justice was now complete.

In an instant, the moment was upon them all. A pulse of the glowing force erupted from between them, soaking into the earth in all directions, like rain being sucked down into a thirsty desert.

Sympathetic vibratory conductive transmissions of thought patterns, using the atomic and molecular sympathetic properties of creation, pulsed within the very rocks upon which they all stood. The most basic atomic and subatomic particles worked in unison as responsive receptors, transmitters and repeaters, rising to a crescendo...like an air raid siren. The **FINAL ALARM** had been sounded.

Every human on the planet was scanned simultaneously...divinely reviewed. It was over in an instant. The sensation of a slight tingle was felt in the cerebral cortex at the base of every brain of every person on the planet...on the land, the sea or in the air.

The countdown had started. Saddam's international cadre of agents followed their instructions. If Saddam's life ended they were to activate their devices of destruction. The media coverage assured that the message was received at the same moment by every agent of death who was still in the field.

There was no time to lose. Saddam's loyal zealots were stationed at any point in time a maximum of ten minutes from their devices.

Once set, the devices of destruction would go off in ten minutes. The reason for the ten minute delay having been built in just in case Saddam wanted to stop the clocks for some possible political reason.

It would have to be assumed that some agents were either closer to their devices than others or at their devices, right then and there.

The population centers were already evacuated for the most part. The people were beneath the earth in large communal assembly structures. Yet, there was still massive human exposure and loss to anticipate.

Large numbers of every plant, animal and insect had been housed in their own evacuation pods. The impact of Saddam's devices upon the environment would be next to total and would be irreversible.

Inventory of souls had been taken. The evil mutation that facilitated and harbored the seed of senseless death and anguish of their fellow man would now be culled out from the population.

As quickly as a match tip being lit then burning itself out, so did bodies in the crowd flare and blow away in a puff of smoke and ash. With the same snapping and searing sound of the match being lit the little pops could be heard.

Screaming and running in all directions, the crowd surged and flowed in panic. The same scene repeated itself throughout the world.

Along a roadside, a lone figure would flare up and disappear...popfff...gone. About a quarter of the crowd in the amphitheater flared. The ratio of those flaring was radically reduced in the general world population.

The **Star Seeker III** hurriedly returned to the area and leveled off at the outcropping. A door slid open as the group of five rapidly clamored aboard. In a heart beat, the escape route snapped shut.

The guards tried to escape with the group. They threw themselves against the now closed side. A few of them flared and disappeared in mid-stride.

Faster than you can say "A Dios" the media and other noncombatants or nonparticipants swarmed back into the sky in their helicopters, leaving all their equipment, intent on finding one of the many subterranean reception orifices in time.

As the Star Seeker slowly rose into the air, a single panicked Republican Guard member launched himself toward the craft's hull and became a flaming projectile in mid air...reduced to smoke and ash before he reached the ground.

Lieutenant Lasamar escorted the group to the bridge's observation window. They were met there by a smiling Captain Senecus. "Mission accomplished!" he boasted.

"No time to talk now. We will be joined shortly by the exodus fleet. They will be undergoing plate reversal shortly. After plate reversal, it might take a few moments for them to break free of the earth's crust. We wish to redistribute the displaced material as best we can. "We wish to scar the planet as little as possible by our leaving."

He added as he went back to his command seat "It won't be long now. Gariedon has been prepared for our arrival."

Star Seeker III went straight up, then glided over the north american continent.

Kevin, oddly enough, was as rested as a frisky child after a nap. He was exhilarated and felt better than he had any right to feel after what they all had gone through.

He looked at the earth and knew in his heart that his loved ones were safe. He prayed that they not be afraid. He hoped that maybe on television, the Tanderoths and his own boys saw that he had gotten away ok...that is, if they had recognized him or Adrian at all.

Unbeknownst to him, Winston Tanderoth and his wife Jenifer had taken their children and Kevin's boys to the marina. It was just a few blocks from their ocean front home. From there, they commandeered Kevin's boston whaler and headed to the inlet.

The six of them were among the first arrivals, scaling up the sides of the roadway to the reception orifice during slack tide. They set the whaler adrift and never looked back...well, perhaps they took a few quick peeks at Old Barney as they disappeared into the reception orifice.

Those few last saddened glimpses of the lighthouse would have to last them a lifetime. Much of what they thought of this area, their lifestyle and, for that matter, of this earth rested within the physical presence of that lighthouse.

It was the standard bearer and symbol representing the life they chose to lead, the physical focal point imbued with their concept of freedom. Certainly the entire area encouraged and represented those feelings.

However, every time they flew near that area and saw Old Barney from the air, every time they crossed over the bridge at Ship Bottom and got that first view of the lighthouse after a long trip down from their north Jersey home, or every time they got near the area by boat...that constant, steadfast monolithic presence could always be depended upon to inspire and remind them that this was one perpetual oasis in the desert of daily tribulation.

To them, that lighthouse was always as constant as a loyal friend. Like two ships sounding their horns as they passed in the night...that was the feeling one got. On the lonely expanses of the foreboding and unforgiving seas, it gave comfort even in a small, yet in a significant way, that there was someone... something out there...a touchstone...a symbol...a presence of hope; like the wave of a hand in passing, along with a friendly smile. That was Old Barney.

That was what they were leaving behind. That is what they had taken for granted and assumed would always be there for them; that anchor, that singular pillar of a wholesome and enjoyable lifestyle that they anticipated being there for generations to come...a lifestyle that assisted parents in passing along an honorable and time proven value system to their children in graphic fashion through observation and hands-on experience.

For example, good honest men made their living from the sea in this area. This was a poignant token representation of what hard work and effort could produce through one's own hands and will. There were no layoffs here. People had to eat. God provided the bounty from which to draw from...a source of clean clear sea life habitat that was replenished by the cycle of life.

A child could experience the good positive feelings derived from the knowledge that he was able to contribute to the family's dinner table, merely by finding a broken clam that a sea gull had dropped, then putting that meat on a hook and then landing a fluke, a weakfish or a bluefish. The fish head then became bait for crabs. In a morning, a young girl or boy could have dinner or a feast of crabs for the family.

The fresh crabs gave friends and family an excuse to get together. They would spread newspaper out over the kitchen table, break out some beer and soda and do what family and friends were meant to do; talk, be with one another, laugh and revel in the company and joy of one another's presence and company...treasured values that still meant something in the town of Barnegat Light...a place where you could still walk at night with your family to the local ice cream parlor and find friendly faces, peace and tranquility.

This is what they were leaving...leaving for all time, because of a charismatic evil agent from hell and shortsighted mislead zealots who found it easier to harbor hatred in their hearts rather than brotherhood.

Winston quietly thanked God in his heart that, even for their brief tenure as residents on this gift called Earth, he and his family had the privilege of experiencing this rare opportunity through the grace of God and by virtue of the miracle of life.

Up in the **Star Seeker III**, Kevin could not have known that all holding areas and exodus pods had projection images relayed to them from the satellite transmissions coming out of Iraq. The children saw everything.

From the vantage point provided by being able to observe Earth's surface from eight hundred miles up, Kevin thought how beautiful this azure gem in the heavens looked. It was so peaceful, belying and shrouding the seeds of the tempest and ruination to come. It was to be a tempest that would scar and corrupt this beauty...this God given resource...for centuries to come. They climbed to an altitude of four thousand miles.

The order had been given for all earth base stations to start plate reversal procedures. In their communal exodus pod, Winston and his wards felt the tremendous antigravitational forces slowly being gathered, concentrated and focused.

The gravity of the neighboring galactic mass as a whole was the external gravity source to be used for the exodus fleet. This source was independent of the earth's gravitational influences. The superstructure shuddered as the scraping and creaking noises of the hull straining against the earth's crust reached their ears.

Adrian, peering from the observation window aboard the **Star Seeker III**, exclaimed with alarm "Look!!! What's happening down there?"

Without notice, just minutes after they had left Iraq, the Earth began to glow with an emerald green hew. No device made by man could have caused this...or at least it could not have been caused by any currently known earth based technology.

Ambassador Fairborne yelled toward Captain Senecus "Moses, Do you know something I don't? What do you make of this?"

"Your guess is as good as mine ambassador" came the reply.

Something even stranger started forming on the opposite side of the planet...something initially obscured from their view. Was it ionized polar gasses? No, it was growing and extending way beyond the boundaries of the earth's atmosphere. It was nebulous, partially translucent, multicolored...fluid in appearance.

"Good God!" Hank Feidor exclaimed in astonishment and awe. Unknown to him, he was right on the money with his comment.

The figure of a bearded man formed behind the Earth. He was lightly clad in a fabric that appeared to be like broadcloth. He appeared to be almost solid, as the seconds passed. It was the figure that appeared after Fairborne's transfiguration during the final planning and briefing meeting.

His hands cupped around the Earth in a caressing gesture as He smiled down upon it. His torso remained obscured, with only His legs, arms, chest and head remaining visible. An asynchronous aura pulsed from His head and shoulders, sending polymorphic rays that leapt from and returned back to His body...like solar flares returning to the sun.

"Quick Lieutenant" ordered Senecus "get this on the scanners and broadcast it to the surface."

The image appeared on every projection wall of every craft getting ready to depart Earth's surface.

Resonating from the very matter of all visible creation in near proximity came His voice, "That which was and is my gift shall remain as my gift. The evil deeds of the would be usurper has been thwarted and turned aside. The abomination, the usurper, has been vanquished for all time.

"In time, again, there may be those who may fall from grace and allow evil to find a footing in their souls. But, now the truth is known and evil's return to prominence will never be allowed by my children to again rise and threaten civilization.

"It will be a mutation of the soul that will be discovered, recognized for what it is and be allowed to live out its corporal existence without threatening my gift to you again. It will never again grow to devilish proportions...to develop into hell's own monster. This never again shall be unleashed upon the family of man.

"The evil instruments and agents of the destroyer have been vanquished along with their leader and director. The poisons have been cleansed from your home. All is as it was...as it shall remain forever and for all time. My gift, this jewel in the firmament, will never again be compromised.

"This is my covenant to my children and to my tribe. May you all live in harmony and peace. May you enjoy and coexist with my creations and fellow creatures, whose rights to exist must never be ignored by you, nor subordinated in any permanently harmful way by your own needs."

His image began to waver as he concluded, "May you individually rise to the limits of your own potentials. May you find joy. May you always know the love that is given to you and that will be yours to share with each other for all time."

The visible figure of what all knew to be the Lord God himself became diaphanous and then dissipated into the ether.

Everyone who had witnessed this visitation knew that the landlord himself had renewed the lease. Not one witness could control their emotions.

Confirmation came from the planet's surface that the cleansing green glow had rendered earth's rivers, streams, lakes and oceans poison free. All nuclear weapons were vaporized; even the ones taken to government storage when some of Saddam's agents were taken into custody.

Ambassador Fairborne urgently and joyfully ordered "Belay the order to depart the planet's surface. Stand down the reversal plates. Further advisories will follow. Send everyone home!" he shouted.

The group of five stood before the observation window hugging one another, sobbing convulsively, unabashedly...uncontrollably...allowing the warm rush of cathartic relief to wash over them.

Adrian said softly, "None of us will ever have to feel alone ever again...thank you God!" as she, Kevin, Hank and the others exchanged embraces...all rejoicing...all in tears. They knew that they counted...that they were loved...that they were part of a very beautiful whole.

-EPILOGUE-

The **Star Seeker III** descended toward the middle of the Pennsylvania farm country and leveled off at about seven hundred feet. It passed over Upper Darby just south of Philadelphia, then entered New Jersey near Camden and Cherry Hill. It crossed over Manahawkin and finally arrived over water at Barnegat Bay, in full view of all citizens.

The people below who witnessed this passage were shell shocked to begin with. They were put collectively into an even deeper awe and shock by this "in person" visitation. There would be many new things the population would learn to get used to in the near future; their soclarian cousins being the most profound of the newness they would have to cope with.

People like to feel in control. This is a universal truth. To give in to a reality, a civilization, a technology that is so far beyond the grasp of the Earth inhabitants' realm of experience would initially cause universal insecurity.

This trauma and the ramifications of these new onslaughts on the psyche of mankind would take a great deal of love, time and patience

The craft lowered to one hundred fifty feet above the water, paralleling the Route 72 causeway about a mile away.

Hank quipped "Whoops...almost no cars. I guess the auto industry is going to have a heyday over the next few years. Buy your stock now."

Kevin joked, "I wonder what the insurance companies are going to say about your handiwork?"

Fairborne interrupted, "We will give earth's industries many new ways to approach transportation fabrication and other areas of manufacture. This is a new dawning. Polluting gas engines will no longer soil the planet. We will help show the way. All in good time. Healing must take place now."

From the observation window as they approached the town of Barnegat Light, Kevin could first see his boat, the **ACT I** at the very end of the pier. The rest of the marina was partially hidden by shrubbery. Taller homes obstructed the view of the street and the marina building itself.

What was also obscured was a welcoming throng of newly impressed fans...people that Kevin had met over the years out on Long Beach Island...an appreciative crowd that needed an outlet for their feelings of relief after what they all had just gone through. They needed a familiar face in the midst of all these revelations; one of their own who had some kind of inside track on what was going on.

"There will be no rest for the weary for the foreseeable future" Adrian observed as she pondered what she and Kevin had to look forward to. She was just glad that she had **something** to look forward to.

She knew they both had a long haul in front of them. Maybe her bosses would cut her loose without too much fanfare and hassle. She prayed that her superiors would be kind and make the debriefing as short and as painless as possible.

After all, they saw the end result. The Soclarians were going to cooperate with all government agencies around the world. What would the big deal be? She was exhausted in every sense of the word.

She reconsidered and mused that she had to give

to Caesar that which was due Caesar before getting back to her own life. She just wanted to have some peace with Kevin. But, she realized that he, too, had responsibilities and obligations, paramount of which was spending some time calming and reassuring his children. Her *quality time* with him and with them...would come soon. She knew that.

The craft made a wide graceful loop out over the ocean and then crossed back over Long Beach Island toward the protected marina just inside the inlet. The craft's bridge remained level as the craft banked.

For visual orientation and balance purposes while in a planet's gravitational field, some chambers within the craft (the bridge included) behaved as large free floating pods, moving within the ship's hull. The pods remained at a constant orientation with gravity's dictates...the walking surfaces parallel to the planet's surface. The hull moved independently.

Even though they had artificial gravity, use of the pods was more desirable when working in close to a planet's surface.

Kevin thought that this would be a great idea for a new ocean liner concept...a whole new type of stabilizer...keep the bottom of the pods super weighted and bingo.

The craft arrived just as the last of the raised roadway disappeared into the original sea bottom under the waters of Barnegat Inlet. People were being discharged through abundant egress locations hurriedly pressed into service. These exits dotted the countryside on the mainland like so many gopher holes.

The space craft stopped and remained motionless over the marina; its engines cut back to the point where a soft hum replaced the sound of the more heightened state of engine readiness demonstrated over Iraq.

"Well pop..." Kevin asked "What do we do now...exchange business cards?"

284

"Kevin, go back to your normal life...as normal as it can be at this point" Hank urged. "Spend some time with your kids. They need you very much at this time...more now than ever before. With the divorce they have lost their world as they knew it twice now. You know that you must now be their strength until they can stand on their own. They'll do it too, they're good strong kids. They'll be good strong citizens when they go out on their own.

"After you spend a few days on the boat, we will be in touch. We, too, have to try to get back to normal, given our new state of prominence and the new reality that this prominence presents.

"Let's all take a breather and relax for a short while. All things will seek their own level. No one is going to rush ahead with anything during the next few days."

Fairborne offered "Established governments will continue to lead and govern. We probably will continue to work through the United Nations. We are going to demand no land nor homeland. Our homeland is on Soclar. We threaten nothing nor anyone.

"Our mission here will continue and we shall continue to be of service and support to the world, just as before. However, the difference is now everyone will know about it. In that light, secrecy will not tie our hands.

"When you joined with us just a short time ago, you left behind a world froth with corruption, of distrust, of moral decay...a world that had pushed its own self-destruct mechanism into motion, creating a downward spiral...creating an irreversible self-fulfilling prophesy...a world of freedom taken to the extreme...a freedom and civilization that became fetid in its own dirty diapers because it did not know how or lacked the conviction to potty train itself. This raised the philosophical and rhetorical question **'WHEN IS TOO FREE**

TOO FREE?' When should a society be saved from itself?

"Now there is a universe of new possibilities, new hope, a new start. May the people of Earth never forget the lessons learned within the last few days and not squander this new beginning through a selectively short memory.

"We have all been given our marching orders from the Boss. We Soclarians are hopeful and confident that now may begin a true basis of kinship between our people...that together, we will be able to go forth into the universe jointly and in brotherhood, as the worthy progeny and representatives that our mutual Benefactor may be proud of.

"This will come to pass, because the light has been seen and the direction made clear. A solid foundation now exists for this probability and eventuality."

Justinian put one arm around Adrian's shoulder and one arm around Kevin's as he escorted them to the center of the ship where they would disembark through the elevator cylinder.

The group of five, joined by Captain Senecus and the Barnegat Light Earth Base Station's commander Leotor entered the cylinder chamber.

The nearly transparent pillar like cylinder descended toward the water. It stopped just a few inches from the end of the floating dock near the **ACT I**. The descent stopped.

Just before the cylinder's door rotated away, Hank whispered to Adrian, "Tell Gerta she still owes me a dance and I'm going to collect".

"I'll tell her, you sly old fox" she responded.

As Adrian and Kevin stepped out and took a moment to get their bearings, the door closed before they could say anything further to their traveling companions. They felt the need to say something more. They felt something was left unsaid.

It was said for them in the faces and warm smiles of their new allies, their new friends as they waved, slowly rising and then disappearing into the **Star Seeker III**. The craft backed off about fifty yards and stayed at the same altitude.

The two turned to see Kevin's sons, Peter and Andrew running toward them, after having been allowed to proceed through a cordon of soldiers. They were escorted by Major Taylor. The Tanderoths were right behind them.

General Edwards and Adrian's boss, a gray suited man with an official looking ID on his lapel, elbowed their way through the throng. They had her mother Gerta in tow.

Gerta pulled free and tried to scream toward Adrian over the clamor and the noise of the waving crowd. The crowd was jubilant...simply trying to get a glimpse of the action. After all, had the Earth ever seen such a day?

"Adrian, Adrian, baby...I'm over here" she called as she ran down the dock.

Abruptly, she stopped and looked up at the observation window of the **Star Seeker III**. There, in full view, was Hank standing in front of a small group of men, with his cherub smile and impish charm trying to mime a dance.

With his right hand over his stomach and his left hand extended out to the side, he swayed. He then stopped and waved, mouthing the words "Hello Gerta".

Kevin dropped to a kneeling position as the boys catapulted themselves into his opened arms. He reeled back from the impact and recovered. The boys buried their heads into either side of his neck and sobbed "Daddy, daddy!...Oh daddy" choking the words through their tears.

They could manage to say nothing else; their blurred eyes speaking volumes, as the tears streamed down their faces. They were safe now. They knew it. They felt it. But, their need was deep and their feelings were just beginning to rise to the surface. Tincture of time was needed now.

Kevin cradled their heads in his arms "Shhh...shhh. It's all over boys. I'm here. It's ok."

He hid his face in their hair, not even attempting to hold back the flow of his own tears, whispering down toward their ears "We're home, we're home my beautiful children, we're home on our beautiful Barnegat Bay...Thank God...Thank you God!"

After a few moments, Kevin stood and met the remainder of the contingent with hand shakes; receiving their expressions of thanks, relief and other comments.

The shadow of the space craft started to move, causing all heads to turn. They stared with undiminished awe as the **Star Seeker III** began drifting upward and east toward the Atlantic Ocean.

The group behind the observation window began waving animatedly and with the smiles and conviction of lost then rediscovered relatives, promising not to make it so long between visits...strongly, deliberately and collectively projecting this into the consciousness of the onlookers.

The crowd waved back in knowing recognition, reassured.

Kevin turned to find the marina manager, Ted Painedast, standing directly in front of him, superimposed against the backdrop of Old Barney...with his red face, white shirt, red shorts...and with his somber, accusatory glare staring him right in the eye.

Suddenly, the frowning down turned corners of Ted's mouth curled upward into a beaming smile, demolishing his severe facade.

Offering his hand to Kevin he said "Well Murdock, you've really done it this time."